Prom Night in Purgatory

~

By Amy Harmon

Cassie ♡

Amy Harmon

1

First Paperback Edition: August 2012

The characters and events portrayed in this book are fictitious. Any similarity to real persons, living or dead, is coincidental and not intended by the author.

Harmon, Amy Sutorius, 1974 –

Prom Night in Purgatory: a novel / by Amy Harmon. –

1st Edition

Summary: Johnny Kinross has escaped Purgatory, only to find himself surrounded by strangers, in a world very different from the one he knew. Maggie O'Bannon must fight for Johnny's love all over again, putting herself at constant risk as she travels through time and space to make things right.

ISBN 10: 1478265574   ISBN 13: 978-1478265573

Printed in the United States of America

That which has been is now;
and that which is to be
has already been.

Ecclesiastes 3:15

~1~
To Every Thing There is a Season

The house was the same, but different. The old swing wasn't old. In fact, it looked as if it had just been hung, so squeaky clean and shiny were the chains that suspended it above the broad front porch. Red and yellow tulips dotted the flower beds, the first buds of spring. There hadn't been any the last time she'd looked. The house appeared as if it had just been freshly painted and the shutters were a gleaming black instead of the peeling flat charcoal they had faded to. There was Irene's car. It was parked haphazardly in the long driveway, as if it had been left in a hurry and was waiting for its owner to return. The chrome glistened, and the pink of the paint looked so new that Maggie wondered that it didn't drip from the doors. Another car passed in front of the house. And then another. There must be a classic car show nearby. A big, black Buick pulled into the driveway behind Irene's Cadillac, and a man Maggie had never seen before stepped out of the car in a huff and slammed the heavy door.

"Irene!" the man bellowed, walking toward Irene's poorly parked car. He was tall and a little heavy set, but he wore his weight well, like a man who was comfortable with himself and accustomed to leading others. His hair was slicked back from his face, waves neatly lacquered into place. His suit was black and almost baggy in its fit, the roomy legs of his slacks pooling slightly above shiny shoes. His white shirt was neatly pressed and his thin red tie disappeared into the V of his big suit coat. He wore a hat like Frank Sinatra's, and it gave him a dapper air. Men looked good in hats, Maggie thought randomly, watching the man stride toward the pink Cadillac.

"She never puts the car away like she's asked, constantly leaving it blocking the driveway," the man mumbled as he yanked the car door open, leaning inside the Caddie's roomy interior. Maggie could see that the keys hung from the ignition. He slid his big frame into the car and pulled the door shut behind him. Maggie wondered if she should stop him or call out for help. He was obviously taking Irene's car. She lurched forward, lifting her arms and shouting. Instantly she stood by the open window of the car, as if propelled at lightning speed to her goal. He didn't seem to notice her standing pressed against the window – and then she wasn't, pressed up against the window, that is. She now sat beside the big man on the bench seat of the car; the high-glossed leather of the seat should be smooth against her thighs, but it wasn't. She couldn't feel the seat at all or her legs that lay against it. As she ran her hand along the dashboard, it was as if she pulled her hand through the air. She couldn't seem to connect with the objects around her. She must be dreaming. Yes. That's what it was. Just a dream. The big man turned the key in the ignition and prepared to drive the car forward, his eyes trained on the garage in front of him. Someone tapped at the window, a sharp rat-a-tat, and Maggie's head swiveled to the left, a movement replicated by the man beside her.

Johnny. He was leaning down to peer into the driver's side window, his dark blonde head tilted to the side, the knuckles of his right hand still pressed to the glass. A small grease stain made a black crease between his first two fingers. The man next to Maggie quickly rolled the window down several inches. An aqua colored truck with bulbous headlights and rounded wheel wells sat at the curb. A flat bed extended from the cab with "Gene's Auto" emblazoned on the side. The truck's horn tooted, and the driver touched his cap and pulled away from the curb.

"Mr. Honeycutt. Sorry to startle you, sir. Gene sent me to pick up the Buick." Maggie's heart skipped and smiled in her chest. Johnny wore a striped blue work shirt with GENE'S embroidered on the pocket. The short sleeves were rolled a little, as if he struggled to conform completely to the uniform.

"Oh, that's right!" Mr. Honeycutt wiped a big hand down his broad face. "I forgot all about that. I did tell Gene to send someone by."

"Would you like us to come back another day, sir?" Johnny's voice was deferential and his manner very businesslike. Maggie stared into his face, wondering why he hadn't even looked in her direction. She waved her hand at him experimentally. His eyes stayed trained on Mr. Honeycutt.

"No…no. Today is as good as any. The keys are in the ignition. The car has been pulling a little to the right. I told Gene. I don't think it's anything a little adjustment can't fix. Change the oil while you're at it, too." Johnny stepped back from the door, and Mr. Honeycutt turned the key off, opened the door, and heaved himself out. Maggie moved to scamper out of the Cadillac after him and was instantly sitting in the big, black Buick parked behind Irene's Cadillac. A few seconds later, Johnny slid in behind the wheel of the Buick. He pulled the door closed and leaned out the open window. His right hand slid up to twelve o'clock on the wheel; his bicep bunched in a hard mound. Maggie reached out to run her hand along it softly but felt only the barest hint of something warm beneath her finger tips and nothing more. Johnny didn't flinch but swatted at his arm, as if he had felt her touch and thought it was the wispy legs or wings of an insect landing on his skin.

"I'll bring it back tonight, sir, unless there's a problem, in which case we'll call you. Should I leave the keys in the ignition or will someone be home to leave them with?"

"Someone will be here, son. Tell Gene hello. He always takes good care of us."

Johnny nodded and waited for the man, who was obviously Irene's father and Maggie's great grandfather, to turn and head into the house. Turning the key and shifting into reverse, Johnny eased the bulky car backward and swung out into the street. Maggie breathed in deeply and smelled Old Spice and the hint of a cigar, just like her great-grandfather must have smelled. Funny... she couldn't feel anything, but she could still smell. Could she smell in all her dreams? Maggie slid over next to Johnny, as close as she could without dissolving into him. She breathed deeply. She smelled citrus and soap and the warmth of sunshine; his scent made her dizzy. Maggie stuck out her tongue experimentally and ran it along the line of his jaw to see if he tasted as good as he smelled. Hmmm, nothing. Darn. She might as well be tasting the air. She whispered into his ear.

"This is a wonderful dream, Johnny. I hope I never wake up." Maggie smiled happily to herself as she drank in his handsome profile, the length of his black lashes, and the straightness of his nose. Johnny worried his lower lip with his teeth and then sang a little, his voice husky and a little off key as he extended his left hand out into the afternoon sunshine and let it stream through his fingers as he drove. "I'm just a fool, a fool in love with...." It was that song. They had danced to that song.

"Ah, Maggie," he sighed. "Where did you go, baby?"

He was talking to her. He had said her name! Maggie struggled to answer, to tell him she was here, right beside him. But she couldn't speak. Her throat was on fire. She wrapped her hands around her neck, as if they could block the pain. Her throat was raw and each breath she took torture. Maggie moaned, and Johnny shimmered next to her. Maggie gasped as something sharp was inserted into her wrist. She held her hands out in front of her, gazing down at them in disbelief. A needle slid smoothly into a pulsing vein below the base of her left palm. Someone said her name, and something icy traveled up her arm from the origin of the inserted needle. She was jerked from Johnny's side, and she grabbed for him futilely as she was sucked through a narrowing black tunnel. Johnny became a rapidly fading point of light at the farthest end. He never even turned his head to see her fly through space.

* * *

The burn in Maggie's throat receded with the cool relief injected into her veins. She heard voices around her, speaking faintly and efficiently. They pulled at her, but she pushed back, eager to fall back into the dream that had given her a glimpse into Johnny's life before Purgatory. He was so real. She refused to heed the voices around her, and they began to fade until they were nothing more than the buzzing of distant traffic. Maggie drifted in a warm, black cocoon and was aware of nothing more.

When consciousness returned, Maggie was in a room she recognized as the room Irene had once decorated as a nursery and then converted into something less painful when the babies never came. She had left it the cheerful yellow that had seemed appropriate for young children but had placed a large bookcase on one wall and had set several plants on the window sills. She had pushed matching chairs against another wall and placed a lamp between them. A fat rug, well made but worn, stretched across the floor from corner to corner. Maggie had often seen Irene in the room reading or working on her needlepoint. She said when Roger was alive it became her private little oasis and he had left her alone there.

Now it was almost unrecognizable. If not for the position of the windows and the size and shape of the room, Maggie might not have known where she was. The warm brown of the wood floors was unchanged beneath the fluffy pink rug that had replaced the heavy oriental in Irene's reading room. Pink flouncy curtains topped the tall windows. A small, white desk sat beneath one, and below the other was a white console proudly displaying a record player with dozens of small round records littering the floor around it. A ruffled pink bed was pushed against the far wall. An assortment of pillows, stuffed animals, and dolls decorated its surface. A little girl, maybe nine or ten, judging from her size, sat on the end of the bed and talked sweetly to a fat bear that she clutched in her hands. Her hair was a soft light brown that just grazed her shoulders, and it was neatly barretted above her small ears. She wore a dress the color of ripe peaches, and her neat white bobby socks and black flats stuck out beneath the skirt that hid her crossed legs.

"Come on, Jamie. You know I need to practice on someone, and if I can't practice on you, who can I practice on? I know you'll feel silly – I'll feel silly too, but if I'm ever gonna marry James Dean I will need to know how to kiss, won't I?" With this convincing argument, the young girl stuck out her lips and laid a very firm kiss on the bear's furry snout. Her eyes were pinched closed, and her lips were pushed out comically. She opened them slowly, and a furrow grew between her blue eyes.

"You're not very good at that, Jamie. You and I will have to practice."

Maggie giggled a little at the serious admonishment. The little girl's eyes snapped up and locked on Maggie in horror. Maggie's giggle died in her head. She hadn't giggled out loud had she? Could the little girl see her? That was impossible. She wasn't really here...this was just a dream.

The little girl's eyes grew wide and fearful. She scooted back on her bed and squeezed her bear close against her skinny chest. She closed her eyes again, but this time, fear was stamped all over her face and her lips weren't pursed for kissing. Instead, they moved in a rushed whisper.

"Ghosts aren't real, ghosts aren't real, ghosts aren't real." After several incantations, she opened one eye as if to verify that Maggie still remained. The blue eye immediately squeezed shut again, and the denials of ghostly existence resumed.

"Is she talking about me?" Maggie thought, stupefied by the thought. "Are you talking about me?" Maggie said aloud, although "out loud" felt different in this dream body. It was almost as if she directed the thought out instead of actually creating sound.

The little girl frowned, and her eyes popped open. She raised one eyebrow slowly, and Maggie had a rush of recognition. Her mother used to do that...raise that one brow ever so slowly, creating an expression that said, "Are you kidding me?"

"Daddy got really mad at me the last time I told him about Grandpa sitting in his chair after the funeral. How was I supposed to know it was a ghost? He looked real to me! Daddy sent me to my room for two whole days after that. I had to eat in here and everything. It was awful! Now whenever I see a ghost I have to pretend that I don't. It's very frustrating." The girl folded her hands in her lap and waited for Maggie to respond. Maggie stared, dumbfounded. This little girl saw ghosts...just like she did. The slim eyebrow rose again, imperiously. Maggie rushed to introduce herself.

"My name is Margaret. But you can call me Maggie. What's your name?" Maggie thought she might already know, but the answer was too crazy to be true, and she waited breathlessly for a response.

"My name is Elizabeth, but you can call me Lizzie." The girl parroted her response in the same cadence

Maggie had used. Maggie tried to school her expression into calm acceptance.

"Is your older sister named Irene?" Maggie wondered aloud, trying to appear casual. She failed. She could see that the girl thought she was being visited by the angel of death.

Lizzie's expression immediately grew guarded, and fear tiptoed back across her features. "Why? What do you want with her?"

"Nothing...I don't want anything." Maggie shook her head as she spoke, underscoring her words. How could she possibly explain? They stared at each other for several long moments. Lizzie was the first to speak again.

"Most ghosts don't usually talk to me," Lizzie said matter-of-factly. "They just walk around doing boring things and pretending I don't exist. It's very rude."

Maggie smiled at that. She would have to agree. "I'm not really a ghost."

"You certainly are...."

"No. I'm not dead. I'm just dreaming. I mean, I don't think I'm dead." Maggie suddenly realized that she could very well be dead. Maybe she had returned to the past because that is where Johnny had existed. If so, she supposed God had been benevolent; wherever Johnny was was where she wanted to be.

Lizzie rose from the bed and walked toward Maggie with a determined set to her chin. She walked with a slight limp, and Maggie noticed her right leg was somewhat shriveled next to the left.

"Did you hurt your leg?"

"I just got my cast off last week. I broke my leg falling out of the tree in our backyard. It was worth it, though. I got to see my mother. She talked to me just like you. And I could see through her, just like you. That's how I know you're a ghost." Lizzie stopped just in front of Maggie and crossed her arms defiantly.

"How do you know Irene? And why are you in my room?" The little girl had some moxie – no doubt about it. She reminded Maggie a little of herself. Maybe being able to see ghosts had steeled their spines and given them courage in the face of the impossible.

"Well. This might sound strange...but, I'm your....your...granddaughter," Maggie finished sheepishly, knowing how ludicrous she sounded. But weren't dreams supposed to be a little bizarre? Without warning, the pulling sensation she had felt as she'd sat beside Johnny in Irene's father's car began to radiate around her. She pushed back against it. She had never known her grandmother. She wanted to stay. The feeling abated a little. She spoke again.

"I live in this house, too...just a long time from now." This time, both of Lizzie's eyebrows rose and disappeared under her curled bangs. The tugging increased around Maggie, demanding that she succumb. She shoved at it again, annoyed.

"My mother was Janice….your daughter." The pull became a vise – an ever tightening clamp. Maggie sucked her breath in sharply and struggled to free herself from the invisible bands.

"Maggie?" Lizzie reached out her hand. "I can barely see you now, Maggie. Can't you stay a while? I'm really tired of Jamie's company. He's just a stuffed bear, after all."

Maggie could barely see Lizzie either. The room had narrowed in diameter, and, just like before, Maggie was whisked away from the past, and the world that held Lizzie winked out like a light.

***

At first she thought it was her dad calling to her, entreating her with the gentlest of voices. She wanted to see him. She wanted to be held and welcomed. She struggled out of the black she was floating in. The voice urged her on. She moved toward it eagerly. She could be with them now…with Dad and Mom, and Johnny too. Oh, please, Johnny too.

But it wasn't Dad. It was Gus. She stopped struggling. She loved Gus, but Gus belonged to a world where Johnny no longer existed; it was a world she didn't want to inhabit any longer. But she had risen too close to the surface, and she could no longer block out the words that poured over her.

"He's gonna need you now, Miss Margaret," Gus said insistently. "He's gonna need you real bad. He's been through hell and back to be here with you. So you need to wake up. You gotta wake up now, Miss Margaret."

The words came again. Gus said Johnny was.....alive? Johnny was here? With supreme effort, Maggie opened her eyes.

"Where is he?" she croaked. Her throat felt like it had been used to sand down an entire gymnasium floor. The pain shot through her and made her shudder and close her eyes once more. She opened them immediately and gazed at Gus. There was a flurry around her as a series of little beeps sounded and two nurses and one doctor came running. The patient was awake. Maggie endured the bustle, poking, prodding, and questions with as little movement and speech as possible. Irene was there, bursting in and rushing to Maggie's bedside. Tears streaked down her soft cheeks. Shad was allowed a little later, but he hung back by the door. He stared at her wordlessly, but she could see the relief in his brown eyes, a relief that relaxed the tightness around his mouth and curved his lips into a small smile. She tried to smile back. Her lips were so dry she could only manage a grimace, so she raised her hand to give him a little wave. The motion caused a tug at her arm and she looked down at the I.V. stuck in her left wrist. It reminded her of the dream. She had been with Johnny, but he couldn't see her. He had been driving Irene's father's car. He had smelled so good, and he was painfully real. The dream was unlike anything she'd ever experienced.

"We'll let you rest, dear. I can see that you're still a little foggy." Maggie realized that Irene was talking to her, and had been talking to her for several seconds. She looked at her aunt apologetically. Shad tipped his head in farewell and Irene and Gus began to follow him out.

"Gus!" Maggie's raspy whisper rose from the bed, compelling him to wait.

"Go on. I'll just be a minute," Gus assured Irene. He waited until they left the room and the door swung closed behind them. He turned and looked at Maggie soberly.

"Johnny," Maggie insisted, her eyes beseeching.

"He's here. Down the hall, actually. He's recovering from a gunshot wound to his chest. He's pretty out of it. I don't know if I can get you in to see him… but I promise you I'll try. He's got a sister…she's looking out for him. I don't know what she's told the hospital staff."

"A gunshot wound?" Maggie scraped out in horror. "Someone shot Johnny?" Then the rest of what Gus said registered in her wool-filled brain. "A sister?" Maggie rasped in disbelief.

"I never told you. I guess I just never thought about it. Chief Bailey and Dolly Kinross had a daughter. You know Principal Bailey?"

Maggie nodded her head, dumbfounded.

"They found him at the school, just lying in the rubble, right where the rotunda stood. He wasn't burned or anything. He just had that wound, and he'd lost a lot of blood. Principal Bailey happened to be there when he was found, and she recognized him. I reckon she's spent her whole life lookin' for his face…and her poor momma before that. She's pretty shaken up, but she's a strong woman." Gus wrung his hands, obviously missing the hat brim he usually abused.

"He's really alive? He's really here?" Maggie felt the realization rise up and tears spill over onto her cheeks.

"He really is, Miss Margaret. As God is my witness, he really is. Praise Jesus," Gus marveled, shaking his head in wonder. "I ain't never seen the like…"

~2~
And a Time to Every Purpose

2011

  Everyone was calling him John Doe. He had stayed silent the first few times he had awakened. At first it was because he didn't know where the hell he was. Shoot, he didn't know WHO the hell he was. He had fallen back into oblivion before he'd had time to ponder anything at all. The next time he was awake for longer. The first thing he was truly aware of was pain. He hurt everywhere, like he had been run over by Gene's tow truck. Gene. He remembered Gene. And little Harv. He'd drifted off to sleep not long after, reassured by the fact that he remembered something and someone. When he woke up again, a woman sat by his bed. The room was dark and no one but the two of them sat amid the bleeping machines that looked like the robots from one of the programs on the television Jimbo's dad had purchased and now proudly displayed in his living room. Jimbo's pop had positioned the set right in front of the windows so everyone who lived on the block would know he had a TV. He left the windows opened when he watched, and sometimes the kids playing ball in the street would abandon their games and listen outside. Johnny had been able to watch it a couple of times. Sometimes the whole neighborhood came over to watch the thing.

At first he thought the woman was his mother. As soon as the thought occurred to him, his mother's face rose up in his mind. The glow of the lights was hardly sufficient to make out the woman's features, but there was something very like his mother in the way she sat, her head nodding in sleep, her neck bowed gracefully in tired supplication. It wasn't until a nurse came in and snapped on the light to check his vitals and poke at him that he saw that the woman was not his momma after all. She was wearing men's pants, and her hair was styled in a boyish cut. The nurse also wore pants….when did that become the norm? Hmmm. He didn't care for it. He had always kind of liked a nurse's uniform; there was something sexy about it. The woman sleeping in the chair bolted straight up and met his gaze in alarm.

"You're awake." Her eyes shot to the nurse. The nurse didn't seem too surprised by Johnny's wakefulness and proceeded to ask him how he felt, if he struggled to breathe, if he thought he could sit up, and a million other mundane things. The nurse was young and pretty, and he smirked at her a little, testing her out. She raised one eyebrow at him disdainfully, and told him she was going to remove his catheter. With a toss of his covers, she unmanned him with a yank.

"Ouch!" Johnny roared. His manhood lay quivering for the lucky females in the room to enjoy. He jerked the blankets back over himself and glowered at the nurse, who fought a slight smile. Gee whiz. The woman had just grabbed his handle without batting an eye. She hadn't even given him time to give her a better first impression. Ah well. She was too old for him. He liked them a little more timid anyway, didn't he? Something nagged at him. A memory of someone...and then it was gone, dissolved into the muddle that clogged his heavy head. He was suddenly dizzy, and the woman who had been sleeping beside his bed jumped up to help him lie back. The nurse patted his leg. Oh, now she was being nice. Too late, sweetheart. She made a few notes and looked up at him again.

"The doctor will be in shortly. Do you think you can stay awake?" When he nodded, she walked out of the room without another word.

As soon as she was gone, the woman beside him began to speak.

"What's your name?" Her voice was calm, but there was a hint of urgency in her tone that forced him to meet her sharp gaze.

"Johnny. Johnny Kinross." It was out of his mouth before he realized that he even knew his name. Johnny.

Yeah. That was it. Johnny Kinross. And his mom's name was Dolly and his kid brother was Billy, and he had the coolest car in the county. And he needed a cigarette in the worst way.

A sharp breath hissed out her parted lips, and her hands gripped the rails on his bed tightly.

"Do you know why you're here?" The urgency was more pronounced now, and Johnny tried to focus. His head had gained at least 100 pounds since he'd opened his eyes ten minutes ago. He was getting tired again. He focused on what she had asked him. He was obviously in a hospital. Some new-fangled fancy hospital, which looked like something from outer space. Maybe he wasn't completely awake after all. Why was he here? His chest hurt like the dickens. He raised his left hand and fingered the bandages on his right shoulder.

"Did I get banged up at the rumble? Me and the guys were outnumbered pretty good." Johnny grimaced, closing his eyes, trying to remember. "Roger Carlton is a snake...."

The woman beside the bed was very pale, and her hands had started to shake, making the bars rattle. She immediately let go and folded her arms tightly around herself.

"Do you remember anything after the.....the rumble?"

Johnny shook his head a little, but his thoughts were interrupted by the door opening. The woman beside him looked as if she would faint where she stood. The doctor seemed to be talking to someone on the other side of the door and was delayed from entering. The woman crouched down very close to Johnny and whispered vehemently.

"Don't tell him anything!" Her eyes were so wide they looked almost comical in her thin face. "Tell the doctor you don't remember your name or anything about yourself or how you got hurt. I promise I'll explain..."

The doctor walked into the room, and she ceased whispering abruptly. The doctor had obviously just come on shift. His hair was slightly damp and his cheeks were ruddy from a recent shave. He smelled like aftershave and antiseptic. A not unpleasant combination, Johnny found. He had a reassuring face and a kind demeanor as he inquired about Johnny's pain levels and checked the wound at his shoulder. He had a chart that he studied for several minutes. When his eyes were averted the woman leaned forward again and this time took Johnny's hand in hers. Her hand was small and as cold as ice. She squeezed his hand tightly, as if to remind him of what she had said. The doctor looked up again.

"What's your name?"

***

Maggie was weak and sore, and too many people hovered and fussed. Irene, Shad, and Gus took turns entertaining her with one-sided conversation to give her smoke-charred throat continued time to heal. She was grateful, in spite of the pain, that she had an excuse to refrain from speech. If she could have, she would have howled with frustration at her weakened state and the conditions that kept her from seeing Johnny. Whenever she got him alone, Gus continued to make excuses as to why she couldn't see Johnny. He told her Johnny was awake now, and reports were that he would make a full recovery. In fact, he was healing so rapidly, his doctors were amazed. When Maggie pressed Gus for more, he claimed he knew nothing. He told her no one except Principal Bailey, Gus, Maggie and Irene knew about Johnny's identity. Shad had some memory of being rescued, but Gus had refrained from explaining anything to him. Gus reassured her that soon both she and Johnny would be released from the hospital, and she would be able to see him then.

"The fewer explanations that have to be given, the better," Gus warned Maggie. "He can't exactly tell everyone he's Johnny Kinross. They'd think he was crazy. Mind you, they'd think all of us are crazy. The best thing we can do for him is to let Principal Bailey do the talkin' and just stay silent and not draw attention to him. She's been around the system long enough to know what strings to pull — workin' with kids as long as she has. She's gonna coach him through, don't you worry."

And so Maggie waited. Three days after she had awakened from her coma, she could wait no longer. That night she bided her time until the nurse on the night shift left her desk. She had been checked on mere minutes before — at night the staff was much more laid back, the rounds fewer and farther between. She figured she would have sufficient time to see Johnny, talk to him, reassure him, and make it back to her room without detection.

Gus had told her what room Johnny was in. She had wheedled it out of him, promising that she would wait for his go ahead. She was breaking her promise. She just couldn't wait any more. She had to see him for herself. She'd had the sneaking fear that it was all just a grand story to pull her back among the living. She was certain that when she was sufficiently healed, Gus would confess that he had concocted the tale for her own good. She had accused him of as much; that accusation finally convinced Gus to tell her where Johnny was recovering. It was only four doors down.

Her heart in her throat, Maggie padded down the hall in bare feet, a robe Irene had brought from home wrapped around her flimsy hospital gown. She had brushed her hair and teeth, but she knew her blue eyes looked too big in her face and her skin was too pale in the fluorescent lights. Nerves skittered under her skin. Johnny was free now. He could go anywhere and do anything. Would he want to be with her still? Would he look at her straight brown hair and big glasses and think he could do so much better than a girl like Maggie? She squared her shoulders and shook off the self-doubt. The door to his room pushed open easily. The bed was perpendicular to the door, and the curtain was partially pulled at the head, making it impossible to see who occupied the space. Maggie froze.

"Johnny?" she whispered. Her heart was pounding so loudly she doubted she would hear him if he responded. "Johnny? Are you awake?" She forced her feet forward and approached the base of his bed. The bed squeaked suddenly, causing her to yelp. Maggie could see that the person occupying it struggled to sit up. A whirring sound commenced and the bed moved, the upper half lifting and halting in an upright position. She still couldn't see his face; the hanging curtain blocked her view from mid-chest up. She tiptoed to the side of the bed and, holding her breath, looked down into his face.

She had wondered if she would be able to see him with her glasses on, or if, like before, he would be visible only when she took them off. However, even with her glasses perched in their usual position on her small nose, Johnny was crystal clear. His hair was pushed off his face, like he had run his hands through it repeatedly. She was a little shocked to see him looking less than perfect – he had never had even a stray hair before. Now it stood up in little tufts at his crown, and his face was creased from sleeping. But that face...it was the same. The same strong jaw and well-formed lips, the same slashing brows and perfect nose. The same piercing blue eyes. Those eyes regarded her now as she regarded him. For a moment, gazing down at his beloved face, she forgot her awkwardness and fear, and she drank him in, every precious detail. She felt her face split into a grin so wide that her dry, cracked lips protested painfully. She pressed her hands to them to ease the sharp pain and soothe their sudden trembling. A sob tore from her throat, and Maggie wondered briefly at the unpredictability of female emotion – smiling like an idiot one moment and holding back sobs the next. She fell to her knees beside the bed and pressed her face against the arm that was unencumbered by his I.V. For several long moments she cried, resting her face against his warm skin and pressing soft kisses into his palm. He made no move to pull away and said nothing but sat silently as she eventually calmed the storm of tears and spoke again.

"Johnny?" she spoke again, her voice shaking with emotion. "You're here. I thought I had lost you." She gripped his arm and raised her eyes to his once more. Slowly, Maggie's euphoria drenched senses started registering several things at once. First, Johnny didn't seem overjoyed to see her. Second, his stare wasn't hostile...but it was guarded and very tense, his lips pressed into a tight line, a deep groove between his brows. She could tell he was waiting for her to continue.

"Johnny?" This was the third time she had spoken his name in the very same manner, but he had yet to move or respond. Something was very wrong. Maggie's hands fell to her sides. She backed away a step. His eyes stayed fixed on her face as he watched her retreat. Maggie felt the tears well up in her eyes again, but this time for an entirely different reason. This wasn't the reunion she had imagined.

The door behind Maggie swung open suddenly, and Maggie turned guiltily, coming face to face with Principal Bailey. Maggie couldn't see her expression; the light behind her threw shadows across her face as she halted in the doorway, clearly surprised to find Maggie in the room. Jillian Bailey looked beyond Maggie to

Johnny, lying as still as a corpse, watching the drama unfolding in front of him. She looked back at Maggie, and then leaned over and turned on the light, illuminating the room in a wash of fluorescent white.

"Hello Margaret," Principal Bailey said in her very official school administrator's voice.

"Principal Bailey," Maggie responded, equally deferential and polite. She tried not to hunch or reach up to wipe her eyes or rub the tear streaks from her cheeks. Doing so would only draw attention to them and further alert the woman of her distress. Jillian Bailey's eyes ran from the top of Maggie's head to her colorfully painted toes. Shad had insisted on painting them purple, gold and green, in honor of the Lakers, and not only was he horrible at staying within the lines, the colors made her toenails look like he had beaten them with a hammer. She curled her toes self-consciously.

"Have a seat, Margaret...or should I call you Maggie?" Principal Bailey's voice had softened, and Maggie was suddenly certain that the woman didn't miss much. She nodded her head toward a chair not far from Johnny's bed and pulled another from the wall, creating an intimate little half circle with the bed. Maggie looked down at her toes, wishing this episode of the Twilight Zone was over. She sat primly on the edge of the chair and folded her hands in her lap, locking her fingers tightly to keep them from shaking.

"Maggie would be fine," Maggie replied belatedly, as Principal Bailey slid into the chair beside her. Maggie stole another look at Johnny, but his face looked carved in stone, his hands lying loosely on the blankets in front of him. What was going on?? Maggie suddenly wanted to shake him or pull at his rumpled hair, anything to shake the frozen look from his face.

"Johnny, this is Margaret O'Bannon – Maggie," Principal Bailey said briskly. "She's recovering from the fire as well. She's a senior at Honeyville High School this year and a very accomplished dancer." Maggie's head started to spin. Why was Principal Bailey acting like it wasn't one o'clock in the morning in a hospital room, like Maggie hadn't been caught somewhere she had no logical reason to be, and acting like Johnny Kinross was a new student in need of someone to show him to his homeroom class?

"Maggie," she continued, "This is Johnny – "

"I know who he is!" Maggie interrupted sharply, her eyes flashing to meet Jillian Bailey's startled gaze. "You know that, don't you? I know exactly who he is." Maggie lifted her chin stubbornly and crossed her arms. Enough of this charade.

Johnny still wasn't saying anything, but his eyes had narrowed and his hands now gripped the rails alongside his bed.

"So who am I?" he queried slowly. The hair on Maggie's arms rose and a shudder ran through her. His voice taunted her with memories of sweet words and quiet declarations. She steeled herself and met his eyes, confusion coloring her voice.

"You are Johnny Kinross."

"And how do we know each other......Margaret?" Maggie gasped sharply. Did he mean to be cruel? Or was he hesitant to reveal himself in front of the woman who watched them in fascination?

"Don't you remember?" She stared at him, willing herself not to betray her devastation. He held her stare silently for several long breaths, and then shook his head once. No. He didn't remember.

"Tell me!" His voice was sharp now, as hers had been minutes before. She stared at him mutely, stunned heat spreading from the pit of her belly to the tips of her fingers. How in the world do you tell someone what he is to you...when he is your whole world? How do you tell him you love him – and that *he loved you* – when he can't seem to remember your name? Maggie was going to be sick. She struggled to her feet, the room spinning and the fear inside her clawing to get out.

"TELL ME!!!" Johnny roared suddenly, his face contorting in anger. Maggie flinched as if he had struck her, and she reached toward him instinctively, unsure of whether to ward him off or pull him close. Jillian Bailey jumped to her feet and grabbed Johnny's hands. He pulled them from her viciously and looked at Maggie again. He pointed at her.

"You know me? You tell me everything you know!" He was no longer shouting, but his voice was emphatic and his eyes were bright with feeling. The finger he leveled at her shook, and he dropped his hands back into his lap, shaking his head with obvious despair.

The door flew open behind them, and all three of them jerked to guilty attention.

"What are you people doin' in here? And what's all the yellin' about!!" A small black nurse flew into the room, shoes squeaking and arms akimbo. She rushed to Johnny's bedside and started looking at his monitors and fussing over him like there had been a murder attempt.

"His heart is racing!! It's the middle of the night, and ya'll are havin' a tea party in here?" She looked at Maggie, stuck out her lips, and furrowed her thin black brow. "And what do you think you're doin' in here, Missy? Visitin' hours are way past...and you belong a few doors down, if memory serves!"

"Please," Jillian Bailey jumped into the fray, "Maggie has been asking to see Johnny for days, and everyone has denied her. He saved her life when the school burned down. She wanted to say thank you and make sure he was okay, right Maggie?"

Maggie nodded emphatically, keeping her eyes averted from Johnny's face. It was all she could do not to run shrieking from the room.

"I found her in here, but I didn't have the heart to turn her away. I'll take her back to her room myself in just a minute. Please, Tima?" Jillian Bailey was in full appeal mode now.

Tima harrumphed and shook her head, making the loops at her ears jangle cheerfully. "Five minutes...you hear, Jillian? And don't think I don't know what you're doin' when you start going all 'Please Tima' on me..." She winked at Jillian to take the punch out of her words and marched out of the room, tossing a hand toward the three of them as if to say "go ahead, I'm through with you." The door swooshed closed behind her.

"Fatima and I were friends in high school," Jillian explained inanely, although no explanation had been requested. Johnny was frozen in stony silence, and Maggie was clinging to her composure with shaking fingers. "I tutored her through English, and she tutored me through math. She never let anyone call her Tima, as far as I know....except me." Jillian smirked a little, and for a minute Maggie saw the resemblance between Johnny and his sister. It was fleeting, but it was there in the way she held her mouth.

Silence descended on the room again, and Maggie felt Johnny's eyes on her like a physical weight. She turned to Jillian desperately.

"How did you know Johnny saved me from the fire?" Her words came out like an accusation, but it was meant more for the boy in the bed than the woman at her side.

"Gus," Principal Bailey answered succinctly. "He told me that Johnny had found Shad and was carrying him on his shoulder when Gus went into the school. If not for Johnny, Shad would have most certainly died. No one would have found him in that locker." She paused and looked at Johnny as if trying to impress what she was saying upon his memory. Then she looked at Maggie. "Gus said you told him that Johnny carried you out as well." She waited for Maggie to pick up the telling of the story.

Maggie nodded briefly. The memory of being swept up in Johnny's arms felt like a mirage, but she clung to it. "He did carry me out! You did!" She looked at Johnny fiercely then, daring him to disagree. "I didn't want to leave you. I told you to let me stay with you. But you carried me out. I don't know how, but you did." Johnny was unfazed by his own heroics. He shook his head once, negating her words.

Maggie gagged on the emotion in her throat, and her eyes began to sting at the indignity of it all. Why did he keep shaking his head? If you truly loved someone, how could you forget?

"You don't remember me? You don't remember anything at all?" Her voice shook, and her stomach heaved in dread.

It was his turn to be fierce, and she could see he struggled to rein in his temper. "I remember everything just fine! I remember going to the new school looking for Roger Carlton. There was a bunch of kids all gathered to see a fight – but Roger Carlton didn't want to fight fair. He set up a little ambush. He messed up my car. I remember Billy running down the hallway waving that damn gun. I remember Billy yelling out. I remember going over the balcony, falling. I remember Billy...." Johnny stopped then and ran his hands up into his hair. The familiarity of the gesture hit Maggie like a physical blow. She gripped her hands tightly in her lap to keep from reaching out to him, to keep from touching him. He wouldn't welcome her touch.

"Billy's dead, isn't he?" Johnny choked out. "I need to tell my momma. She's not gonna take this well."

Maggie's lips trembled, and the tears swam in her eyes. Oh, dear God! He was just realizing they were gone?! Oh, Johnny!" She hid her face in her hands, overcome with sympathy. This wasn't happening.

"Johnny...." Jillian Bailey stood and touched his shoulder. "Momma already knows. All of that happened a long time ago."

"What the hell are you talking about?" Johnny was yelling again, so loudly the entire hospital would be coming down around them. "None of this makes any sense! I don't know you! I don't know HER!" His eyes flew to Maggie, who had reached for him again, needing to comfort him, needing to touch him. "I don't know where I am or what I am doing here!" Maggie dropped her hand and reached for the bars on Johnny's bed. Her legs trembled and her heart bled.

The door banged open again, and this time Fatima wasn't alone. A bevy of medical people swarmed the room.

"OUT!" Fatima roared, pointing at the door. "Jillian! Take that girl back to her room." Johnny had pulled his IV out of his wrist, causing blood to stream down his raised arm, and he was attempting to pull the bandages from his shoulder. Someone pulled Maggie from Johnny's side, yanking her hands from the bars that were supporting her. Fatima bodily restrained Johnny as someone injected something into him. His shouting and struggling lessened almost immediately. Jillian Bailey wrapped her arms around Maggie's shoulders and led her from Johnny's room. Maggie collapsed onto her bed and sobbed. Jillian Bailey sat beside her, crying quietly with her, until the sun nuzzled its way into her hospital room, slipping golden fingers through the slats in her blinds and reminding her that life continued, whether or not Johnny had lost his.

***

Maggie begged to see Johnny again, regardless of his feelings for her. His despair and fear made her almost crazed with worry. He was alone, his entire world gone, and Maggie knew acutely what that felt like. Alone without a friend in the world. She would be Johnny's friend, even if friendship was all he wanted. She pleaded with whomever would listen, beseeching them to allow her access to him. Finally, toward the end of the next day, Jillian Bailey came back to her room and shut the door firmly behind her. She looked dead on her feet.

"Maggie," Jillian Bailey sat on the foot of her bed. "I know you're asking to see Johnny. I know you have feelings for him, and you're worried about him. You can't see him right now, though. He doesn't remember you, and he doesn't want to see you."

Maggie nodded, taking the blow in stride. "I won't ask him for anything or make him uncomfortable. I just want him to know he isn't alone."

Maggie swallowed the tears in her throat and kept her face composed. She was good at that. Many years of being disappointed and rejected had made her an expert. She'd never been hit or slapped or abused, but she'd been shunned, neglected and ignored. One year she'd been placed with a new foster family right before the holidays. They didn't want their "family" time at Christmas "interrupted", and they didn't want extended family who would be visiting to feel "uncomfortable." So she had spent the holiday in her room, listening to sounds of revelry and laughter floating up the stairs from the gathering below. It had sounded like fun. They had brought her a plate of food on Christmas Eve but had almost forgotten on Christmas day. She had many stories like that one. Lonely was something she was intimately familiar with, and something she didn't want Johnny to suffer from, even if she wasn't his preferred company.

Jillian Bailey nodded, and her eyes searched Maggie's blank face for several seconds. "I don't understand how any of this happened. But it did. And I promise you I will do everything in my power to help him and to take care of him as long as he needs me to.

He won't be alone." Her tone was tender as she reached for Maggie's hand.

"I'll be waiting," Maggie whispered, and her composure cracked the smallest bit. "Will you tell him? Tell him I will be here whenever he needs me."

Jillian nodded and rose from Maggie's bed. The next day, Maggie was released from the hospital.

~3~

A Time to Be Born

Bobby and the Bell Tones were pretty good. They looked slick and professional in their matching light blue sport coats and jaunty black bow ties. The guy at the mic could really sing, and they played all the crowd-pleasers, with enough slow numbers that the boys could hold their girls every other song. Johnny arched his back and tried not to pull at the collar of his too-tight bow tie. His white sports coat was too hot, and he longed for denim and boots. Tonight he was slicked up and pressed into the fancy duds his momma had insisted he wear. He had thought he should make a statement and wear his leather jacket to the Prom, but Momma nixed that idea.

The cheerful pink carnation pinned to his lapel defied the heat of the overcrowded, over-decorated gymnasium. The room had been transformed into a water world for its "Under the Sea" theme, complete with fountains and aquariums. Huge fishing nets hung overhead, filled with seafoam green balloons that were clearly meant to look like bubbles. Giant glittering starfish hung precariously from the nets, and the entrance had even been made to look like the gangplank of a sunken ship. Irene Honeycutt's daddy had given the prom committee, of which Irene was president, a healthy donation, and they had put it to good use. So often the band was the thing they scrimped on, but not tonight. The kids were dancing their socks off.

Johnny hadn't really wanted to go to the Prom, but Carter had a thing for Peggy Wilkey, and he had begged Johnny to ask her so they could double date. Johnny had asked Carter why he didn't ask her himself. Carter moaned and claimed his momma said Peggy was a tramp and he had to take his cousin because she would never get asked. Johnny liked to dance, so he'd taken pity on Carter; plus, Johnny liked Peggy, and he knew her daddy would hate it if he asked her. Peggy's daddy was a cop, and he was always pulling Johnny over for the slightest thing. Johnny figured making the old man sweat a little was just payback, and it was nice to stick a thumb in his eye when he got the chance. He watched as Carter swung Peggy around the dance floor, Peggy's pink dress swinging around the two of them as they moved. Carter's cousin Nancy didn't look too happy about it, but at least she'd gotten to come. She caught him looking at her and immediately elbowed the equally glum girls sitting at her sides. Their heads swiveled toward him and they straightened their backs and fluffed their skirts in syncopated rhythm. Then they all stared at him like a pack of piranhas. Johnny rapidly shifted his attention elsewhere.

Irene Honeycutt tapped her feet and looked longingly out at the dance floor. Roger Carlton was surrounded by a bunch of his friends, chatting away, ignoring his date. Johnny had already asked Irene to dance once, just to get under Roger's skin. He started forward to ask her again when he saw the girl. She was in fire-engine red, and her dark hair was long and unbound, waving past her shoulders and swooping across one eye, creating a peek-a-boo effect. None of the girls wore their hair long these days. They all wore it in pinned curls and shoulder length styles with curled bangs. This girl's hair looked like that movie star that Momma liked – the one from the 1940's...Veronica Lake. She wasn't very popular anymore. Momma said Veronica Lake had a bad reputation for drinking too much and getting married and divorced too many times. Momma said if it was a man drinking too much booze and spending too much time with the ladies, no one would mind. In fact, he would probably be more popular! She defended Veronica Lake like it was something personal. Johnny shook his head, banishing thoughts of his mother and her own flawed reputation.

The new girl looked like she had come alone. She walked down the gangplank entrance and paused, as if trying to figure out what to do next. She clutched a little silver handbag in her pale hands. Johnny's eyes traveled from her hands to her smooth bare shoulders and down her slim form encased in red. The bodice was tight, and his eyes lingered where they shouldn't. The skirt was a very full tulle -- that's what Peggy had called it-- as was the style of most of the other girls' dresses, but no one was wearing red. All the other girls were wearing different pinks and pastels. This girl stood out like a sore thumb...or a rose among carnations. The girl seemed to suddenly register this fact, and she looked down at her dress and back up again, out at the swirling shades of pale. She turned slightly, as if trying to decide whether to leave the way she had come. Johnny couldn't let that happen. He started to walk toward her, weaving in and out of the dancing couples.

When he was about halfway across the floor her eyes latched onto him, and he saw the color rise on her cheekbones and her hand flutter to her chest. She watched him like she knew him, like she expected him to be there. He knew he'd never seen her before...he would remember if he had. She looked a little like Irene Honeycutt in her coloring and the wide blue set of her eyes. He wondered briefly if they were related. And then all thoughts of Irene Honeycutt fled. The girl smiled at him, and his heart hitched and his step faltered. He stopped several feet in front of her, and for the life of him he couldn't prevent the smile that spread across his own face in response. His usual swagger failed him. He felt like he was twelve years old.

"Hi," she said sweetly and smiled again. She looked at the dance floor and back at him. "Are you going to ask me to dance?"

Johnny held out his hand, and she walked forward and slid hers into it. Her hand was smooth and small, and he had the inexplicable urge to grip it tightly so she couldn't slip away. He led her to the dance floor just as the music kicked up into a rollicking swing. Damn. He wanted to pull her close, not swing her around. He turned to ask her if she wanted to wait this one out. One look at her, and he knew what her response would be. She was practically vibrating with the music, her eyes sparkling, waiting for him to engage. He hoped she could dance.

Without a word, Johnny took her little purse and shoved it into the inner pocket of his tuxedo jacket. She couldn't dance with that thing in her hand. She didn't protest but gave him both of her hands and lifted her eyes to his. And they began to move. Oh yeah, she could dance. It was like she knew what he was going to do next, like she understood his timing and had danced with him before. He spun her around, pulling her in and out, and watched her in amazement as she matched him step for high-paced step. The kids around them started to take notice, and the space around them widened, clearing their way for more ambitious steps. Her long hair streamed around her, and her skirts flew around her slim legs as her feet dared him to keep up. He tossed her up, and her legs snaked from side to side and up into a hand stand and quickly down before her skirts revealed more than she would have liked. There was a gasp and a smattering of applause, and Johnny swung her around his hips like a hula hoop. She laughed out loud and whirled back into his arms like it was where she belonged. The music ended with a crash of cymbals, and their audience whooped and hollered. Johnny thought he heard Carter and Jimbo taking credit for some of his moves. He laughed and looped his arms around his partner's waist, pulling her into him. The music cooperated, and the Bell Tones began a slow doo-wop as Bobby crooned his affection into the microphone. She raised her eyes to his, and his breath hitched once more. Her eyes were so blue and welcoming, and he desperately wanted to kiss her. Man, he was known to move fast, but not this fast! He had met her only minutes before, and here he was, wanting to kiss her in the middle of a crowded dance floor. Her lips were parted in a smile, and her slim arms were embracing him in a dance that felt suddenly too intimate and yet not nearly intimate enough. She raised her chin the slightest degree, and his eyes dropped to her mouth. She breathed his name. "Johnny."

His eyes closed as he felt her whisper cross his lips.

"Johnny...."

And then she was gone. His arms still held the memory of her form. His face was flushed from the exertions of their dancing. He could still hear the song they had moved to echoing in his head. His eyes snapped open, and he shot up in his bed, only to cry out as the pain in his chest and right shoulder awoke right along with him.

"Johnny?" It wasn't her voice anymore. He wondered at what point it had changed. The woman who professed to be his sister stood at the side of his bed.

"Your heart monitor started beeping like you were in cardiac arrest. I'm sorry I woke you...It just scared me. You must have been having quite the nightmare."

Johnny almost laughed at the sheer irony of her words. The nightmare existed only when he opened his eyes. He refrained from commenting though. It would only sound like a complaint, and he knew she was only trying to help him. She had barely left his side, and for all the confusion and anger he kept hurling her way, she never lost her temper with him or addressed him in frustration. He had done what she had told him, only because he didn't know what else to do. He claimed he had no memory of who he was, and she had done all the rest, running interference with his doctors and making sure he was taken care of.

She looked like his mother. She wasn't glamorous or beautiful, but the resemblance was still there. She looked like Billy, too. Her hair was dark like his had been, and she had the same cowlick in front. This made it easier to accept that she was family...and harder to accept that they were gone. Johnny slid back down to a prone position and stared at the ceiling. The late afternoon sun peeked beneath the blinds at his windows, reminding him that he slept constantly. They said it was a normal part of the healing process, it must be working, because he was healing fast. He couldn't care less about that. He just welcomed the escape sleep provided from the despair that was every waking moment. He slid his eyelids closed, willing himself to return to the dream.

It had been a dream, after all. He recognized the mystery girl now that he was awake. It was her, the girl who had sobbed her heart out at his bedside the day before. The girl he hadn't been able to remember. Margaret. Maggie. In the dream she hadn't worn glasses, but it was her. The prom had been real though - - down to the smallest detail. He remembered it all clearly. After all, it had only been a few months ago. He stopped himself then. According to him, that is. It wasn't 1958 anymore. Jillian Bailey said it was now March 5, 2011. That would make Prom 1958 an event that had happened almost fifty-three years ago.

He had taken Peggy Wilkey. She had worn a pink strapless gown that displayed her generous cleavage to perfection. Carter had just about died when he had seen her, and he had spent the whole night trying to woo her, despite the fact that he was supposed to be showing his frumpy cousin a good time. It was all the same as in the dream: the people, the fishing nets and glittering starfish, the discomfort of his tie and his wish to be free of it. All of it the same....except for the girl, except for Maggie. Funny, in his dream she had been wearing the dress Irene Honeycutt had worn. He remembered that dress. Nobody else had worn red. Pastels were the flavor of the occasion, and Irene had shown up in that little number and tongues had wagged and wagged. Irene had wilted under the scrutiny. He had thought she looked wonderful, but apparently she wished she had chosen differently.

In his dream, Irene had worn a fluffy peach dress with little bejeweled straps. He had danced with her, just like he had in real life. The song was even the same. Just the dress was different. Strange, that. Why would his subconscious mind dress Maggie in Irene's dress and place her at the prom? He could still see her, standing there with her long hair and that red dress, like she had become part of the memory.

***

"He doesn't remember me," Maggie spoke the words that had been bottled up inside her since she had been released from the hospital the morning before. "It's like none of it ever happened, Gus. It's like he fell from the balcony in 1958 and woke up in 2011. The years in Purgatory are gone, wiped away – and the only thing that's left is the time that passed while he was there." Maggie and Gus bounced along in Gus's old truck, Gus at the wheel, Maggie leaning against the passenger door, staring out into the late afternoon sky.

They were alone for the first time since she'd arrived home. Irene had sent them to the store to pick up a couple of things for dinner, and Shad was out with some new friends. His star had risen since he'd survived the fire at the school. He'd been invited to several parties and been begged time and time again to share his tale. He and Gus had agreed to leave Johnny's part in the story out of the retelling. In Shad's story, he had forced his way out of the locker, only to collapse before he'd exited the school. His grandpa then acquired hero status when he had found Shad and carried him out to fresh air and safety.

Gus reached over and grabbed Maggie's hand, holding it tightly in his. He didn't say anything; he just held her hand. His sweet gesture was her undoing. Maggie felt the dam burst, the disappointment and disbelief pouring out as the tears came. Gus pulled to the side of the road, threw the truck into park, and pulled her close. He wrapped his arms around her and soothed her with a gentle, "there, there, Miss Margaret."

"I....th-thought it...it...w-was a mir-miracle," Maggie gulped, clinging to Gus's wiry arms.

"It is," Gus responded quietly. "It is a miracle."

"No it-it...isn't." Maggie struggled to push herself upright, to look into Gus's face. "It's just another form of purgatory...don't y-you see? It's a n-nightmare for J-Johnny." Maggie scrubbed her face, trying to make the tears stop flowing. She breathed in and out several times, fighting for dominion over her despair. She didn't speak until she felt exhaustion start to douse her raging emotions, and her tears slowed to a stop.

"You know how they say be careful what you wish for?" Her voice was so soft it was amazing Gus even heard.

But he did hear, and he nodded, his dark eyes full of sympathy.

"I wished so hard that Johnny could have a second chance….that we would have a chance. I think I made it happen, just by force of will. Now the universe is laughing…and I am once again the butt of the joke."

"I think sometimes we do make things happen….just by wantin' 'em bad enough. That doesn't mean things is gonna be easy, though, even when you get what you want. Life is work, girl. Love is work. Plus, fallin' in love is fun. Ain't nothin' like it. Just think, you get to fall in love with Johnny all over again."

"I never fell out of love with Johnny."

"But you're acting like it's over," he rebuked softly. "Love isn't pretty, Miss Margaret. I think that's why so many people don't make it. They don't appreciate the hard times. They expect it to be all airbrushed and touched up like the pictures you see in them magazine ads. Why, just the other day, I was looking at some pictures in a magazine my daughter Malia left laying around."

"Gus!"

Gus leveled a look at Maggie that had her biting her lip and trying not to laugh, as heartsick as she was.

"There was an article showing how they made the models in the pictures look a certain way. They trimmed off a little weight here and there, touched up a blemish, even made their womanly assets look bigger, and when it was all done, the woman didn't even look like a woman anymore!"

"Womanly assets?"

"You know what I mean, Miss Margaret," Gus chided. "They made the woman look like a doll - all fake and plastic, with her face painted on." Gus sighed dramatically, as if someone had taken a marker to the pages of his Bible. "When my wife Mona got cancer, she lost a lot of weight. She used to have beautiful curves and thick curly hair. Her hair fell out when she went through chemo. She cried and told me she didn't think I would love her anymore." Gus's voice had grown soft, and his eyes were bright with the painful memories.

Maggie squeezed the hand that still held hers, comforting him in return. Gus sat without speaking for a time.

"The truth is, Margaret, I just loved Mona more. I saw her strength and her patience, her gentle heart, and her love for me and her desire to shield me from pain. All those things were more beautiful to me than her curves or her pretty hair. All those wonderful traits were on display like they'd never been before, and she took my breath away. I loved her more when she died than I did the day I married her. The woman I married was beautiful, but the woman I lost was stunning.

"Don't forget your miracle so quickly, Miss Margaret. The hard times are often the best times, 'cause they draw you closer. You should be singin' hallelujahs from the rooftops - celebratin'."

Gus's voice was gentle, and Maggie didn't take offense. Though she thought she had reason enough to *want* to forget, she wouldn't forget her miracle - not now, not ever. Even though he had forgotten her.

~4~
A Time to Plant

"Maggie?" Irene started, dishing up a small portion of her famous coleslaw. "Remember a few months ago when we cleaned up the attic and donated all that stuff to Goodwill?"

Maggie nodded absently, wishing she could find a place to dance her despair away. She ached for the escape and considered removing her bed from her room to give her more floor space. Since the school had burned down and she'd been released from the hospital, she hadn't danced once. She needed it more than the food Irene kept piling on her plate. She needed it almost as desperately as she needed Johnny.

"We didn't by any chance give away a record player, did we?" Irene worried. "I don't remember seeing it. I promised the ladies at the historical society that we could have it for our auction coming up here in a few weeks. It should be worth something. It still works just fine, and it has all those old 45s in perfect condition." Irene sighed. "I got nervous all of a sudden that maybe I'd had one of my senior moments and given it away without thinking."

Something niggled at Maggie, and she sat for a minute, trying to pull it forward. "I know we didn't give a record player away...but I don't remember seeing it either. Whose record player was it, Aunt Irene?"

"It was Lizzie's. She loved it. It was in her room upstairs until she got married and moved out. When Roger and I moved back into this house after Daddy died, it was still there, right where she had left it. When I made that room into a nursery, I moved it upstairs into the attic. It hasn't been used since – but it still worked when I moved it up there so....Maggie? Are you all right, dear?"

"Did she used to have a bear she called Jamie?" Maggie blurted out.

Irene blinked once, twice, and then stuttered out, "Why....yes! She did. She named him after James Dean...." Her voice trailed off.

"What Maggie? What is it?"

"I saw her....I mean, I think I did. When I was in a coma....I had a dream. At least I think it was a dream. I was in her room. The record player sat under one window. There were records on the floor. She was sitting on her bed, talking to the bear. It was so funny that I laughed. She saw me. She thought I was a ghost...."

Gus and Irene were staring at her, their spoons halfway to their mouths. In unison, they set their spoons back on their plates.

"She saw you?" Irene squeaked.

"Yes! We talked for few moments and then....something pulled me away. Gus pulled me away. He was telling me to wake up, that Johnny needed me. She, Lizzie, called after me, and told me to stay." Maggie's eyes were unfocused, looking beyond Gus and Irene, remembering how real it had all been. "It wasn't the first time, either. The other time I was with Johnny – riding next to him in your daddy's big black car. A Buick?" Irene's jaw dropped.

"Daddy did have a big, black, Buick....but why would Johnny be driving it?"

"He was taking it to Gene's for a tune-up....I think. I remember feeling so happy, wishing I could stay right there beside him...but he couldn't see me like Lizzie could. Although he did say my name..." Maggie's voice trailed off in puzzlement. She had forgotten that part.

"Lawdy, lawdy," Gus marveled with a short whistle. A deep frown curved his mouth, and his eyes were wide with fear. "You best be careful, Miss Margaret."

"Careful?....Why?" Maggie and Irene both gazed at Gus in surprise.

"This all reminds me of my grandma. She saw ghosts…just like you do. Just like you, she claimed most the time it was like she was seein' somethin' from the past, someone doin' somethin' they'd done many times. Or she'd see somethin' happen that had a great deal of emotion attached to it…battle scenes, things like that. She said sometimes the things she saw were so real that she almost forgot where she was, like she got pulled into their stories. One time she was traveling North with my grandpa….this was in the early nineteen twenties or so, mind you…long past the days of the Underground Railroad. You know 'bout the Underground Railroad, Miss Margaret?"

Maggie nodded her head. "It was a network of routes and safe houses and people that helped runaway slaves get to the free states and Canada, right?

"That's right, during the early to mid 1800's," Gus agreed, nodding with her. "My grandma and grandpa ended up staying the night in a home that had been along one of those routes. For some reason or other, my grandma couldn't sleep that night. She was restless and she didn't want to disturb my grandpa. She thought she could step outside and get some fresh air, maybe walk a little bit." Gus suddenly stood up from the table, as if the story was making him nervous. He paced a little and then bade them to follow him to Irene's little front sitting room. When they were all seated, he continued his story.

"A short ways behind the house there was a big, dried up creek bed. The folks my grandparents were stayin' with said it'd been dry all summer long, but that night, when my grandma slipped outside, she thought she could smell water. The moon was full, and it was one of those nights where everything is all bathed in moonlight; she said she could see almost as well as if it was day.

"When she got down to the bank of the creek my grandma said it was dry, just like the folks said it would be....but she could still smell the water." Maggie felt the hair on her neck prickle. She had forgotten how she had been able to smell Johnny and the scent of cigars and cologne in Jackson Honeycutt's car. Maggie forced her attention back to Gus, almost afraid to hear what he had to say next.

"Grandma said she closed her eyes, breathing the smell in. She said it smelled so fresh and cool...but then she smelled something else. She said it was a smell she didn't immediately recognize. She sniffed the air, and suddenly she knew. She said it was a sharp, ripe scent...like someone who has worked long hours in the sun. But it was more than just the smell of sweat and labor...It was the smell of fear." Gus's hands began to shake a little bit, and he clasped them around the armrests on the old chair. He rubbed the worn fabric with the tips of his long fingers and took several deep breaths. Gus looked up at Maggie then, and Maggie felt a frisson of alarm. Gus was frightened by what he was saying.

"When my grandma opened her eyes, she saw them. There were three women, two men, and a handful of children walking up the creek bed. My grandma said she cried out in surprise, but they didn't seem to see her. She said they were maybe ten yards downstream when suddenly she noticed there was water in the creek. It came up to the knees of the men and women who were walking in it. The children were holding the hands of the adults and had to struggle a little to keep upright. A light breeze was blowing toward where my grandma stood, and she caught that scent again....the smell of raw terror. Their clothes didn't match the time period, and my grandma realized she was seeing something that had happened long ago. They were moving quickly, as quickly as the water would allow, and my grandma watched them as they neared and then passed her and walked out of sight beyond the bend in the creek.

"She realized they was slaves...runaway slaves. My grandma says she felt a connection so strong that she was sure someone in that little group had to be kin. She said it was almost like she could hear another heartbeat, and it called to her own. She didn't want to leave. She said she wanted to run after them, that she almost couldn't bear to stay behind.

"Then she heard another sound, and it made her blood run cold. She heard dogs. She said the baying sounded like it was comin' from everywhere at once. And then, just like with the water in the creek bed, one minute it wasn't there and the next it was. She said there were men on horses with dogs, obviously trying to run down the runaways. But unlike the slaves, the dogs could see her. They veered off one side of the bank, across the water, and up onto the side of the creek where she stood, watchin' all of it happening maybe seventy-five years after the fact. The men on horseback followed the dogs. My grandmother began to run. She turned back toward the house, screaming for my grandpa, and suddenly..."

Gus stopped and mopped his forehead, which glistened with a light sheen of sweat. "Suddenly she couldn't see the house no more. It wasn't there. She could feel the dogs closin' in, and she heard one of the men cry out and knew that he had spotted her too."

Irene was suddenly clasping Maggie's hand tightly in her own, and her eyes were as wide as saucers.

"My grandma was wearing a long white nightgown with a shawl wrapped around her. She said the ends of the shawl must have been streaming out behind her because she felt when one of the dogs caught a piece of it, and it was yanked from her shoulders. She stumbled a bit and another dog was immediately at her heels. One dog sunk his teeth into the back of her leg, and she screamed for my grandpa again. She said she knew she was done for...and in that moment she saw my grandpa's face in her mind and held on tight to his image, wishin' for him like she'd never wished before.

"And then he was there, grabbin' her up in his arms..." Maggie and Irene breathed out in unison, one gusty sound of relief. "The dogs were gone, the men on horses, nowhere to be seen. Grandma had awakened the whole house with her screams. Grandpa apologized to everyone and hustled Grandma back to their room with some excuse as to why she was outside screaming bloody murder."

"So it was just....a vision?" Irene asked timidly.

"Of sorts..." Gus nodded. "But when they got back to the room, my grandma's nightgown was soaked through in back from the knee down."

"So there had actually been water. She actually saw the runaway slaves walking in a creek filled with water," Maggie whispered.

"It wasn't soaked through in water, Miss Margaret, it was soaked through in blood. Grandma had a huge bite mark on her left calf. She showed me the scar many years later when she told me this story. She hadn't just seen a vision, she'd been there. For that moment in time, she wasn't just an observer of the past, she was a full-fledged participant.

"My grandma always wore a St. Christopher medal that my grandpa gave her around her neck. She told me St. Christopher was the patron saint of travelers." Gus paused and looked at Maggie. "She was a traveler of a different kind, I s'pose. She said there were places that pulled at her, as if the layers of time were very thin, and if she wasn't careful she would fall right through and find herself in another time completely."

"What did she mean by 'layers of time?'" Maggie was spellbound by the direction the conversation had taken.

"She believed that time wasn't a big long line of events. Grandma said time was like layers of thin cloth folded back and forth, one layer above the other, accordion style. She said sometimes certain events seeped through from one layer to the next, creating a stain that was visible even on the uppermost folds. Visible to some, at least."

"So something happens in the past -- a powerful event or something that is repeated enough to create a...a stain and that stain seeps through to the present?" Maggie pondered aloud.

"That was her theory. It made sense, especially given that she was constantly seein' people and things from the past. She steered clear of places that were part of her family history. She felt like the blood connection with an ancestor, combined with a location where that ancestor had lived, created a conduit – a place where the layers of time were so thin as to be precarious to someone with her gift."

Gus stood and walked to Maggie. Leaning down a little so he could make eye contact, he spoke very slowly and succinctly. "You have her gift, Miss Margaret, the same gift as my grandma. It is a gift YOUR grandmother had, as well. Your grandma lived in this house, and you live here now. That's some mighty thin layers..."

"This house could be a...conduit?" Irene fluttered her hands in front of her face, as if she'd just been told the house was haunted. She looked ready to collapse, and Gus reached for her hands apologetically. He soothed and shushed, reassuring Irene that the house was nothing of the sort, but he looked at Maggie over Irene's bowed head, and though he said nothing more to her on the subject, his eyes spoke volumes.

~5~

A Time to Cast Away

"He wants to see you, Maggie." Jillian Bailey stood at the door and hunched her shoulders against the March winds that signified the last gasp of winter. April would be here shortly, and soon Honeyville would be awash in spring. Maggie wished it would hurry. She was cold all the time, inside and out. With spring came graduation, and May couldn't come soon enough. She had no desire to leave Irene, but Honeyville had become a very painful place to be.

Maggie rose and came to the door. She still wore the clothes she had worn to bed. It was still fairly early for a Saturday morning. Jillian Bailey looked tired and thinner than the last time Maggie had seen her. I guess having your brother rise from the dead had that effect. For Lazarus it had only been days....for Johnny it had been decades.

"Did he tell you why?" Maggie asked quietly, looking into the woman's weary face. Hope was threatening to well up inside her heart.

"No. He just asked me if I knew where to find you." She hesitated a moment. "He rarely asks for anything….so when he does, I like to help him if I can." Maggie felt the grip of the guilt and pain she always felt when she thought of Johnny these days.

"If you want to grab your coat…I can take you right now." Principal Bailey looked so hopeful. But Maggie didn't want to ride with her. She would see Johnny, but she wanted to be able to leave if and when she needed to, without having to ask for a ride home

"I need to jump in the shower and get dressed…I'll be there in an hour. You can tell him I'll see him then."

Jillian looked as if she wanted to protest but then nodded her head briefly. "All right. Just…please, don't take too long. The fact that he wants to see you is a good sign, I think. I don't want him to change his mind before you get there."

Maggie nodded and shut the door behind Johnny's careworn sister. She ran for the stairs, pulling her things off as she went. Less than 45 minutes later, she was showered, dressed and blow-dried, and grabbing the keys from the rack. She wore the same blue jeans and purple shirt she'd worn that day in the school mechanics shop, the day she and Johnny had shared their first kiss. She hesitated for a moment, an idea popping into her mind. It couldn't hurt. She raced back up the stairs and wrenched up the lid of her window seat, lifting Roger Carlton's old scrapbook up and out. It might give Johnny some answers...or some proof of what had happened in the years he had lost.

Jillian Bailey lived in the same house she had been born in. It was a tidy bungalow with a wide front porch and a garage that had been added on in more recent years. The grass was neat, and the flowerbeds had been cleared of winter debris, the dirt turned in preparation for spring flowers. Irene said it had been Clark Bailey's childhood home as well. He had lived there as a bachelor and then when he'd married Johnny's mother it had become their home, the home they had raised their daughter in. Maggie wondered if Johnny would find remnants of his mother there and if it would bring him comfort. She hoped so. She slid into the drive . Belle the Caddie had run perfectly since Johnny had given her the tune-up. She wondered if she should tell him about it.

"He's in the garage," Jillian Bailey said without preamble as she opened the door to Maggie's knock. "Walk around to the side and give the door a good rap. He's got some music on in there....so if he doesn't hear you, just go in."

The music was some sort of thrashing metal band from the eighties. Maggie couldn't name the band. If it wasn't music she could dance to, she usually wasn't interested. She wondered why he'd chosen it; it was so different from the music he liked. Johnny didn't answer when she knocked. She pushed the door open and walked into the dim light of the large garage. A sensible tan Camry sat in the farthest dock with its hood opened wide. Nearest to Maggie sat Johnny's Bel Air. Maggie gasped and walked around it, marveling at the care that had obviously been taken to keep the car in such good condition.

"It's your car!" Maggie cried excitedly and looked around for Johnny, glad they would have something to talk about. He unfolded himself from under the hood of Jillian's Camry. His shirt had a little grease at the hem where he had probably wiped his hands without thinking. He had gotten a haircut since she had seen him last. The style was slightly modified from its original 50s look, but it didn't change his appearance all that much. He wore jeans, and Maggie noticed how he rolled the bottoms in a thick cuff – 50s style. His shirt was a plain blue tee that he'd tucked into the jeans that rode his hips. He was thinner, but he moved effortlessly and seemed completely healed from his ordeal. He nodded at the car and then looked back at her soberly.

"How do you know it's mine?" Johnny replied softly.

"You told me," Maggie offered, just as quietly. "An oil man from a couple of counties over forgot to put his brakes on when he went to spy on his wife at the reservoir. It rolled right into the water and sunk like a box of rocks. He told you if you could get it out, it was yours. You, Carter, and Jimbo got it out. You took it apart, cleaned it, and rebuilt it the summer before your senior year." Maggie ran her hand along the sleek black side and stopped in front of the hood, which was raised just like the Camry. She tried not to look at Johnny, but she couldn't resist. She tried not to smile at his surprised expression. He grunted but didn't comment on her obvious knowledge of his history.

The silence in the garage became cloying, and Maggie struggled to find something to say, anything to say.

"What do you get when you offer a blonde a penny for her thoughts?" Maggie asked randomly.

"Huh?" Johnny shot a look at her from under his hood.

"It's a joke." What do you get when you offer a blonde a penny for her thoughts?"

"What?"

"Change," Maggie supplied, waggling her eyebrows. Johnny stared at her for a moment and shook his head. Maggie tried again.

"What do you call a brunette with a blonde on either side?"

Johnny didn't reply.

"An interpreter," Maggie answered, a little less cheerfully this time. Johnny didn't even look up from the car's engine.

"What did the blonde say when she looked in the box of Cheerios?" she said, her voice subdued. This was her favorite one. It used to be his.

No reply again.

"Oh, look! Donut seeds..." Maggie's voice faded off.

Johnny slammed the hood and wiped his hands on a nearby rag.

"Did I used to laugh at your jokes?" he asked brusquely.

"Only the blond jokes. I used to tell knock knock jokes but you told me they were terrible." Maggie smiled at the memory. Johnny had liked the blonde jokes, and Maggie had searched for them, sharing new ones with him every day. She had even started calling them "Johnny jokes" because he was himself a natural blonde.

"Let's hear one."

Maggie thought for a minute. "Knock, knock."

Johnny raised his eyebrows impatiently, waiting for her to continue.

"You're supposed to say, 'Who's there?'" Maggie prodded.

"Who's there?" Johnny parroted.

"Sarah." She waited. "Say Sarah who."

"Sarah who?" Johnny droned.

"Sarah reason you're not lettin' me in?"

Johnny rolled his eyes, and Maggie giggled a little, relieved he was at least participating somewhat.

"Yeah. That's pretty bad. But I can't imagine I liked the blonde ones much better," he grunted sourly.

Maggie tried not to let his dismissal bother her.

"Why is it so hard to believe that you and I were friends?" Maggie said quietly. She approached him and stopped, shoving her hands into the back pockets of her jeans.

"I don't know, Margaret." He leveled his gaze at her again. His eyes were like blue ice. "Maybe because I was born in 1939 and it's now 2011, and I still don't look like I'm a day over nineteen." Johnny's voice was laced with sarcasm. He walked toward her, still wiping his hands on the rag. He stopped about a foot in front of her. "Maybe it's hard because I don't know where the hell I've been for the last fifty odd years and nothing and nobody that I knew is still around to explain it all to me." His voice had risen considerably, and his face was flushed.

He crossed his arms at his chest and looked her over once, and then again, resting his gaze on the glasses perched on her nose. "And maybe it's hard to believe because I don't remember you, not at all…"

"You don't have to be a jerk," Maggie shot back, crossing her own arms. "Is that why you wanted to see me? So you could tell me again how forgettable I am?" Maggie pushed her glasses farther up on her nose, though they really hadn't slipped at all. She felt the tears threaten to spill over, and she rebuked herself silently but firmly. She would not let Johnny Kinross see her cry over him. Not again. She had *some* pride.

He didn't deny her accusations or defend himself. He just stared at her mulishly for a second and then spoke again.

"So, Margaret –"

"Maggie!"

"Maggie. You are the only one who seems to know what I've been doing or where I've been all this time. And I sure would like to know. I thought maybe you could tell me." He attempted to sound flip, but there was a layer of strain that underscored his nonchalance. Maggie's heart softened toward him the smallest degree.

"All I know is what you've told me," she said, somewhat begrudgingly. "I moved here almost a year ago. I started working at the school last summer. I noticed things right from the beginning, but they seemed natural enough...I thought it was Gus."

"Thought it was Gus doing what?"

"Gus is the janitor...the older man who visited you a couple of times at the hospital?"

Johnny nodded once.

"I thought it was Gus playing the songs from the 50s when I would work alone. One day I actually saw you in the hallway. You scared me. Then another time I fell into the dumbwaiter shaft, and you saved me. I didn't know who you were, but Gus told me that the school had a.....a ghost. He'd seen you in the school off and on for the last fifty years, ever since your disappearance the night your brother died. The first time he saw you he told the police, and they searched the school. It wasn't until later that Gus realized his mistake. He thought you were dead.....that you were a spirit haunting the school. The problem with that theory was that I had touched you, and I knew you weren't a ghost. I learned as much as I could about the tragedy and your disappearance, and then I came to the school and I...." Maggie gulped a little, wondering if he would think she was crazy. Probably not, considering his very existence was proof of something seriously bizarre.

"You what?"

"I went to the school and I....started talking to you, calling you. I asked you if it was you who had saved me that night. I ended up in the rotunda...the place where you and Billy..."

"Died?" His tone was caustic, like she had said something incredibly offensive. He wasn't making this easy.

"Fell," Maggie retorted sharply. "You were suddenly there. Just...out of nowhere...there. You talked to me for a minute. You were amazed I could see you, and I frankly was amazed as well. I have seen ghosts before.....but never like you. You could see me too; you were aware of me, and you still had a physical body. At least, it felt that way..." Maggie halted again, unsure of where to go next and needing desperately to sit down. There was a folding chair propped against the wall, and Maggie sank into it gratefully. Johnny leaned back against the door of the Camry and stared at her through narrowed eyes.

"I had a body....but no one could see me." It wasn't a question, but a recap.

Maggie nodded. "You said that you thought you'd been trapped between Heaven and Earth. You told me after you fell from the balcony you could see Billy lying beside you. You could see that he was gone." Maggie could feel the grief rising in her again. But this time it wasn't for her own pain but for his. Her voice shook slightly, but she didn't let herself stop. He stiffened at the obvious emotion in her voice but didn't react as she repeated the horror of what he had gone through.

"You said you could feel death's pull. You knew you were dying. You told me you knew you had to fight it. You didn't want to leave your mother. You didn't want her to suffer the loss of two sons, even if you were the son....she was left with. See, you blamed yourself that Billy was dead. You were filled with guilt and pain and you fought...well...death." It sounded overly dramatic, but there were no other words to describe what Johnny had told her. "You told me you refused to die. Then you felt a...a cracking – and there was a burst of light. The next time you became aware, policemen were there. Eventually, even your mother was there, but nobody could see you or hear you. They took Billy's body away at some point, and you tried to follow him, but you couldn't leave the school. It was like there was no world beyond the doors – just black. You said you were trapped there."

"All this time?" Johnny's voice was an incredulous whisper. "How can that be? I remember falling. I even remember what you've described....the feeling of fighting death. But that's all. I woke up in the hospital like it had all just happened. I even had the gunshot wound."

"You had no wounds in Purgatory. That's what you called it. Purgatory. You didn't even have a drop of blood on your clothing. Your clothes and body didn't wear or soil; your hair was always perfectly in place. You weren't really human – but you weren't an angel either. You could do some amazing things, with just a thought. You told me energy wasn't created or destroyed, it was simply redirected. You could harness energy. You could even heal! Here! Look at this." Maggie stood and, yanking the sleeve of her purple shirt above her elbow, turned her inner arm out for Johnny's perusal. The scar from her burn was a slightly raised pink half moon against her pale skin. "I burned myself....and you pressed your hand over the burn...and healed it."

Johnny reached out, running his fingers along the puckered edges of her scar. His touch was light, but Maggie felt it to the tips of her toes. She missed the Johnny who loved her! Oh, what she wouldn't give to have him back! The longing hit her like a gale-force wind, and she shuddered involuntarily. She pulled her arm away and turned from him. She needed to leave. She couldn't do this.

"Maggie." This time Johnny's voice was soft, and for a moment he sounded like the old Johnny. "What else? What else could I do? How did I spend my time?"

"You said you read a lot. You even read to me, sometimes."

Johnny raised his eyebrows and snorted in disbelief. "I hate to read. Try again, sweetheart."

Maggie stiffened and raised her chin slightly, a look Johnny was quickly coming to recognize as her battle stance. "You told me that, too. You also told me you'd read almost everything in the school library. You said it was better than boredom."

He didn't respond to that, and Maggie turned, pacing away from him for a moment.

"Have we ever danced?"

She spun around and looked at him, her mouth agape. "Why? Did you remember something?"

"Have we ever danced?" he shot back, repeating the question.

"Yes," Maggie breathed. "We've danced. I love to dance. You said you used to watch me. Then one night you actually danced with me. You're a good dancer. Do you remember that?"

He turned away and braced his hands on the hood of the Camry. "I had a dream where I was dancing with you....but it wasn't the way you describe. In the dream it was still 1958. Everything in the dream was true to life – except you. But it hasn't faded like dreams do. It feels like a memory. But how could that be? Unless you were around in 1958?" He looked at her and raised one eyebrow in question.

She shook her head. "No." Only in her dreams.

"Yeah. I didn't think so." He leaned under the hood and began to scope out the inner workings of the Camry. Maggie watched him for a minute. Maybe, like her, he had heard all he could for the moment.

"I brought something for you," she offered after several minutes.

He didn't respond but kept tinkering with this and that.

"It's a scrapbook from the years you were gone. It belonged to Roger Carlton. He could never come to grips with your disappearance; he was a little obsessed with it."

"How did you get your hands on it?"

"We found it a while back. He's been dead over a year now. He was married to my aunt....Irene Honeycutt. I think you knew her."

"Irene Honeycutt is your aunt?" His voice was incredulous, and he stood up so fast he banged his head on the Camry's raised hood.

Deja vu slammed into Maggie. They had had this conversation once before, only that time it had involved Irene's car. The words were almost exact, including Maggie's next response.

"My great aunt. Her sister was my grandmother."

"Your great aunt..." Johnny repeated slowly. Maggie remembered how he had tweaked her braid the last time. She guessed that part of the conversation would not repeat itself.

Johnny slowly straightened and walked back to where Maggie held the big book out in front of her. He took it from her gingerly and began to flip through the pages slowly, one by one. He sank into the chair Maggie had vacated, so Maggie rummaged around until she found a bucket she could sit on and pulled it close to him, watching him as he read, following along as he turned the pages of the worn scrapbook.

He stared at the headings and the pictures, shaking his head in disbelief. His breath came faster and faster, and Maggie feared he would hurl the book across the garage. She reached to take it from him when suddenly he flipped to the back where the pictures were inserted in neat little rows.

"Where did he get these?" He traced the picture of himself standing with his mother and Billy at graduation. "I haven't even seen some of these."

"He had police reports and all kinds of stuff. Irene hadn't never seen the book. We're not sure where he got them."

"Look at that....that's me and Peggy at the Prom." His voice trailed off as he stared at the picture. "There's another one – you can see Carter there in the background. He sure had a thing for Peggy. I think that's your aunt right there." He pointed at a photo, and Maggie leaned toward him to look. Sure enough, the photographer had captured a group of young people in sports coats, bow ties, and ball gowns sitting around an oval table with a seashell centerpiece. Irene was smiling brightly into the camera; Roger had his arm slung possessively around her shoulders.

"Huh…" Maggie frowned. "She told me her dress was red. I could have sworn she said red. This photo may be black and white, but that dress definitely isn't red."

Johnny jerked the book from her hands and stared down at the photo. His eyes widened perceptibly as he drank in the details of the picture of the smiling teens. He sat frozen for several heartbeats and then slammed the book closed and tossed it rudely at Maggie. Jumping up from the chair, he paced back and forth between the two cars with their mawing hoods, his hands shoved deep in his pockets. He was a bundle of nervous energy, and everything she said just seemed to make him angry.

"Johnny?" Maggie asked softly. He didn't respond. After a moment she resumed talking. "I don't know what to do or say. You saved Shad's life…Gus told you about that, didn't he?" Johnny jerked his head in affirmation. "And you saved my life. Something happened that night; somehow you escaped Purgatory. I can't explain it, but…." Maggie took a deep breath and plunged on. He deserved to know how she felt. "I think you made a choice. You chose life and all the ugly hard things that go with it, even though Heaven would have been easier."

Johnny had stopped pacing and was facing her, his feet spread, his hands clenching the greasy rag like it was a lifeline. Maggie looked down at her own hands so she wouldn't have to watch him watching her. She didn't see him cross toward her, but suddenly he was there, in front of her. He tossed the rag to the floor and reached for her, gripping her by the shoulders and pulling her to her feet. Johnny's eyes were bright with unshed tears, and for a moment Maggie thought he would break down. His hands were big, and it hurt where his fingers dug into her flesh. He was almost panting as he spat out his next words.

"You think I chose this life?" Maggie stared at him stonily, willing herself not to flinch.

"Did I love you, Maggie?" She didn't respond.

"Did I love you?!" Johnny cried. She nodded mutely, and shut her eyes against his belligerent gaze.

"Did I kiss you, Maggie?" his voice dropped to a whisper. Maggie's lips trembled at the mocking in his voice.

"Yes. You did!" Maggie meant to mock back, but her voice betrayed her and broke on the last word, revealing her hurt.

He pulled her close to him then and buried his face in the crook of her neck. He folded her in his arms so tightly she thought she would have to push him away to breathe....and she didn't want to push him away, though she knew he held her not out of love, but out of desperation. Johnny lifted his head and whispered hoarsely, his eyes on her mouth, his lips only inches from hers.

"If I kiss you now, do you think I'll remember? Do you think the world will suddenly make sense? That I will remember that choice? That maybe the last fifty years will come back to me?"

Maggie glared at him, willing him to release her, yet wanting him to kiss her, and hating herself for it. Johnny gripped her even tighter in response. Then he dipped his head until his lips brushed hers softly, so softly. Maggie shuddered and he stiffened. She thought surely now he would push her away. Instead, he lowered his mouth again, this time parting her lips with his and holding her face in one of his hands. Johnny's kiss was warm and insistent, and it was at once familiar and yet completely brand new...his lips on hers, his taste in her mouth, his scent engulfing her. For a moment, she melted into him, letting the fire in her belly burn away the pain, letting him kiss her, and kissing him back. But there was no love in his kiss. And that made him a stranger; it was a stranger's kiss. The realization hurt her pride, and Maggie fought her way out of Johnny's arms and pushed him away as angrily as he'd pulled her to him. He let her go, and for several minutes neither of them spoke.

It was Maggie who finally broke the silence and approached him once more, shoving her hands into her pockets, mirroring his stance. "I'm so sorry, Johnny. I know you don't want to be here. I know none of this makes sense. The craziest part of it all is….you were willing to *give* your life for me…what was left of it at least. But as much as I want you, I can't expect you to *live* your life for me, or to live your life with me. I wanted to be with you so bad. I would have stayed with you in that school, because I was more afraid of losing you than I was of the fire. I thought it was the only way we could be together. But you wouldn't let me stay."

Johnny turned away from her, rejecting her, dismissing her appeal. Maggie felt her heart shatter. She finished her plea in a broken whisper.

"But I would have chosen you too; and I *haven't* forgotten. Not one second. Not one minute. Not one kiss." And then, picking up the scrapbook from the concrete floor and setting it in his hands, she turned and walked out of the garage. She walked away from the Johnny who no longer knew her or loved her, out into the grey future to the car that had weathered the decades while Johnny wandered in Purgatory. He didn't come after her.

~6~

A Time to Build Up

Johnny had treated Maggie badly. He wasn't sure why. She had made him angry. Again, he wasn't sure why. Maybe it was the fact that she knew him – or some version of him – that he couldn't remember or hardly believe. When she told him he used to read to her, he had almost laughed out loud. He didn't like to read. In fact, he hated it...didn't he? The problem is, as soon as she said it Johnny remembered just the previous day when he had been wandering though Jillian's house, at a loss of what to do with himself. He'd had the sudden urge to pull several books down from her overflowing shelves and dive in. He had even grabbed a copy of a book called *A Tale of Two Cities*, and before he had even opened it, he knew what the first words were...verbatim. He had opened it fearfully and read in growing horror. He knew the story.....with his eyes closed. He may have known more, but he'd flung the book across the room, breaking its binding. The cover had fallen off, and Jillian had looked pained when he'd shown her. It was one of her favorites, apparently. He had felt like a heel. Then she told him it had once belonged to him. She said his mother had given it to him for graduation. There was an inscription inside the front cover.

May, 1958

To Johnny,
> *May it always be the best of times,*
>> *Love, Momma*

Since he had been released from the hospital he'd spent most of his time in the garage with his car. Jillian had said his mother had never been able to part with it. She had kept it all these years – having Gene give it periodic tune-ups, keeping it in running shape. It was the only time he'd felt a glimmer of happiness since this whole horror show had begun. Plus, it had given him something to do. Then he had spent his time looking under the hood of Jillian's car. There was no carburetor, and everything was smaller. Jillian said many things were computerized in cars nowadays. Then she had to show him a computer. When he'd touched it, a spark shot out from his finger tip and it had shorted out. Jillian had groaned. She'd been able to get it started up again, but as soon as he had touched it, it shorted out once more. He'd decided to stay away. He had been careful to not mess with her car – other than to change the oil and just look. So far the car still worked – computer and all, although he had been told he now had enough money to buy whatever he wanted, including a new car if he destroyed Jilllian's.

Chief Bailey, with funds from Mayor Carlton and assistance from the the president of Honeyville Bank and Trust, had helped his mother set up an account that would provide reward money for information about his disappearance, and would also collect interest and be available to Johnny if he ever came home. Dolly Kinross had always believed he would. When it became her responsibility, Jillian Bailey had minded the money religiously. She had happily informed Johnny it was now his. There was over a million dollars in the account.

Now his thoughts slid back to Maggie. She wasn't the kind of girl he usually went for. She wore big glasses, and she seemed kind of feisty. He'd always liked his ladies blonde, agreeable, and a little on the full-figured side. Maggie's hair was dark and her frame maybe too slender, although he'd had to readjust his thinking when he'd seen her today. She moved like a dancer; she was graceful and lithe, and if he hadn't been so distracted and irrationally angry, he might have liked to just watch her move, surreptitiously of course. She was funny too. His mouth twitched a little, remembering....donut seeds. He had been in no mood to give into her attempts to make him smile, but he smiled now as he thought of her dopey jokes.

He hadn't meant to grab her, or to kiss her for that matter. He had wanted her to tell him what she knew. But everything she said just made him more confused. He felt so out of control; and she was so infuriating, the way she looked at him like she understood what he was going through. Worst of all, she was in love with him. He could see it all over her face. And then he had seen that picture in the book she'd shown him. The picture of Irene in what appeared to be a peach dress, just like in his dream. Not red. And Maggie had commented on it too. All at once he had been suspicious that the universe was playing tricks on him, like his existence was just a wall of cards and any minute it would come crashing down and he would lose another fifty years.

It was then that he had grabbed Maggie and held on. He had mocked her and teased her. But it was to cover his fear and to give himself an excuse to hold her tighter. She had felt good in his arms. Her taste was sweet on his lips, and he had forgotten for a moment that none of it was real. She had pushed him away, but not without kissing him back first.

She said she loved him. She said she would help him. But Johnny was fast coming to the realization that he was way beyond help. He was in quicksand up to his neck, and he was sinking fast. He almost welcomed the thought of oblivion and wished the end would come quickly.

***

Since the night of the fire that destroyed Honeyville High School, the town had scrambled to make arrangements for the 600 students that had been misplaced by the fire. Before the fall of 1958 and the erection of the new school, Honeyville High School had been located on Main Street. The original buildings still stood, but they had been renovated and were now used as city buildings, including a library, a senior citizens center, and a courthouse. The old school gymnasium had been used as a recreation center for the past fifty years, getting a face-lift every so often to keep it safe and habitable.

The school board and Mayor Pratt, along with the teachers and administrators of the high school, decided the best course of action would be to move the students back to the "old" high school for the time being, as it was the only facility large enough to accommodate the entire student body.

A new courthouse and county jail had been completed earlier in the year, and the city had planned on demolishing the building that had housed both the court and the city jail, now almost 100 years old. Instead, the space was reverted back to a high school and all the city functions were moved to the new court house, along with a few trailers and portables for the police station and other various displaced city offices. The people of Honeyville would have to do without a library and a rec center during school hours. The original high school cafeteria had been remodeled into a senior center long ago, so the old folks were misplaced during the day as well, relinquishing their space for its original purpose. In just a matter of weeks, a temporary high school was pulled together, and Maggie and her classmates were back at school. There were no lockers, very few computers, lots of thrown together work spaces and mismatched desks, but it was functional, and Maggie was glad to get back to some sort of steady routine.

Gus had moved to the new/old school with the rest of the high school staff, and Maggie still cleaned after hours, collecting trash in strange rooms and unfamiliar hallways, trying to pretend nothing had changed. But things had changed; Maggie felt the shift within herself was almost as noticeable as her altered surroundings. Maybe it was the age of the old school, or Maggie's heightened sensitivities since the fire, but on more than one occasion she had seen glimpses of people and events long since past. There were no lunch ladies at the temporary Honeyville High cafeteria – the facilities weren't sufficient, so students just brought lunches from home, but Maggie had seen a lunch lady with a white kerchief covering her hair, wearing a truly ancient pair of sturdy shoes and an apron covered dress, dishing up huge portions of nothing on tray after tray to kids who no longer lined up at her cafeteria window. One morning before dance practice, she'd seen a boy in canvas sneakers and outdated shorts standing at the free-throw line, tossing up a ball that made no sound as it bounced off the gymnasium floor. The frequency of the sightings was unnerving, but Maggie attempted to ignore them as best she could. Usually, they blinked out in a matter of seconds, and Maggie was never truly frightened by them.

Dance team practices resumed, but the team now had to meet before school in the old gymnasium, and many of the girls complained about the rough floors and poor lighting. Maggie didn't care as long as she could dance and, in dancing, lose herself for an hour or two. Region competition came and went, and then state. Then morning dance rehearsals were no longer scheduled as the end of the year drew close, but Maggie continued to come early before school, turning on the music and finding solace in the movement and a measure of joy in the quiet of the old gymnasium.

That morning she docked her iPod in her portable player and warmed up to a random selection, moving with whatever came out of the speakers. When one of

Johnny's old favorites filled the room, she moved to turn it off, hating the rush of emotion the music caused, hating that the song was ruined for her.

But she hesitated a breath too long, and the melody wrapped itself around her, almost begging for a second chance, and she found herself swaying in surrender. Up on her toes and down on her knees, stretching her limbs in silky supplication, she moved over the old wooden floors where many had danced before her. Her eyes were closed, allowing her to concentrate on the movement, and she didn't see the room around her shift and slide into some place new, but she heard the music swell and change as the song came alive in living color.

Suddenly, figures were swirling around her, faces smiling, skirts billowing, couples spinning and twirling to the music she had lost herself in. She stood under a huge fishing net filled with balloons and dripping with silver and gold stars. A band in matching sport coats sang to her left, but the sound she heard was not in sync with the moving lips of the lead singer or the flying sticks of the cheerful drummer, as if the soundtrack of time was disconnected with the picture playing out in front of her. It made her slightly dizzy, and she turned from the band, looking out across the floor that was now filled with ghostly dancers. A banner hung on the back wall proclaiming the theme of the occasion. "Under the Sea – Prom 1958."

Maggie gasped and began searching the faces around her. He would have been here. The figures dimmed, and Maggie feared the vision would suddenly cease. Desperate, she pulled her glasses from her eyes, clutching them in her hand. Sure enough, the figures sharpened again, their faces as clear and their clothing as vibrant as if they were truly present. Was that Irene? A girl in fluffy peach sat by herself at a table with a huge shell centerpiece. She looked like she wished she wasn't there. Maggie's breath caught, seeing her aunt as a young girl. Her hair curled around her shoulders, and jewels sparkled at her ears and wrists. She was lovely. She fiddled with the drink in front of her and stared out at the dance floor longingly. A couple joined her at the table, and Irene's eyes lit up and her face and hand motions became animated as she spoke to her friends. Then several couples danced between where Maggie stood and Irene sat, blocking her view. Maggie commenced searching for Johnny once more.

There! Against the back wall, standing beneath the banner. Something about the figure was familiar. Maggie leaned this way and that, searching for the boy beyond the milling apparitions. All the boys were dressed in white jackets and black pants, making it difficult to distinguish one from the other. There he was again. It was Johnny! Maggie angled for a better look. A blonde girl with a truly magnificent cleavage was standing close to him, holding onto his lapel and smiling up at him flirtatiously. Maggie's heart twisted painfully in her chest, and she wished she hadn't been so eager to identify the familiar face. She gripped her glasses tightly. Johnny may not want her anymore, but she didn't think she could watch him with another girl, even if it had all been long ago.

A tall, sandy-haired boy with an easy smile and the requisite white jacket appeared beside Johnny and whisked the buxom blonde from Johnny's arms and out onto the dance floor. The boy laughed back at Johnny as if he'd scored the winning shot. Johnny just smiled and shrugged as he watched the couple twirl away. Suddenly he froze, and he seemed to be looking right at her. Maggie turned, trying to determine what held him transfixed. She couldn't see beyond the couples surrounding her, and she turned toward him again.

He seemed to be looking at her, but he wasn't the only one staring. Irene's eyes were trained on her as well, a slight furrow between her slim eyebrows. Roger Carlton stood behind Irene with his hands braced on her chair, and he straightened, his eyes narrowing in recognition, as if he had just noticed her too. Surely they weren't looking at her!

Maggie looked down at the clothes she was wearing and then back up again, almost dizzy with the illusion she was witnessing. She was still wearing snug black dance shorts and a bright pink sports bra, with a thin white tank over the top. Her feet were bare and her hair was bound back in a long ponytail, and if she were actually visible, the whole room would be gawking. But the couples dancing around her seemed completely unaware of her presence -- as was always the case in her visions. One couple danced so close she should have been able to feel the swish of the girl's skirt and the brush of their bodies moving past. She felt no such thing. Yet Johnny was transfixed, staring at her as if he couldn't look away. He'd started making his way toward her, moving between the tables that lined the dance floor.

Maggie turned again, scanning the room for what could have so captured his attention. A flash of red caught her eye, and she strained on tiptoe to see beyond the dancing crowd. A girl in red stood in the entrance to the gym. Maggie sidestepped another couple attempting the jive and strained to get a better view. Johnny continued to move toward her, and had Maggie not seen the girl in red, she would have sworn he was looking at her. Her heart pounded in her chest, and she rubbed her hands anxiously on her dance shorts.

He was ten feet away. Gus's fear-filled eyes rose up in her memory, his warning sounding like a clanging bell in her head. *"Be careful, Miss Margaret. My grandma wasn't just an observer of the past; she was a full-fledged participant."* Maggie closed her eyes, shutting out Johnny's approaching figure, pressing her hands to her face, willing herself away from the dizzying promenade taking place around her.

"Maggie?" Johnny's voice was filled with question as his hands settled on her shoulders.

Maggie cried out and stumbled back, her legs tangling beneath her. Johnny's arms slid around her, and her eyes shot to his. He steadied her, his body firm and solid against her chest. Maggie's eyes dropped to his shoulders encased in black cotton. No white sports coat, no perky pink carnation.

"Maggie?" He said her name again, and his eyebrows were drawn low over his sky blue gaze. "Are you all right?"

Maggie pulled free of his arms, looking around the empty gymnasium, where every trace of glimmering stars and glittering people had dissolved into the quiet present. She stood beneath the basketball hoop where she had seen the ghostly boy diligently practicing his shot. Her iPod made a new selection, a Katy Perry song with an addictive hook -- definitely not 1958.

"Maggie!" Johnny shook her a little, and his voice rose in concern.

"What are you doing here?" she blurted out and pulled away again, but she felt her legs wobble beneath her. She slid ungracefully to the floor and pulled her knees to her chest, breathing deeply and trying to gain her bearings.

He didn't answer her immediately but squatted down beside her, reaching out to tilt her chin toward him.

"Your pupils are so big your eyes look black," he scolded, as if she had any control of what her pupils did.

"I'm fine," Maggie protested, pulling her chin from his grasp. "Just give me a minute to catch my breath."

"You're definitely not fine," Johnny argued.

Jillian had oh-so-innocently told him that Maggie danced before school started every day. He knew Jillian thought he owed Maggie an apology, although she had never said as much. She just kept dropping little bits of information, bringing Maggie's name into the conversation, mentioning her dance team's victory at their recent competition, telling him what a "lovely girl" she was.

Then last night Johnny had dreamed about Maggie again. They had been dancing on a beach, the moon lighting the sand and shimmering off the water. Music had drifted down around them, and he had felt almost weightless, suspended in the sweetness of her smile, the feel of her arms around him, the slide of the silk bodice of her dress against his open palm. He woke up with her name on his lips and such an aching yearning to see her that he had showered and come to the school, planning to watch her from a distance without revealing his presence. He had told himself once he saw her the feeling would abate.

Johnny had heard music from the hallway and he had hesitated, worried that he would give himself away when he opened the old gym door. Luck had been on his side because the door was propped wide and he slipped inside, the early morning shadows and the poor lighting of the ancient gymnasium providing sufficient cover. Maggie had been facing the opposite direction, moving to a song he had never heard before. He leaned against the metal bleachers and drank her in -- a lithe form in clothing designed to move but not to entice, though he found it did both. She took his breath away. The realization was met with swift resistance. He didn't want to like her. He didn't want to need her.

Then the music changed, and Maggie stopped, turning as if she didn't like the selection. It was a song Johnny had liked from the moment he heard it: the Skyliners singing "Since I Don't Have You." It was a brand new song his senior year in high school. He had probably danced to that song in this very gym, surrounded by his friends. Maggie spun, and for a minute he was sure she had spotted him. She threw herself into the song, long limbs and sweet curves calling him to dance with her. He had found himself moving toward her, wanting to join her, wanting to close his eyes and move to the memory encased in the song. And then she had stopped, as if she'd forgotten the steps.

Johnny had stopped too, suddenly awkward and afraid, not knowing how to explain himself. But Maggie had looked right through him. He froze, watching her as she seemed to be lost in thought, her eyes shifting here and there like she was taking in the details of the empty room. A small smile had played around her lips, and he had thought maybe she was playing with him. He moved toward her again, and this time her eyes had locked on his. She had looked down at her clothes and then behind her, as if she couldn't believe he was looking at her. He had said her name but she didn't respond. She had rubbed her eyes, almost as if she couldn't believe he was there and he had said her name again, reaching for her as she swayed and staggered dizzily.

Now Maggie was looking at him as if she were losing her mind. Maybe she was... although Johnny wouldn't swear by his own sanity.

"I'm fine," she said it again, this time with more conviction. "You just startled me." Maggie got to her feet defiantly and walked to her blinking music player. She pushed a button and silence filled the space where the music had been. Johnny didn't comment but let her retreat, wishing he had stayed in the shadows.

"Why are you here?" she asked again, and her voice was small, as if she didn't really want to know.

"I came with Jillian." Okay that was a lie, but he wasn't about to tell her he had dreamed about her and couldn't stay away. "I just wanted to see the old place." Another lie; he didn't care if he ever saw the old place - which had gotten significantly older since he'd last walked the halls. "She told me you might be here." At last the truth, but where did he go from here?

Maggie nodded, waiting for him to explain further. He shrugged, pride warring with principle.

"I'm sorry I kissed you." He was so full of shit; that was the one thing he wasn't sorry about. "I mean, I'm sorry I...acted the way I did, that day in the garage. I asked you to come, and then I was a jerk. I'm sorry."

Maggie seemed surprised by his admission, and her face relaxed into a smile. It warmed him, seeing the pleasure his apology brought her.

"It's okay. I understand," she said softly. "But thank you."

A loud bell clanged through the gymnasium like a runaway train, and Maggie and Johnny both jumped. Maggie cursed under her breath and seemed to realize she had lingered too long.

"I have to go..." she stuttered, grabbing up a duffle bag and forcing her music box inside of it. "I'll see you soon...okay?"

Johnny nodded, and watched Maggie run from the gymnasium on light feet, leaving him alone, standing in a place that echoed with a million yesterdays. He thought he glimpsed a flash of red near the far entrance, but when he turned his head there was nothing there.

~7~
A Time to Break Down

Teenagers spilled out of the brightly colored doors, several of them congregating on parked cars and leaning out of open windows. A huge burger, fries, and a shake topped the establishment, which used to be called The Malt. It had been renovated and expanded over the years, and it was now called Shimmy and Shake, because in addition to providing ice cream and food, there was a big, loud, old-fashioned jukebox off to one side and a small dance floor to make good use of the tunes. Everyone just called it Shimmies, and it was the place to be if you were above the age of fourteen and below the age of twenty- five. Families usually didn't come inside to eat; it was too loud. Instead, they pulled up to the drive thru and left the dining room to the younger generation.

Maggie had been there a couple times with Shad. He liked to go out on the dance floor and try to impress the ladies with his skills, which might have worked if he'd *had* any dancing skills. Shad had been on her case since she got out of the hospital to "hit Shimmies." She had used every excuse in the book, but after school that Friday, he had wheedled and begged her to take him, and now she was here, tired, hungry, still a little freaked out from the ghostie episode in the gym yesterday, and definitely not in the mood for Shimmies. But it *was* Friday night, and she really had nothing better to do.

As soon as they had walked in, Shad was off to work the room. At the moment, he was entertaining some new friends with a wild tale, his mouth working overtime, his hands flying with descriptive enthusiasm. The kids around him were laughing and listening, and Maggie felt a measure of relief that Shad was enjoying his new-found fame. Maybe it was because the jerks who had locked him in that locker and then forgot he was there when the school was on fire had made him their new pet. It was amazing what a guilty conscience could do. Their attention had drawn the admiration of others, and in just a matter of weeks since the fire, Shad was living in a whole new social hemisphere.

The smell of french fries and meat sizzling on the grill had Maggie's stomach grumbling loudly, and she was thankful for the music that pounded throughout the room, disguising her famished state. It was still early -- barely six o'clock -- and the place wasn't full, but it would be soon. Maggie sank gratefully into an empty booth on the edge of the dance floor. She hadn't even picked up the menu when she saw Johnny's car pull into the lot. It was the last place she thought she would see him.

Johnny climbed out of the Bel Air and shut the door slowly. His eyes were wide as he checked out the cars littering the space – everything from trucks with monster wheels to VW Bugs but all of it a novelty. The girls spilling out of a few of the vehicles were almost as mind boggling. For a minute, Maggie imagined how strange everything must seem to him. The fashions had definitely changed. Dara Manning and several of her equally blonde friends chose that moment to pull up in Dara's red Mustang convertible. The took the only spot open in the whole lot, mainly because it was marked Handicapped. That didn't stop Dara, and she and her friends checked their lipstick and fluffed their hair as Johnny checked them out. Maggie could hardly blame him – there was an awful lot of skin on display, but she suddenly really wished she wasn't there.

It took about two seconds for Dara to notice Johnny. Her brows shot up, and she said something under her breath to Carly Nelson, sitting beside her in the passenger seat. Carly's head swiveled around, and Johnny, as if realizing he had totally lost his cool ogling everyone around him, turned and walked to the door without a backward glance. Maggie felt silly sitting all alone in the red booth and wished she had thought to head to the bar when she'd seen Johnny. Of course, he spotted her as soon as he walked in. He didn't wave or nod, and he took in the joint for several long seconds before he headed her way.

Maggie tried not to squirm but did anyway. Johnny slid into the booth across from her, assuming she was alone. Of course she wouldn't have a date! She was in love with him, as he well knew. She sighed crossly and grabbed a menu for something to do. She would let him be the first to speak since he had joined her...without an invitation, she thought with a mental snarl.

The menu she held in front of her nose didn't stop her from seeing Dara and her friends crowded around the jukebox. They were taking turns posing and tossing long looks over their shoulders at the cute new guy none of them knew. Dara caught Johnny's eye and mouthed the word "Hi." Then she tossed her hair as she turned back toward the jukebox display, leaning over more than she needed to. Johnny just shook his head and looked back at Maggie. Maggie just pushed her glasses higher on her nose.

Music with a steady, throbbing, beat suddenly erupted from the jukebox, and several kids cheered and jumped up, filling the dance floor. Dara and her friends took center stage and began a series of semi-choreographed moves apparently designed to attract male attention. Maggie turned away, wishing their food would hurry up and arrive. Johnny watched the action on the dance floor for several minutes, while Maggie stared out the window into the deepening shadows.

"Hey, Mags." Shad stood at her side, shifting from foot to foot, his eyes darting to Johnny and then away again. "Scoot over baby." And without waiting for her to respond, he crowded in next to her, jostling her until she shifted over enough for him to sit on the bench without sitting in her lap. His eyes never left Johnny's face. His body was vibrating like a tuning fork, and his feet and fingers tapped non-stop against the table and the floor, making Maggie long to grab his hands and press them flat and stomp her feet on his toes to quiet them, even for a second. Shad looked jealous, afraid, and uncomfortable all at once. He couldn't take his eyes from Johnny. Apparently he remembered some things about the night of Johnny's rescue, and Gus had filled him in on the rest. She and Shad had never discussed it. Maggie assumed Johnny was just more than Shad was willing to accept.

"So.....you're the guy Maggie's got the hots for." Maggie rolled her eyes and dropped her head into her hands. Leave it to Shad to just come right out with it. From her dejected position, she couldn't see Johnny's response, but she felt his interest pique like a blow torch aimed right at her face. Her neck and cheeks flamed hot.

"Johnny Kinross - in the flesh." Shad was warming up to the subject now, his lines right out of a poorly-written, made-for-TV movie. "You're Johnny Kinross, right? I mean...I never saw you. But I think we had a pretty good relationship." Maggie sputtered, a laugh erupting from her chest. Shad swiveled his head and gave her his "Shut-up-woman!" lips and his "domineering male" chin thrust. He was talking again before Maggie could give him her "you've-got-ten-seconds-to-vacate-the-premises-before-I-cut-you" glare in response.

"My Grandpa Gus says you can't remember anything." Shad was banking on that much, Maggie thought wryly. "I just wanted to say thank you and let you know that I got your back." Shad extended his hand across the table, waiting for Johnny to grasp it. When Johnny did, Shad maneuvered his hand into a series of hand shakes that had Johnny fighting not to smile. Maggie felt a small measure of gratitude to Shad for that much. It didn't last long.

"Oh, and Johnny? Maggie is my girl. Sorry, man. I'll forgive you this time, 'cause you didn't know better. But this?" Shad pointed from Maggie to Johnny and back again. "This here? This ain't happ'nin' - clear?"

"Shad!" Maggie was no longer grateful or amused. Johnny looked like he was going to explode, however. His face had gone almost as red as hers had been minutes before, but it wasn't from embarrassment. He was laughing at her. Shad was as clueless as ever, and he turned to Maggie then, sliding his arm around her shoulders.

"Do you wanna dance, Mags? I got something good coming up after this!" Shad waggled his eyebrows suggestively. She shrugged Shad's arm from her shoulders and would have turned him down just for being such a pain, but then she caught Johnny's expression as he turned his head to stare out across the dance floor. He looked out at the writhing figures, at Dara as she ran her hands through her hair and strutted around the floor. Then he eyed Maggie doubtfully. He slid his hands along the back of his plastic seat and smirked the smallest bit.

"You said you love to dance, right Maggie? Let's see you. Go on now. Your boyfriend wants to dance."

Maggie felt her temper flare and burst in her skull. What was with him? He seemed to relish making her feel completely undesirable. What? Did he think she couldn't dance? Did he think mousy Maggie with her big glasses couldn't do the same moves Dara and her trashy trio were doing? He didn't find her attractive? Fine. She would show him a thing or two.

Maggie shot to her feet, shoving Shad out of the booth and setting her glasses on the table. She didn't look at Johnny as she walked away. Instead, she called over her shoulder, "Don't wait for me....I might be a while."

Shad had chosen her favorite song, thank God for small miracles. It was several years old, but the driving beat and the funky base line were hypnotic and gritty, and she threw herself into the song, pulsing and popping with the rhythm, prancing around the floor as if she owned the place. Shad tried to keep up, but knew within seconds Maggie was in rare form. Instead, he hollered and raised his hands, the first to form a circle around her. By the end of the song, Maggie had quite the audience. Take that, Johnny Kinross. She raised the damp hair off of her neck and spun a little, soaking up the whoops and whistles around her, dropping into a sloppy curtsy, blowing a big air kiss to all the admiring bystanders.

She walked triumphantly out of the dancing throng to see that the table she and Johnny had occupied was empty. Maggie whirled, wondering if Johnny had so disapproved of her display that he had left Shimmies. But no...she could see his car through the windows, still parked in the same spot. She sat down in dejection. So much for showing Johnny how attractive she could be. "Showing someone" wasn't effective if he didn't care enough to watch. Her eyes wandered around the dining area, wondering where Johnny was, feeling silly sitting alone, especially after she had just called so much attention to herself.

Her eyes lit on him seconds later. He was standing in the entrance to the hallway that led to the restrooms, eyeing the assortment of pictures that adorned the long wall. Maggie continued to watch him, studying him as he drank in the history of the Shimmy and Shake. He hardly moved, and after two or three minutes, Maggie felt a frisson of alarm. Relinquishing her prime booth and swinging her purse over her shoulder, Maggie wove her way to his side.

Johnny was standing in front of an old picture of his mother and Chief Bailey. In fact, all the pictures along the wall were quite dated. Maggie had never noticed the picture before. She'd been to Shimmies a few times, and whenever she'd walked down this hall it had been with the intent to pee, not to peruse. The shot was a cute one, though. The Chief had his arm around Dolly's Kinross's shoulders, and she was smiling up at him sheepishly. The picture next to it was a picture of another couple standing in front of Shimmies on opening day, big smiles on their faces and balloons billowing around them. There was something familiar about the two, and Maggie looked closer, trying to place them.

"Do you know these people?" Maggie asked, tapping the glass lightly. She glanced up then, looking into Johnny's face for the first time since she had joined him at the wall. His face was wet with tears. The shock of seeing him that way made Maggie gasp audibly. He turned abruptly and walked out of the Shimmy and Shake. Maggie hesitated briefly, and then ran out after him. She would call Shad later. She followed Johnny to his car and was surprised when he beat her to her door, opening it for her before she could open it herself.

As soon as Maggie sat down, an image of Johnny sitting by another girl, here in his car, flashed on the periphery of her vision. The busty blonde had her arms wrapped around his neck, and she was sprawled against him. He was kissing her soundly. Maggie gasped and snapped her eyes closed, willing the ghostly replay away. Johnny slid in beside her and gunned his car, screeching out of the lot as curious bystanders stopped to watch.

He pulled out of the parking lot and onto Main Street. They rode in silence. Maggie gnawed at her lower lip, wishing he would talk to her, knowing he wouldn't. She waited until he had pulled in front of Irene's house. She hadn't told him where to go. He made a move to get out, most likely to open her door, as it seemed to irk him when she did it herself. She took a deep breath and plunged in.

"Who were those people in the pictures?" She couldn't comfort him if she didn't know. For a minute she thought he wouldn't answer. Then he sighed, and his voice shook slightly.

"My momma and Chief Bailey."

"I recognized them," Maggie paused briefly. "Who were the others?"

Johnny leaned against the steering wheel, peering out at the full moon that was rising in the sky, casting a soft white light down on his upturned face. Maggie was grateful for the illumination; it made it easier to read his emotions. He seemed devastated, not by the picture of his mother but by something else.

"The one in front of the restaurant was Carter and Peggy. Apparently they own the place. There were several pictures of them. The last shot was them on what looked like a fiftieth wedding anniversary celebration. They must have gotten married in the fall after we graduated. I had a feeling they were hiding something. I think Peggy was pregnant."

Maggie stayed silent, waiting to see if he would continue. He didn't. She thought of the blonde she'd seen in her vision of the prom, and the girl she'd seen him kissing in his car for that brief second before she'd closed her eyes to the ghostly replay.

"Did you love Peggy? Is that what's bothering you? That she married your friend?"

Johnny laughed, a humorless snort that negated her supposition. "No. I didn't love Peggy. She was always Carter's girl, though it took her a while to figure it out. I just tried to help them along."

"So.....you're glad?" He didn't seem glad. Maggie was a little lost, and she feared he would put an end to her questioning before she got some answers. At the moment, she was striking out. "So what upset you so much...back at Shimmies?"

He looked out the far window, depriving her of his profile. She had almost given up when he resumed speaking.

"There were pictures of a couple of guys I knew. It looked like they were in the army or something. There was a newspaper article framed up too. It had a list of names. I knew almost all of them. The article was about men lost in a place called Vietnam." Johnny turned stricken eyes on her. "Was there a war?"

Maggie felt his despair wash over her. She nodded, realizing suddenly what was coming. "Yes. There's been more than one, but...yes. The Vietnam war started in the sixties and lasted into the seventies." At least she thought it did. She was much more familiar with the wars in Iraq and Afghanistan, the wars of her generation.

"The article was about a monument they were going to erect here in Honeyville. Jimbo's name was in the article. He's gone, Maggie. And Paul Harper, and Grant Lewis...and so many other names I recognized. They're dead...." Johnny suddenly slammed his hand into the dash, causing her to jump in surprise. "What the hell happened, Maggie? Why am I here?"

Maggie struggled to find words and then abandoned her attempt as Johnny continued.

"I've missed my whole life, the life I should have already lived. The people I care about are old or....dead!"

The silence inside the car was thick and stifling, Johnny's words sucking all the oxygen from the space.

"The people I care about are old or dead too," Maggie whispered.

Johnny barked out an incredulous laugh and shot a stunned look at Maggie. She stared back, daring him to challenge her statement.

"It's not the same thing!" Johnny looked like he was about to break something, but Maggie held her ground. His eyes blazed in the dim light, and his jaw was clenched hard enough to shatter his teeth.

"I know. It's not," she soothed. "But alone is still alone however you come by it. And you and I really aren't all that different."

Maggie reached out tentatively and smoothed the hair from his brow, resting her hand alongside his face. His eyes closed briefly, and he pressed his cheek into her hand for less than a heartbeat. Then he pulled away with a groan, and Maggie's hand dropped back to her lap.

"Ah Maggie. Just go...just...please, go. I apologized once, and I don't want to have to do it again, but at this point the only kind of comfort you can give me does not involve conversation."

Maggie's heart stuttered and then sped up at the implication of his backhanded offer. His eyes met hers defiantly.

"Go!" he ordered. He leaned across her to open the door, and then he shoved it wide. Maggie burned where he'd brushed against her. He looked away, waiting for her to exit the car.

Maggie slid out without another word, shutting the door behind her.

It wasn't until Johnny had pulled away that she remembered Irene's car was still at Shimmies. Sighing, she began the long walk back to the place she started from, in more ways than one.

***

Maggie worried about Johnny all day Saturday. She slept restlessly, ate poorly, and generally couldn't get his distraught face out of her head. It's easy to stay away when you're pushed, easy to believe you're not needed or wanted. And it was even easier to imagine that Johnny would do fine without her. He was strong and capable and more resilient than anyone she knew. But it wasn't easy to stop loving him, not easy at all. So she worried.

Finally, by Sunday afternoon, she decided she would just stop in and check on him, put her mind at ease, and quickly retreat. It had rained steadily all day, and Maggie swerved to hit every puddle she could on the way to Jillian Bailey's house, just to distract herself. When she reached the Bailey bungalow, she hopscotched through the water to reach the front steps and, taking a deep breath, rapped several times on the door. She shoved her hands deep into the pockets of her jean jacket and braced herself for an answer.

But Johnny wasn't home. It was Jillian Bailey who answered the door. Maggie had psyched herself up for nothing. Jillian sniffed experimentally out at the saturated air and then inhaled deeply, closing her eyes in appreciation.

"I've been waiting for the rain to stop so I could sit out here and enjoy the aftermath." Jillian sank down on the top step of her little porch and patted the spot next to her.

"Sit with me for a minute, Maggie."

The concrete was slightly damp, but Maggie acquiesced, perching on the step and pulling her knees in close to her chest so she could prop her chin on them.

"I thought after the last time you came that you might not come again," Jillian confessed and shot a sympathetic look Maggie's way.

"He was in rare form after you left. I couldn't even get him to come in for dinner, and he kept that music on until all hours of the night, even though I know he doesn't care for it. I finally understood what it was like to actually raise a teenager and not just send them home at the end of the school day."

"He apologized....but I definitely don't seem to have a calming affect on him, that's for sure," Maggie added, and smiled ruefully to ease the sting the words left in her heart. "That's actually why I'm here. I saw him Friday night. He gave me a ride home." Although she hadn't actually needed one, Maggie added silently. "He saw some pictures at Shimmies that upset him. I wanted to make sure he was okay."

"Ahhh, so that's what set him off," Jillian sighed.

"He says everyone he knew is old or dead."

"He's right, Maggie. They are."

"I told him everyone I care about is old or dead too, though that isn't entirely true. I care about him."

"He cares about you too, Maggie," Jillian supplied softly.

Maggie bit her lip to stop it from trembling. Why was it that kindness reduced her to a puddle? Call her names, reject her, neglect her, and she could handle it, but say something kind or sympathetic and she was defenseless.

"He calls your name in his sleep," Jillian continued. "He may push at you and pretend that he doesn't want you, but there's a reason you don't have a calming affect on him. You've gotten under his skin."

"He calls my name?" Maggie exclaimed, shocked.

"He may not remember you here," Jillian tapped her head, "but he knows you here," she settled her hand on her heart. "He's not really fighting you, he's fighting the contradiction. Although it probably feels that way."

Maggie's chin trembled again, and she fought for composure. Jillian seemed to understand and gave her a moment to regroup.

"My mother always said he would come back." She deftly turned the subject away from Maggie. "She made arrangements for him. She wouldn't even refer to him in the past tense and wouldn't allow me to, either. It drove my dad nuts, but he loved her, so he tolerated what he thought was a mother's inability to let go."

"But she was right," Maggie contributed quietly.

"Yes....she was. I wonder how things would have been different if she'd been able to move on. But she never could. She wasn't a bad mother, but she was distant and distracted. She even named me Jillian in honor of them--John and William combined." Jillian shrugged like she'd come to terms with it. "My dad loved her madly, and she loved him, but she wasn't ever what I would call a happy woman, though she devoted herself to making him a happy man."

"Your dad was a good guy, wasn't he?"

"He was the best." Jillian spoke fiercely, and it was her turn to get emotional. "He looked for Johnny too, you know. He said there were just too many loose ends. It always ate at him. I wish they could be here now. I hope somehow they know, wherever they are."

"And Billy?"

"And Billy." Jillian smiled a little. "Billy didn't haunt my mother the same way Johnny did, though she grieved for him too. Whenever she talked about Billy she could smile. Death is a pain that we can heal from. Not knowing is an open wound that never heals."

"It's the not knowing that is making this so hard for Johnny," Maggie whispered.

"But that's where you come in." Jillian reached for her hand. "You are the miracle that will fill in the blanks..."

"I can't make him remember."

"But you can help him forget."

~8~
A Time to Mourn

Two days later, Johnny was waiting for Maggie when she exited the school. She was tired and hungry; lunch had been hours ago, and her afternoon janitorial duties had taken longer than usual. Her feet were sore, her back was stiff, and her glasses had been giving her a headache since the morning of the ghostly promenade in the school gymnasium. Maybe it was because she had been too nervous to take them off, even when she slept; they seemed to keep her in the present. She slipped them off now and rubbed the bridge of her nose wearily, closing her smarting eyes to the blushing pink of the sunset.

"Do you need a ride?" he said, his voice coming out of nowhere.

Maggie's heart leaped in traitorous joy at the familiar voice and then plummeted almost as quickly when reminded of the unrequited nature of her feelings. Her eyes snapped open and her head shot up to see him leaning against the pole she'd chained her bike to almost ten hours earlier. He looked like an ad from a fashion magazine, so nonchalant and carelessly good looking against the backdrop of the setting sun.

"How did you know where to find me?" she stuttered out ungraciously, slipping her glasses reluctantly back on her nose. She preferred the days when she could only see him without her glasses.

He shrugged noncommittally, not breaking eye contact, but not answering her question. "Do you need a ride?" He said again.

"No, actually."

"Come on. I'll take you home."

I don't need a ride. That's my bike." Maggie pointed to the bike at his feet. He didn't look down at the bike, which made Maggie think he was aware all along that it was hers.

"It'll fit in my trunk."

"No, thank you. I'll ride it home. It's a big bike."

"It's a big trunk."

Maggie stared at him, confused by his sudden appearance and his even more sudden interest in spending time in her company.

"Why?"

"It was made that way. Most of the cars made in the '50's had decent sized trunks."

"Ha ha, very funny. That's not what I meant and you know it. Why do you want to take me home?"

Maggie almost smiled at his dry attempt at humor. But she didn't. It still hurt too much to look at him, to be near him, and her smile stayed dormant.

"I want to talk to you."

"I had the very distinct impression the last time we were together that I made you angry. Plus, I'm thinking your driver's license is long expired. You shouldn't be driving."

"Ha, ha, very funny," Johnny mimicked her. "Have you always been such a goody-two shoes?"

"Nobody says goody-two-shoes anymore!" Maggie said crossly and walked to her bike, squatting beside it to undo the lock.

"Maggie," he coaxed. "Maggie?" She really tried not to look up at him. "How do you drive a blonde crazy?"

Maggie's head shot up, and her eyes locked on his.

"You put him in a round room and tell him to sit in the corner," Johnny quipped, but his eyes were serious.

"Not bad, Kinross. Did you make that up yourself?"

"It's not really a joke, I guess." Johnny shifted his weight. "It's the way I feel...like I'm stuck in a place with the wrong instructions. I'm making a mess of things." He halted, shrugging his shoulders. "Come on, Maggie. I'll buy you dinner. Whaddayasay?"

Maggie sighed and stood, pulling her bike upright as she did. "I don't know if my heart can take it, Johnny. Plus, I eat like a horse. I doubt you're prepared for the price of today's cheeseburgers."

Johnny gazed down into her upturned face for several long heartbeats. "My heart's a little battered too, Maggie." His voice was low and soft, and Maggie's anger dissolved like a snowflake on her outstretched tongue. His heart was battered too. She groaned and shook her head. He'd lost everyone and everything. They had a great deal in common, didn't they?

"All right," Maggie surrendered, her voice pitched on a level with his. "Lead the way."

Johnny took her bike without further comment and pushed it to where the Bel Air was parked at the curb. He popped the trunk, slid her bike in, and closed it without a word. Maggie didn't wait for him to open her door but, like most girls of her generation, opened it herself and slid inside. For a moment, she was alone in the interior of the car. She breathed in deeply, letting his scent wash over her. She thought of the blonde girl with big breasts she'd seen kissing him the last time she'd sat in Johnny's car. She wondered if she would ever be able to ride in his car without seeing that kiss. It must have been some kiss to be stamped on the interior like it was.

"You okay?" Johnny asked as he slid in beside her and turned the key.

"I'm definitely not the first girl that's ridden in this car."

"Huh?"

"I just saw....I mean...never mind."

Her voice was sharp, discouraging a follow-up question, and they rode in silence for several minutes.

Johnny flipped on the radio and a song with a driving beat filled the car and shook the dash. He flipped it off almost immediately. Maggie reached out and turned the radio back on, turning the knob until she found what she was looking for.

"There. Is that better?" Elvis begged her to not be cruel, and Johnny visibly relaxed.

"I feel like I haven't eaten a cheeseburger and a shake for years..." Johnny's voice trailed off. Maggie giggled and then thought how inappropriate laughing was. None of this was funny in the slightest. But when she looked at Johnny, amazingly enough, he smiled with her, his dimples making their first appearance since Purgatory. Maggie gasped at the jolt of electricity that smile shot straight through her belly. She was in such trouble!

They went to Shimmies again, but this time Johnny pulled into the long line at the drive thru, and Maggie breathed a sigh of relief. She was too tired for drama, and Shimmies was full of teen angst. Maggie took one look at the menu board and knew what she wanted. She always got the same thing. Johnny was still reading the menu, a frown of disbelief between his brows. She guessed that the prices were a tad bit higher than he was used to. Oh well, she'd warned him, hadn't she?

"Do you need me to buy?" She asked softly. Johnny shot her a look that would have caused her to shrivel up and die had she not grown a rather thick skin over the years. Still, she cringed a little bit. He clearly took her offer as an insult.

"I've got plenty of money... but it had better be a darn good burger. The last burger I ate cost fifteen cents."

"Fifteen?" Maggie squeaked.

Johnny tossed his heads toward the window at the gas station they could see across the road. The fuel prices were displayed on a large marquee. "A gallon of gas used to cost me a quarter. I can't believe people are still driving cars at these prices." He looked back at her, his expression unreadable. "You already know what you want?" He changed the subject abruptly.

"I always get the same thing."

"Not too adventurous, huh?

"Life is disappointing enough without having to take chances on your food. I always go with the sure thing."

A waitress skated up to Johnny's window and crouched down so she could see into the car, her pad and paper poised and her eyes drifting over Johnny curiously. Whenever it got really busy, Shimmies sent a girl out to the drive thru on skates to take orders. It gave the place a car hop kind of feel.

"Ready guys?" The waitress popped her gum.

Johnny tipped his head at Maggie and she rattled off her standard cheeseburger, french fry, chocolate shake request.

"Make that two of the same," Johnny added, his eyes lingering briefly on the girl's very short shorts, and then looking away quickly. The girl didn't miss the look, and skated away with a little extra swing in her hips. She even glanced over her shoulder to see if he was watching her. Maggie was pleased to note that he wasn't.

"None of the girls wear enough clothes," Johnny murmured, almost to himself.

Maggie raised her eyebrows. "And you don't like that?"

"Surprisingly enough, no, I don't." Johnny sat back in his seat and looked around, his face contemplative. "Some of the mystery is lost if it's all on display. Half the fun of getting a present is unwrapping it. If you already know what's inside, why bother?"

They ended up eating their dinner at the little park located about a block off Main Street. Johnny said the park had been there for as long as he could remember. The playground equipment had been updated, and he claimed the trees were much larger than they used to be. He stood beneath one giant oak and tipped his head back, as if trying to count the highest leaves. The sun had set, and the evening shadows merged and touched; the gray of twilight lay softly all around them. They ate in reflective silence, before Johnny spoke up randomly.

"So you always get the same thing?"

"What?"

"You said life was disappointing enough without having to take chances on your food. You said you always go with the sure thing."

Maggie shrugged, dipping a fry into her shake. "When I find something I like I tend to stick with it. Less risk that way, I guess."

"Huh. I guess that makes sense."

Maggie shrugged, using nonchalance and bravado to cover what had been a very unsettled life.

"Your mom and dad aren't around?"

"They died when I was ten. I've spent the last few years living in different homes. It hasn't been too bad."

Johnny looked at her gravely, his mouth drawn into a long line. He didn't challenge her.

"I got to come live with Irene after Roger died. He didn't want her to take me in. I think she would have anyway, but worried that he would make my life miserable...more miserable than not having a home at all."

"Roger Carlton messed up both of our lives," he bit out.

"Roger Carlton messed with many lives," Maggie retorted, her thoughts on Irene.

"It seems kind of unfair that you know so much about me but I don't know anything about you," Johnny remarked, changing the subject. Maggie was glad. They had had the conversation about Roger before, whether Johnny could remember it or not.

Maggie ducked her head. She didn't tell him that once he had known everything about her. "You probably know more than you think."

"Well, I know you like to dance."

Maggie nodded and held up a finger. One thing.

"And you're good at it."

Maggie smiled, shrugging, but she lifted another finger. Two things.

"Oh, please. You know damn well you're amazing. You don't think I watched you the other night? The whole place was glued to your every move," he paused.

"I was egging you on, you know. I wanted you to go out there. I wanted to see you..."

"You did not!' Maggie interrupted hotly. "You didn't think I could. You think I'm unattractive and boring."

"Keep tellin' yourself that, Maggie, and I'll keep telling myself that, and we'll both be happier in the long run."

Maggie jumped to her feet, abandoning her dinner and the boy who seemed intent on hurting her feelings, for the safety of the swings. She had barely gained any height, when strong hands gripped her waist as she descended and pushed her skyward once more. Johnny continued to push her higher and higher as Maggie closed her eyes and let the wind she'd created dance in her hair and lift her into the night. After a while, Johnny stopped pushing, and Maggie reluctantly slowed, looking around to find him.

He sat on the swing to the right of her, but he wasn't swinging. He sat with his long legs spread before him, his arms bent and hanging loosely from the chains.

"I wasn't a sure thing," he commented as she slowed to a stop.

Maggie tried to make out his expression in the darkness that had deepened while she had swung.

"No,....I guess not," Maggie agreed. "You were a risk."

"And you're not a risk taker."

"It wasn't a conscious choice, really. In some ways we needed each other. But I didn't fall in love with you because I needed you."

"No?" Johnny's voice was soft.

"No. I fell in love with you because you were good and brave, and you laughed at my jokes, and you made me feel beautiful, and for a million other reasons. It would have been easier to pretend I couldn't see you. But I've never been able to pretend with you. Maybe that's what loving someone does; it strips us of our defenses. I've spent the last eight years pretending I'm fine. I can't seem to pretend anymore." Maggie began to swing again, but Johnny stood and held the chains, hindering her efforts. He stood behind her so Maggie couldn't see his face as he began to speak.

"Today, I rode down Main Street and all over the town, up and down streets that look almost nothing like the Honeyville I remember. The house I lived in isn't even standing anymore. There's a big apartment building there. I went to your house today, to Irene's house. I just parked my car and sat. It's one of the only places that still looks the same. Older, a little worn-out....but still here. Your aunt saw me. I think I scared her to death. She just stood there, staring at me. I don't know who was more surprised. Yesterday, she was a beautiful girl. She looked a lot like you." Maggie swung her head around to meet his gaze. He met her eyes and then looked away again, resuming his watch of the moon.

"Yeah, you're beautiful. And you damn well know it. I'd have to be blind not to see it. Even Irene couldn't hold a candle to you." Maggie sat in stunned silence, all other thoughts fleeing from her girlish brain with his stunning admission.

"Yesterday she was a beautiful girl," he repeated, "and today she's an old woman." His voice was loud in the quiet, and harsh, and Maggie flinched at his cold pronouncement.

"Irene walked out to the car, and I got out. She just looked at me. She thanked me for saving you. Her hands and her voice shook. I didn't know what to say. I can't remember saving you, so it seems wrong to take any credit for it."

Maggie's heart grieved for what he had lost, and what she'd lost as well. He had loved her. He had wrapped her in his arms in a fiery inferno. And he couldn't remember.

"She was afraid of me. And I don't blame her." Johnny looked at her then, defiance and sorrow warring across his handsome face. "I'm afraid too. All my life, when things got hard, I just pushed back, worked a little harder, got mad, used my fists, whatever. But this is something else. If it was just the sadness, or the guilt, or missing my momma and Billy and wishing I could see them again, I think I could learn to live with that. But the fear, the not knowing who I am or what I am -- I don't know how to fight it."

Hardly daring to breath, Maggie stood and turned to face him. The swing still hung between them, but she leaned through it and wrapped her arms around him, laying her head lightly on his shoulder. Johnny was about as stiff and welcoming as a wooden plank, but she didn't move or release him. After a moment, she felt the tension in his shoulders lessen, and he sighed, the sound broken and regretful. His arms rose and encircled her. When he spoke again, his voice was almost tender.

"That morning in the gym, when I was watching you dance -- for a minute it all felt so familiar, and I could see how loving you might be. I understood how I could have fallen for you."

Maggie held her breath, burying her face in his shoulder, wishing she could just stop time for a moment, wondering how loving someone could hurt so much. She could feel the hesitation in him and knew he had more to say.

"But none of this feels real. I just want to wake up and have it all be over. If this were 1958, and I was just a guy and you were my girl, it would be different..."

Maggie started, pulling away from him with a gasp. Her head spun, as if time had turned over. He had said the very same words to her the night of the Winter Ball, when it had been just the two of them, dancing to songs nobody ever danced to anymore.

"Maggie?" Johnny stopped mid-sentence when she pulled away, and he looked down at her, questioning. The moon played across one side of his face and left the right side in shadows, making him look more ghostly than he ever did when he'd haunted Honeyville High.

"If I were just a guy, and you were my girl, I would never let you go," Maggie repeated softly. "You've said those words to me before. But it's never going to happen, is it? You're not just any guy, and I will never be your girl."

Johnny stared down at her for several long seconds. She stared back, and above them the wind moaned mournfully through the trees. The sound echoed the longing in Maggie's heart.

"I just want to go home, Maggie," Johnny's voice was barely louder than the wind. "I just want to go home."

~9~
A Time to Weep

It was much, much later when Maggie was awakened by the sounds of bumping and dragging above her. Her room was just a short flight of stairs below the large attic filled with decades of Honeycutt memorabilia. She lay in bed, listening, still too sleepy to be frightened, yet unable to ignore the fact that something or someone was in the attic. When she had dragged herself in from Johnny's car earlier that night, she had avoided Irene because she didn't want to share her pain and knew she couldn't hide it. She had avoided even her own reflection because she knew it was written all over her face. She had crawled into her bed, and Irene had stuck her head in after a while. Irene hadn't said anything, and Maggie had feigned sleep. Irene had stared for several long moments and then pulled the door shut again, sighing a little as she did.

Now, several hours later, Maggie was pulled from sweet oblivion and felt resentful of the boogie man who had disturbed what little peace she had left. Tossing off the blankets, she grumbled to her bedroom door and wobbled up the stairs to the attic. The stairway was lit, and Maggie could see that the lights in the attic were also blazing.

"Aunt Irene?" Maggie rubbed her bleary eyes and looked at the disorder around her. Just a few months ago she'd organized every inch of the space. Now it was a disaster. Boxes were overturned and dresses pulled out of protective zippered linings. A few hats had been tossed helter skelter, and in the corner, with tears streaming down her face, Irene Honeycutt sat on a faded love seat in a gauzy peach formal, hair done and make-up on. Thoughts of Dickens' Miss Havisham from freshman year English rose unbidden in Maggie's head, and she shuddered a bit at the comparison.

The dress was loose at the bust; Irene's frail shoulders and shrunken chest didn't fill it out as well as her younger self. The waist was pulled tight, where age had thickened her youthful form, but she had managed to zip it, even still. She looked terribly uncomfortable.

"Irene?" Maggie said again, trying not to overreact at finding the bride of Frankenstein crying in her attic in the middle of the night.

"Hello, dear," Irene burbled, attempting cheeriness and normalcy, and failing miserably. "I was just wondering if I could fit into this old thing...I was up here looking for Lizzie's record player. I don't know what I've done with it."

"You're all dolled up. Make up and hair at three a.m., Auntie?" Maggie sat down next to Irene on the dusty love seat and reached out to finger the skirt of the peach confection.

"Go ahead, say it, I'm a silly old woman!" Irene tried to smile, but her words ended in a sob, and she mopped at her eyes with an old flannel doll blanket.

Maggie didn't respond to that. Irene wasn't silly. She was sad and obviously troubled about something. Maggie wondered if it had anything to do with seeing Johnny Kinross back from the grave, sitting in all his youthful glory in front of her house earlier in the day.

"This is beautiful. Is it the dress you wore to the prom? I think I recognize it from one of the pictures in Roger's scrapbook."

"It's funny...I remember wearing red to the prom. I came up here looking for the dress. I know I have a red dress."

"So you didn't come up here looking for the record player?" Maggie poked at her and tried not to smile.

Irene shot her a look that indicated she thought Maggie rude for pointing out her lie. Her tears stopped falling, though, and she smacked Maggie lightly on the arm.

"Smarty pants!" Irene huffed, and Maggie snickered, making Irene smile a little too.

"I remember this dress now. I really am getting old. I did wear this. I had purchased the red dress, but at the last moment I got cold feet. Lizzie, my little sister, informed me that no one would be wearing red and I would feel silly. She was right. It was the only time I ever took fashion advice from a ten-year-old. The funny thing was another girl at the prom was wearing a red dress just like it. I'd forgotten all about her. She stood out like a sore thumb, but she looked wonderful. Johnny danced with her..." Irene's eyes filled with tears once more, and she stopped talking and suddenly stood. "That dress is here somewhere."

Irene started pulling dress bags from a long, free-standing rack, unzipping them like she was on a quest. Maggie scurried after her, tidying up the abandoned and discarded articles of clothing Irene left in her wake.

"Here! I knew it was here somewhere," Irene cackled gleefully, and wrenched an armful of red from a dress bag smashed between two others. Irene's curled and pinned coif was now a rat's nest, and her eye makeup was smeared, but she seemed extraordinarily pleased with herself, so Maggie didn't comment.

"Look at it, Maggie! It's gorgeous. And here are the shoes and the clutch! I never even got to wear this!" Irene wailed mournfully. Struggling out from the disarray she'd created, she headed down the stairs, the red dress hanging over one arm, the shoes and the little silver purse clutched in the other. Maggie looked around in despair. Shaking her head, she left the chaos for another day and pulled the long strings on the weary bulbs, covering Irene's mess with darkness. Gingerly she made her way down the stairs and went in search of her aunt. She couldn't very well go back to bed when Irene was having a major melt-down.

She found Irene in her bedroom, sitting at the ornate vanity in the corner, fixing her smudged makeup and smoothing her ruffled hair. Maggie hadn't spent any time in Irene's room, and she looked around at the girlish abode with troubled eyes. The big mahogany bed had a wilted canopy above it with long curtains that could be closed at night. The spread was a faded rose color with matching pillows and a yellowed lace bedskirt hanging below it. The furniture was well made and delicate. A small lady's writing desk with a slim cushioned chair adorned one wall. Pictures framed in roses covered the dresser and vanity. Even the wall paper was a faded pattern in pale pink. Maggie couldn't see anything of Roger's in the room and wondered if they had slept separately.

Maggie sank down on the bed, and a hint of lavender and talcum powder rose from the rumpled sheets.

"Has this always been your room, Aunt Irene?" Maggie questioned softly.

"Hmmm? Oh, no. Not always. When Roger and I moved back into the house after Daddy died, we shared the master bedroom. When Roger died, I moved back in here. Gus and Shad and a few others helped me move all my things from the attic. It looks almost like it did when I was a girl. I love it. It makes me feel young again."

Maggie watched her aunt for a minute more. Irene repinned some loose hairs and powdered her nose. Then she stood and reached for the red dress that was laying in a heap on the thick beige carpet.

"Auntie? Why are you doing this?"

Irene froze, halfway through trying to unzip herself from the peach formal to don the red. Her hands fell back to her sides, and she looked at Maggie with sorrow-filled eyes.

"Is it because you saw Johnny today?" Maggie continued gently. "He told me he came here because it was one of the only places that still looked the same."

Irene crumpled weakly onto the vanity bench, her shoulders bowed in dejection. After a moment she nodded her head in surrender.

"When I saw him, I forgot for a moment that I no longer looked the way he does. He hasn't aged a day. I was frightened because none of it makes any sense. It wasn't until he had gone, and I'd stopped shaking, that I came into the house and caught sight of myself in the entrance hall mirror. For a moment I didn't recognize myself, Maggie. My reflection was that of an old woman, and I realized, maybe for the first time, that my life is....over. I won't fall in love again. A man won't look at me with passion in his eyes. I won't ever be kissed the way a woman wants to be kissed, ever again. I am an old woman. But I don't feel old inside. Inside, I am still beautiful and young. I'm still the girl who wanted to wear this dress but lost courage at the last second."

Maggie slid off the bed and knelt at Irene's feet. Sadness made her heart heavy and her head drooped into Irene's lap. Why was it that human beings constantly grieved for what they couldn't have? She was no exception. She lifted her head and tried to smile.

"Let me help you put on the red dress. You should get to wear it at least once."

Irene smoothed Maggie's hair and gazed down into her face, a face that reminded her so much of herself many years ago. She shook her head slowly.

"No...I don't think I want to see myself in it after all. I'd much rather see how you look in it, Maggie. It will do my heart good to remind myself that once upon a time I was as young and beautiful as you are now. Come on. Let's have a look."

Maggie reluctantly stood and, dropping her pajamas, stepped out of them and pulled the red dress over her head and down her body. She smoothed the thin straps onto her shoulders, and Irene zipped the back in one swift pull. Maggie spun and, seeing her reflection in the vanity mirror, smiled with pleasure. She had always been a little uncomfortable in red, as if it drew the kind of attention she'd rather not have. But she should wear it more often. Her skin glowed against the vivid hue, and her eyes were lit up like Christmas lights. Her hair was rumpled from sleeping so she reached for a brush on Irene's vanity and brushed her hair to the side. She had gone to bed with it damp, and it had dried in heavy waves, giving her an old pin-up girl look.

"Take off your glasses," Irene demanded. "Let me do your eyes. You know they say a girl can never wear too much blue eye shadow!"

"No! Aunt Irene!" Maggie objected, pulling away.

"I'm teasing! Wrong decade, Maggie!" Irene chortled at her own joke and proceeded with a surprisingly light hand to line and shadow Maggie's eyes. Stepping back, she clucked over her handiwork. Then she reached for a tube of deep red lipstick and demanded that Maggie pucker up.

"Now. You take your lipstick and put it in your little purse....see? Right here." Irene produced the little sparkly silver purse she had discovered in the attic. She unhooked the clasp with a snap and dropped the little gold-plated lipstick tube in the bag.

"It's the perfect size. Look, you could even fit your glasses inside." Irene demonstrated the convenience of the little clutch. Then, clicking it shut, she handed it to Maggie.

'You are now ready for the dance. Now let's see you twirl!" Maggie stood, and stepping into the matching shoes, she twirled for Irene. She immediately found herself giggling with delight. Girls never outgrew playing dress-up.

Irene clapped and giggled right along with her. "The hair is different than mine would have been. It wasn't really in fashion to wear it long. But you and I definitely could have passed for sisters." Irene began to hum and, extending her arms to Maggie, began spinning her around the bedroom in a dizzy dance to her off-key tune.

Around and around they went until Irene got quite breathless and collapsed onto her bed, her dress poofing out around her, revealing her skinny legs and old-lady knees. Maggie curled up beside her and stared at the high ceiling as she waited for Irene to catch her breath.

"We girls danced together all the time when I was young," Irene sighed. "You do it nowadays, and people call you mean names, but we would jive and jitterbug and swing together all the time. The fancy dresses kind of get in the way, though." Irene giggled again, and at that moment she sounded very much like a seventeen-year-old girl.

"You should have worn this dress, Auntie," Maggie murmured. "The peach is beautiful, but maybe the red would have forced you out of your shell."

"Aw, Maggie. I was never in a shell. It was more like a self-imposed cell. I don't think anything could have altered the path I was on. Not even a bright red dress. I think back on those days. What if I hadn't married Roger? What if I'd gone to New York and studied fashion like I secretly dreamed. What if I'd gone to Paris for the summer after I graduated like my daddy promised me I could? I look back and think what an absolute ninny I was."

"Why didn't you do those things?"

"I didn't understand that the choices we make stay with us forever, Maggie. My daddy always spoiled me. He gave me everything I wanted. But most of all, he adored me. I took it for granted. I just thought everyone would treat me that way. I didn't know how precious his love was. Then Roger came along, and he was rude to me, made me cry, treated me quite badly. We called it playing hard to get. I was intrigued by him. I made it my goal to make him want me -- to be his girl.

It was a game to me. It wasn't until after we were married that I realized that Roger would never adore me. He might have loved me; I actually think he did in a way. But he would never think I hung the moon like my daddy did. He would never treat me like I was a treasure, because to him, I wasn't. I had no value to Roger beyond the pretty face and the Honeycutt name. And now, here I am, seventy-one years old, and the choice I made at seventeen is the choice I still have to live with today. So many times I could have left. But I had lost all confidence in my ability to make good choices. I didn't have any education or world experience, so I stayed. And I gave my life away."

For a long time, neither of them spoke but lay, watching the ceiling fan whirring its peaceful tune. Time was a greedy banker who never paid interest.

"Johnny feels like his life was taken away...." Maggie whispered, slipping her hand into Irene's. "I know it's not the same...but he has his whole life in front of him and doesn't want it. You have your whole life behind you and wish you could have it back."

Maggie waited, wondering if she'd said something wrong, but Irene didn't reply. Propping herself up on her elbow, she peered down at Irene. She was asleep. A delicate snore escaped her open mouth, and Maggie shook her head fondly and pulled a coverlet over the two of them. There was no way she was getting up for dance practice in an hour. Or school for that matter. Lying down again, she drifted off to sleep, her head filled with images of Johnny and Irene, young and carefree in 1958.

***

Maggie awoke to the sound of a vacuum cleaner and a cheerful disc jockey counting down in another room. She felt like she had been asleep for a only a short while, but from the amount of sunshine streaming in the windows, it had been a lot longer than that. Irene no longer lay beside her, but the peach formal was laid across the bed. The bed was neatly made beneath her. Huh? How had Irene managed that?

"Note to self," Maggie said out loud, struggling to a sitting position. "Prom dresses are not for sleeping." The red dress was cutting into her sides and making her legs itch like she had rolled in grass. The thin bejeweled strap of the silver clutch was wrapped around her wrist; she even had the red shoes on her feet. Looking down at them, she felt a little like Dorothy in *The Wizard of Oz*. She clicked her red heels together a couple of times and said the required line about there not being any place

144

like home. Climbing off the bed, Maggie attempted to straighten and smooth the wrinkled dress.

"Where are my pajamas? This dress has gotta go." Maggie searched the floor for the pjs she had dropped the night before, but they were nowhere in sight. Irene must have picked them up. Catching her reflection in the mirror, Maggie yelped in surprise. The ruby lipstick Irene had applied was smeared around her mouth, and her eyes looked like she'd gotten a bit carried away with the whole smokey-eyed look. The smokey part extended about an inch below each eye.

Her hair was a lion's mane, and Maggie reached for Irene's brush with the inlaid mother-of -pearl handle. It gleamed as though Irene had randomly decided to polish the silver upon awakening. Next to the brush lay the matching mirror and comb, and a perfume bottle with a bulbous diffuser was placed nearby. Lipsticks were scattered here and there, and a photo of a young Roger was placed in a position of prominence on the far left side. Maggie picked it up and studied it for a moment; strange, she hadn't noticed it last night. A little note was wedged into the ornate frame of the oval vanity mirror and Maggie leaned in for a closer look. It wasn't a note after all, but a ticket stub from a movie theater called the Marquee. The ticket stub didn't look much different than a carnival ticket - it just had the name of the theater and the price of the ticket printed in the corner - $0.60.

She'd seen the remains of the old theater downtown. The long vertical sign still remained, jutting out from the side of the abandoned brick building. The Marquee windows had been broken and the movie posters removed long ago. There had been a fund raiser hosted by the Honeyville Historical Society to refurbish the old theater not long before the fire that had destroyed Honeyville High. The project had been put on hold, however. Irene said the money raised would now go toward building a new school. She said it had been one of her favorite places growing up, and she was disappointed that she might never see it restored.

The vacuum started up again somewhere else in the house, and Maggie turned away from the mirror, puzzled by Irene's sudden need to pull out all her old things and display them like she was seventeen again. A ribbon of fear wound its way around Maggie's heart. She needed Irene to keep it together; Irene was the only person Maggie had left in the world.

Maggie walked toward the bedroom door and tripped, her heel catching on the edge of the heavy rug that was spread across the wooden floor. Wait. There *was* no rug in this room. Irene's bedroom had beige carpet that she fussed over incessantly. Maggie stared down at the gaily patterned rug -- roses and vines intertwining in a repeating pattern across a pale pink background. She looked around the room again, trying to find an explanation for the impossible. The door to the heavy wardrobe stood wide, giving Maggie a glimpse at the clothing inside. Tops and skirts stuck out in messy disarray, and pearls and shoes were strewn on the floor nearby. None of the clothing was familiar. The lamp sitting on the bedside table was different too. Last Christmas, Gus had given Irene a gold reading lamp that she could turn on simply by clapping. Irene had thought it the most exciting thing she had ever seen and had gleefully clapped the little lamp off and on, over and over, like a kid in a toy store. She had placed it by her bed; it had been there last night. Maggie had clapped it out, relieved that she wouldn't have to get up. And in the corner, a record player in an ornate console, not unlike the one she had seen in Lizzie's room, stood open and ready, a record docked on the waiting turn-table.

Maggie reached for the door, the heavy knob smooth and familiar against her palm, soothing her in a way only tangible things can. There had to be an explanation. She would just go find Irene. She walked out into the long hallway and proceeded down the stairs.

She noticed immediately that the house had a new sheen, an air of vibrancy and wealth that made her doubly suspicious that she had awakened in a different

147

house. The wood floors gleamed, and the runner centered on the stairs was plush and new. The banister beneath Maggie's hand was smooth, and a hint of lemon oil rose as she ran her hand along its surface. At the bottom of the stairs was a table and a stiff-back chair that Maggie had never seen before. Around the corner a phone was anchored to the wall. It looked like something used only for decoration. The rotary dial protruded above the rectangular brass box, and the ear piece, at the end of a long cord, was attached on the left side. Maggie touched it gingerly. It rang suddenly, a shrill clanging in the quiet hallway, and Maggie sputtered and screamed, jumping a foot in the air. Footsteps started down the stairs. Maggie looked up to see sturdy shoes, nyloned legs, and a full yellow dress covered with an apron. Not Irene. Maggie raced through the short corridor and into the kitchen. Her heart raced as she looked at the white cupboards, so familiar yet so wrong. The counter tops were a cheerful red formica, the floor linoleum in a marbled pattern of red and beige. Not Irene's kitchen. Somebody had baked bread, and the loaves were cooling on a cloth on the wooden table that was centered in the large space.

Maggie felt the way she had the time she had mistakenly walked into the men's bathroom at school. All the dimensions were the same: the corners, the mirrors, and the colors were identical, but the function and fixtures were all wrong. And everyone inside was a stranger. At the time, it had taken her brain a moment to compute and inform her of her mistake. When she realized what she had done, she'd been almost as horrified about going back out as she was about staying put.

She looked out the kitchen window that overlooked the front porch. Rose bushes lined the walk. That was the same. There was the front porch swing. Check. A long pink Cadillac pulled into the drive. Irene was home! She would explain. Maggie watched as the car came to a jerky stop halfway between the house and the garage. Three girls in skirts and blouses and cardigan sweaters in varying colors and similar styles piled out of Irene's car. They were laughing and chattering, and Maggie frowned in dismay. The girl with the dark hair and the familiar gait led the way up the front steps like she owned the place. They were coming inside!

Maggie raced through the kitchen, praying the phone call that had summoned the strange woman had ended. The corridor was empty, and Maggie took the stairs two at a time, flying out of sight just as the front door swung inward, granting entry to the trio of teens that spilled inside. A door opened to her right, and a little girl of about ten stuck her head out as Maggie reached the upper landing.

"Lizzie?" Maggie cried.

~10~
A Time to Sow

The little girl's eyes widened in horror, and her jaw dropped in preparation to scream bloody murder. Maggie sprang forward, wrapping her arms around the little girl and dragging her back into the room beyond. She slammed the door with her rear-end and sank to the floor, the little girl still clutched in her arms, her right hand clamped tightly against her mouth.

"Please don't scream! I'm not going to hurt you. I don't know how I got here, but I will leave just as soon as I can figure out how to get home...okay? Just please don't scream! I don't want them to call the police and throw me in jail. I promise I'm not a crazy woman. I've just misplaced my.....umm, my house, see. I've just lost my.....my sense of direction, yeah! That's it. I've just gotten turned around. Maybe I was sleep walking and came into your house....." Maggie stopped. The little girl wasn't fighting anymore. Instead, she was gazing at Maggie with extreme interest. Her eyes had resumed normal size and had lost their horrified glaze. Maggie hesitantly removed her hand. When the girl made no attempt to alarm the house, Maggie dropped her arms and released her altogether. The girl sat up and folded her legs beneath her. Her soft brown hair was pulled back in a messy ponytail, and she wore a silky pair of pale green pajamas with cropped pants and short sleeves. They looked like something Doris Day would have worn....or maybe Carol Brady, although Maggie thought her decades may be a little off. Maggie wished she had a pair. The dress was really starting to chaff.

"I remember you..." the little girl whispered. "You're Maggie. You called me Lizzie. You remember me too, right?"

Maggie almost moaned out loud. It was all too much. Instead, she nodded her head. "Yes. I remember you. How's Jamie?"

Lizzie's one eyebrow rose and her nostrils slightly flared. "My bear?" she said incredulously. Stupid question, apparently.

"Lizzie? Will you pinch me please? Really, really hard?"

The little girl looked pleased by Maggie's request, the way little girls are when given a chance to get even. She reached forward and, grabbing a small section of skin, pinched Maggie's arm enthusiastically.

"Ouch!" Maggie gasped, slapping her hand away. "Okay. Yep. Definitely not asleep."

"Last time I could see through you!" Lizzie cried and pinched her again. When Maggie swiped at her she froze, listening.

"Irene's coming!!" she hissed, her eyes widening like before. "Why in the world are you wearing her dress? She's gonna go ape!"

Maggie scrambled off the floor, smoothing the dress and trying to come up with a plausible explanation. The truth was, Irene said she could wear it. Somehow, she didn't think that would fly.

"Stay here. I will take care of this!" Lizzie poked her head out the door, waving Maggie out of the line of sight.

Maggie hugged the wall behind the door and watched through the crack that was created when Lizzie opened it a little wider.

"Hi, Shirley! Hi, Cathy!" Lizzie chirped in her best annoying-little-sister voice. "Are you guys gonna try on your dresses? Can I watch?"

"Hi Lizzie," one of the girls replied cheerfully. The other reached out and smoothed her hair. "Are you feeling better? Irene said you've been sick."

"I'm fine. Nana says I can't miss any more school, though. I milked that sore throat for all it was worth."

The two girls looked at each other and laughed at Lizzie's blunt admission. Irene's friends were both pretty, and though one was dark and the other a redhead, there was a resemblance in their smiles and in the tone of their laughter that had Maggie guessing they were sisters.

"Lizzie?" Irene came out of her room and into the hallway, a perturbed frown on her face. Maggie stared in amazement. Aunt Irene at seventeen was very lovely indeed. She was slim and stylish, and her eyes were a soft blue, her skin a pearly white, and her brown hair perfectly flipped and held back by a thick white headband. Irene's tearful countenance filled her memory. *"I am an old woman. But I don't feel old inside..."*

"Lizzie?" Irene had stopped in front of Lizzie's door, her arms folded, her hip popped to one side. "When I left today, both of my dresses were laid out on my bed. Now the red one is gone, and it looks as if SOMEONE has been bouncing on my bed." She tipped her chin to the side and raised her brows at her little sister.

Lizzie pursed her lips and thought for a moment. Maggie held her breath and hoped her grandmother knew how to tell a convincing story.

"Oh that. I think Nana said something about the red dress needing to be pressed or aired out. She said it smelled like armpit sweat...or something."

The three teens gasped, and the girl named Shirley covered her mouth, trying hard not to laugh. Irene growled deep in her throat.

"Lizzie!"

"Oh come on, Irene!" Lizzie said, mimicking Irene's stance. "You know you aren't going to wear the red dress. You'll feel silly in it. Cathy and Shirley are both wearing pastels, right?" Cathy bobbed her head in agreement and added that she was wearing "mint" and Shirley was wearing "blush." Maggie almost snorted and pinched her nose to keep the giggle from escaping.

Lizzie continued her campaign. "You look marvelous in the peach dress, sissy! Did she show you, girls?" Lizzie looked at the sisters who shook their heads in unison. "Irene! You have to show them! My sister is the most beautiful girl in the world." Irene's eyes softened, and her folded arms dropped to her sides. She smiled and dropped a kiss on Lizzie's head. One minute flat, and Lizzie had Irene right where she wanted her.

"Come on! Let's go!" Irene clapped her hands excitedly and spun toward her room, her friends following close behind. Lizzie closed the door and sighed gustily, making her bangs rise and fall on her forehead.

"Whew! I thought we were goners, for sure. Stay here! I have to make sure she doesn't change her mind. Just in case, take off that dress! My robe is hanging on my closet door. It's too long for me, so it should do until Irene leaves and we can find you something in her closet." With that, Lizzie was gone, shutting her bedroom door firmly behind her.

Without wasting a second, Maggie struggled out of the red dress and dropped it to the floor with a sigh. She had on a pair of pink bikini panties and that was all. Somehow she had slipped through the layers of time and found herself with nothing more than a pair of undies and borrowed formal wear, and a lot of good that did her! The red shoes and the dress belonged to Irene, the young Irene! She shook the frightening thoughts from her head. Dwelling on her predicament would only cause her to close her eyes, curl up in the fetal position, and scream hysterically.

She found Lizzie's robe and pulled it on, thankfully belting the soft flowered cotton around herself. It was too short, and the sleeves hung several inches above her wrists. But her pink panties and bare chest were covered, and for now that was enough. She wished she could sneak down the hall to the bathroom, but didn't dare. She would just have to hope Lizzie made short work of Irene and her friends. She picked up the red formal she'd stepped out of and shook it briskly. Luckily, it didn't seem all the worse for wear. The skirt was gauzy, and the creases weren't very noticeable. She hung it in Lizzie's brimming closet, hoping that Irene wouldn't discover it there and accuse Lizzie of theft. She worked it into the back of the closet; these girls seemed to have plenty of pretty things. Irene's declaration that her daddy had spoiled her seemed to be true of Lizzie as well.

Lizzie's room was exactly as she remembered it from her coma "dream." Maggie was now convinced it hadn't been a dream at all. She had actually been here, at least in spirit. Lizzie remembered her, too. Maggie shuddered to think what would have happened if she hadn't.

After a while, she heard voices in the hallway and dove behind the bed, squeezing her eyes shut as if that would help to disguise her. But the voices went past, and she heard the clippety cloppety sound of feet bounding down stairs. A moment later it was silent, and Maggie rose tentatively from the floor.

The door shot open, and Lizzie flew in, her eyes bright with victory. "Maggie?" Her eyes found Maggie immediately, and she launched into an explanation of all that had transpired since she left the room.

"....so the Russel twins invited Irene to sleep over, and they're all going to help each other get ready for the prom at their house tomorrow. Daddy is out of town, so it's just me, you, and Nana! Nana believes everything I say. I'll just tell her you're a cousin. You can sleep in Irene's room if you want or the guest room upstairs...or Daddy's room!" Lizzie laughed as if sleeping in her father's room was the most outrageous thing she had ever heard. It would be pretty weird.

"Wait...wouldn't your Nana know that I'm not family? I mean, if she's your grandmother..." Maggie's voice trailed off at Lizzie's confused expression.

"She's not my grandmother! She was hired to be my nanny when Momma died. I started calling her Nana. Now she's kind of a housekeeper too. She lives here with us. Her room is downstairs. She might wonder about you, but she'd never say you couldn't stay, and you look enough like us that she won't question it. Plus...you'll eventually go back to where you came from, right? Last time you only stayed for twenty minutes or so. Can you try to stay longer this time? I'm bored." Lizzie flopped on her bed, illustrating her claim.

"Elizabeth Honeycutt...you are something else." Maggie smiled down at the precocious child and shook her head in wonder.

"Yeah, yeah, yeah." Lizzie waved the compliment away, but Maggie noticed her cheeks pinked with both pleasure and maybe a little embarrassment. "The Russell twins said they could only handle me in small doses, which is why they all decided to sleep at their place. I was trying to be obnoxious, just to get rid of them."

Maggie laughed and plopped down beside her new friend. "You're talking about Shirley and Cathy, right? They're twins?"

"Nah, not twins. Just sisters. Cathy's older. She was born in September and Shirley came along nine months later, in June. So they're in the same year at school and everything. I think they prefer to be called twins. It seems to embarrass them that they're not. Shirley said once that her parents reproduce like rabbits. I asked her if they had any new baby bunnies for sale, but then Irene made me leave her room," Lizzie remembered with a forlorn expression. "Anyway, they're Irene's best friends."

Maggie giggled. Who was it that said every generation thinks they invented sex? Things weren't so very different in the '50s it seemed. "I liked them. I wonder why Irene's never mentioned them?" Maggie mused thoughtfully.

"You know Irene?" Lizzie frowned.

"Yes. I live with her. She's my great-aunt. Just...a long time from now, that's all."

"Do I live with you too? Am I a grownup like Daddy? Am I beautiful? Did I marry James Dean? If I didn't, I hope I at least got to marry Johnny...."

Maggie felt a familiar tug from somewhere deep inside and gasped a little, recognizing the sensation and what it might portend.

"Lizzie. I don't think you and I can talk about this. I won't be able to stay for long if we do. Does that make sense?"

Lizzie sat up and peered into Maggie's eyes. "You'll disappear?" she whispered, distracted from her line of questioning.

"Is that what happened last time?" Maggie queried softly.

"Yes. You just faded away."

"I don't want to fade away...not yet." Thoughts of Johnny surfaced to the forefront of her mind. She wanted to stay a little longer. She needed to stay a little longer. She didn't know if she could change anything, but she wanted to try.

"What year is it, Lizzie?" She hoped the question would not make her disappear.

"It's 1958, silly," Lizzie said, dumbfounded.

Maggie nodded, strangely comforted by Lizzie's response. If Prom 1958 was tomorrow night, Johnny would be there. A realization shook her suddenly. Irene had said there had been a girl at the prom in a red dress, just like hers. Could it have been Maggie? Her mind tripped and stuttered over the possibility. She felt a wave of disorientation wash over her, and she pushed the thoughts away, worried they would pull her under. She smiled brightly at Lizzie, willing herself steady.

"I am silly, huh? I'm also stranded in your house with no clothes and no money, and I'd like to stick around for a while, if that's okay with you."

"Neat-o! Let's find you something to wear. And let's go have an ice cream. I'm tired of being cooped up in my bedroom. It's almost dinnertime, and I've been in my pajamas for three days!"

Maggie begged for the bathroom and a toothbrush and met Lizzie in Irene's room when she was finished using the toilet and scrubbing her face with the cold cream she found in the cabinet. Lizzie was already dressed and had laid out an outfit on the bed, complete with a bra with cone shaped cups that looked more suited to Wonder Woman than a pretty seventeen-year-old like Irene. Maggie looked at it doubtfully. The panties laying beside it would cover her belly button.

"I think you should pull your hair up in a ponytail. It won't look quite so babyish that way. And here's a hair ribbon that will match your sweater." Lizzie seemed so pleased with herself that Maggie decided not to complain about the underwear, or the comment that her long hair was "babyish."

"While you get dressed, I will run downstairs and take care of Nana. She can give us some of her grocery money, and we'll have dinner at "The Malt.""

Lizzie buzzed out of the room and Maggie proceeded to pull the borrowed clothes on. She pulled on the bra and panties, feeling like she'd stepped into a commercial for synchronized swimming. She chortled at her bullet shaped breasts, outlined perfectly by the fitted blue sweater Lizzie had picked. The blue polka dot pants were high waisted -- they had to be to cover those giant undies. They looked like capris....or cropped equestrian pants. She slid her feet into the white flats and dutifully pulled her hair into a high ponytail, tying the ribbon around the elastic band.

Twirling in front of Irene's mirror, she wondered if she would dare leave the house this way. She picked through the makeup on Irene's vanity, finding an eyelash curler, an eyebrow pencil, and a round tin of eyeshadow that slightly resembled what she used in 2011. There was a little brush and a rectangular pan of something that said "Maybelline." She stared at it, puzzled. She decided to leave it alone. Instead, she lined her eyes with the black eyeliner pencil and dabbed on a little shadow. She applied some red lipstick, which seemed to be the only shade Irene had.

She supposed she would do. It was then that Maggie realized not only did she not have her glasses here in 1958, but she didn't seem to need them. She spun around, focusing her eyes on every corner of the room and then swinging back to her befuddled reflection in the mirror. Crystal clear, all of it. It didn't make any sense. But at least she wouldn't go stumbling around while she was here, squinting and bumping into things.

"I've got two dollars! We're going to eat like kings! We even have enough for a show!" Lizzie burst into the room waving the money around in her hand and dancing around. "Nana gave it to me! She thinks I am meeting Eileen and Lucy. I decided not to tell her about you until tomorrow. Don't worry. I'll sneak you in tonight. She doesn't come upstairs after bedtime unless I screech like a banshee, which I sometimes do. Seeing ghosts isn't always the funnest talent." Lizzie slipped her hand into Maggie's and proceeded to pull her out the door and down the stairs, never even pausing for air.

"You can ride Irene's bike. She never rides it anymore, not since Daddy bought her a car. You do know how to ride a bike, don't you?" Lizzie walked to the garage and opened the door, flipping on the light to brighten the interior. Within seconds, Maggie had assured Lizzie that she did indeed know how to ride a bike, and they were off down the street, heading downtown for supper in 1958.

It was a good thing Lizzie was with her because although the general layout was the same and she recognized some of the homes, the spaces between the homes was larger, and much was missing from the landscape. Main Street was decidedly different. Although many of the buildings were the same, the businesses they housed had almost all changed. There was a huge drugstore, a J.C Penney and Co. department store, a jeweler that had a giant cartoonish picture of a diamond and "Watch Repair" emblazoned below. There was a barber shop with the twirly red and blue striped pole and men in hats going in and out of the establishment. There was a furniture store that didn't exist in modern day Honeyville, either - it had televisions and toasters in the windows with a banner that shouted that they now carried the "Crosley Automatic -- the world's first fully automatic television with five electronic wonders at your fingertips." A bank on the corner of Main and Center Street, with a massive clock jutting out from the sign declared it "A great time to save."

There was a courthouse with stately pillars that must have been torn down before Maggie ever arrived in Honeyville. It sat next to Honeyville High which looked old even in 1958. No wonder they were building a new one. Maggie wondered if she would have a chance to go see it, and if the construction was finished. It had just been completed in the summer of 1958 when Billy and Johnny fell from the balcony. Maggie pushed those thoughts away.

Everywhere she looked were old/new cars and people in the costume of 1950s America. Maggie felt like she was on a movie set, and her eyes whipped back and forth at one wonder after another. One department store had "5 cents to $1.50" in thick gold lettering above its large windows, and like every female in history who smells a bargain, she was tempted to browse, just for a minute. Maggie thought of Johnny driving up and down the streets, comparing Honeyville then and now, and felt a surge of melancholy, finally understanding exactly how different the two towns really were.

"Hey, Dizzy Lizzie! Who's your babysitter?" Lizzie had crossed the street and swung off her bike in front of The Malt, Maggie close behind her. Maggie gawked at the group of boys piling out of a big blue Lincoln and almost crashed Irene's bike into the side of the diner. She let out a screech and at the last minute managed to brake and step off without making a fool of herself. She didn't look at the boys, but primly hitched her bike on the rack and pretended disinterest in a young Roger Carlton and his three friends.

"She's not my baby sitter, Roger!" Lizzie retorted hotly and stuck her tongue out at one of the boys, who promptly stuck his out in response. Roger slapped the back of his head and sighed. The boys wore V-necked sweaters that revealed the collars of their white undershirts. They all had identical haircuts as well --

buzzed sides with a short flat top. The three seemed to take their cues from Roger, and when he crossed his arms and smiled at Maggie, they repeated the action almost immediately.

"Introduce me, Lizzie." Roger had a toothpick in his mouth that he slowly moved from one side to the other. Maggie had seen him three times now, and she liked him less each time, if that were even possible. Her heart pounded at his proximity, and she felt a little sick to her stomach. His hair was dark and his eyes green, and he was undoubtedly handsome - and very sure of himself.

"I'm telling Irene that you were staring at our cousin with drool on your chin, Roger," Lizzie said snidely, looping her arm through Maggie's and pulling her into the Malt Shop. That seemed to bring Roger up short. It was one of his friends who called out after them.

"Does the cousin have a name, Dizzy?"

"Do you have a brain, Larry?" Lizzie replied, and Larry's friends guffawed at her wit. Maggie decided she definitely liked her grandmother.

"Inquiring minds want to know!" another boy yelled out.

"Her name is Maggie, okay? Now go away!" Lizzie grumped, and they walked into The Malt. It wasn't much to look at, really. It was shaped like a long train car with small windows running all along the side. Inside, the roof was domed and a long line of stools connected to an even longer bar ran along one side with narrow tables and metal chairs running along the side with the windows. A soda fountain, complete with pull levers, occupied one side of the counter, and grey menus with three red stripes along the top and three red stripes on the bottom were spread here and there for easy access. Big grey and red squares criss-crossed the floor, and a jukebox played songs in the corner. A man in a big white apron and a white cap dispensed soda and barked out orders to the kitchen behind him. There were a couple of waitresses in grey dresses with rounded white collars, little caps, and white ruffled aprons manning the tables. The place was brimming with teenagers.

Lizzie hopped up on a stool and pulled Maggie along, tapping the shoulder of the fellow sitting between the only two empty stools and asking him politely if he would "scoot over so she and her friend could sit together."

He slid to his right agreeably, and Lizzie patted the stool he had vacated, indicating that Maggie should sit. She did so and was trying not to be too noticeable about staring at everyone and everything when Lizzie informed her that she would order for both of them.

The two boys to her right were discussing a ball player's salary, one exclaiming that "before you know it, athletes would be making more than the president!" She giggled a little at that, and one of the boys looked up at her in surprise. Maggie's giggle died in her throat. She recognized him. He glanced away immediately, blushing furiously, apparently unaccustomed to eye contact with girls.

It was Billy Kinross. She was sure of it. Same glasses and short spiky hair with the cowlick in front. He had a splash of freckles across his nose, and he wore a short-sleeved dress shirt and khakis. He reminded her a little of Wally Cleaver.

"Lizzie," Maggie leaned toward her young cohort and whispered into her ear. "Who is the boy two stools down on my right?"

"That's Billy Kinross. Why? Do you think he's cute? If you think he's dreamy, you should see his brother."

Maggie couldn't very well respond that she knew exactly how "dreamy" Johnny Kinross was. She didn't need to; Lizzie had simply paused to take a slug of her pink, foamy malt. Maggie pulled the strawberry confection to her own lips and drank thirstily as Lizzie swallowed and continued, her top lip mustached in milky pink.

"Billy is in here all the time, lucky duck, because his mother works here. I think he gets his dinner free."

"His...mother?" Maggie swung her head around, looking for the two waitresses. "Is she here now?"

"Prob'ly. Billy doesn't come unless she's here. No free food that way." The man in the white cap and apron set baskets brimming with food and lined in red tissue paper in front of them. Maggie's stomach growled loudly, and Lizzie snickered into her hand.

"Can I get you ladies anything else?" the man asked with a rosy- cheeked grin. Maggie thanked him politely as Lizzie dove in, but his attention was drawn almost immediately to something going on beyond them. Maggie swiveled in her seat to see what had narrowed his eyes and robbed him of his cheerful smile.

Roger Carlton sat at a table with his three friends, but his arm was clamped firmly around a waitress's trim waist, and his other hand had captured one of her hands in his. The waitress was trying to extricate herself while still maintaining the facade that nothing was amiss, but her discomfort was obvious. Maggie didn't have to see her face to know it had to be Dolly Kinross. She was a platinum blonde, and her hair was rolled and pinned in curls around her head. Maggie could only see her profile, but she could see how nicely the dress hugged her hips and how youthful her figure was. Roger Carlton seemed to have noticed as well. Funny, Maggie had been given the impression that he was angry with Dolly Kinross for having an affair with his father. Maybe that wasn't why he was angry at all.

The man behind the counter called, "Dolly...order up!" although no order had been called from the window behind him. The woman freed herself and turned away from the boys. Roger watched her walk away, and his face held a strange expression. He caught Maggie staring at him, and his face smoothed immediately. He gave a little wave, and her heart gave a dread filled twist. She turned away from him quickly. As she turned, she noticed the episode had not escaped Billy Kinross either. His cheeks were ruddy again, and his eyes were on the counter-top, his hands fisted and white. Dolly Kinross slid behind the long counter and shot a grateful look at the man in the apron. He shook his head at her and turned away. She smiled and shrugged and, leaning forward, pinched Billy's cheeks, causing him to lift his sullen gaze.

"Eat up, Billy. I get off in a few minutes. Can you walk down to Gene's and ride home with Johnny?" Her voice was musical, and there was the slightest gap between her front two teeth giving her a winsome look. Deep dimples appeared at each side of her mouth. Johnny had those dimples.

"Aren't you comin' home?" Billy asked, his voice low and wary.

"In a while, darling." She glanced away then, and busied herself removing her apron. "Don't worry about me." She sat a brown bag on the counter in front of Billy. "This is for your brother. Make sure he gets it now!" Dolly Kinross let herself be distracted, and she hustled away. Billy sighed mightily and grabbed the bag, sliding off the stool as he did. He sneaked a glance at Maggie without turning his head, his eyes darting sideways. He ducked his head when he again caught her looking at him.

"Gee whiz, Maggie!" Lizzie breathed between bites. "Stop staring. You're acting like you've never seen a cute boy before."

Maggie twisted back around on her stool and stared at the food she hadn't even touched -- food she no longer had any appetite for. She was almost nauseous with the knowledge she carried. She knew what would happen to Dolly and Billy, to Johnny, even to the little girl who sat next to her. She knew their life stories, their heartaches, and the day each one died. Could she change any of it? Did she dare? What if she made things worse just by being here?

She wanted to run down the street, screaming after Billy, warning him of the perils to come. And more than anything else, she wanted to find Johnny and lock her arms around him, convince him that she loved him, and never go back home. Could she? Was it possible that she could stay and save him from Purgatory all together? Would time go on in the future without her? Or would it remain suspended until she returned, or until she caught back up with it?

~11~
A Time to Keep

When Lizzie and Maggie left The Malt, the sun was setting, and as long as Maggie's eyes stayed trained on the horizon, she could almost believe she was in the same Honeyville, in spite of all the changes in the last 53 years. Maggie convinced Lizzie to ride farther down Main, past Gene's Automotive. But the place was locked up, and the plaque on the door read "closed." There was no sign of the Kinross brothers or Johnny's car. Maggie felt a surge of panic. How could she shrug her shoulders and pedal meekly back to her house, to Lizzie's house, knowing that at any minute she could be whisked back to where she had come from.

"Are you okay, Maggie?" Lizzie said softly, straddling her bike next to Maggie, who sat staring dejectedly at the quiet automotive shop.

"I am in love with someone who doesn't know I exist," Maggie tried to laugh at what she'd meant to be an inside joke, but the laughter stuck in her throat.

Lizzie looked at the automotive shop and back at Maggie. Lizzie Honeycutt was many things, but dumb wasn't one of them. "You're in love with Billy Kinross? Already?"

"No. I'm not in love with Billy." Maggie smiled ruefully and turned away from the empty storefront, climbing back onto the seat of her bike and positioning one foot on the ground and one on a pedal.

"Johnny?" Lizzie squeaked, as if Maggie had just confessed her love for the King of England. "You love Johnny Kinross?"

Maggie felt tears prick her eyes. It seemed Johnny was out of her league even in 1958. She started to pedal back down Main Street, Lizzie trying to keep pace behind her. She knew her way home, but the return trip was not as filled with wonder and excitement as the trip to town had been. Maggie felt a sluggishness in her muscles and a fatigue in her weary head that had her fearing her time was closing fast. When they reached the house, she climbed the stairs and fell across Lizzie's bed, barely able to keep her eyes open.

"Maggie?" Lizzie's voice was small and scared, and Maggie opened her eyes with great effort. "Are you sick?"

"No, Lizzie. I don't think so. I just think I might not be able to stay much longer." Maggie felt Lizzie pull off her shoes and cover her with a light blanket. "Please don't go yet Maggie. I'll be right back. Hold on, okay?"

Maggie nodded a little, her head feeling like it weighed eighty pounds. In what could have been only a minute or two, Lizzie was back. She crawled up beside Maggie on the bed and, snuggling close, tucked her hand inside Maggie's.

"I've told Nana that I'm feeling tired; I have been sick after all. I told her I was going to bed. She is waiting for the *Mod Squad* to come on. I don't think she'll move from the sofa for the rest of the night. I am going to hold your hand while you sleep. I'm going to hold your hand so tight that you won't be able to go."

"Thank you, Lizzie," Maggie sighed.

"I was thinking. You have to stay at least one more day. If you're going to make Johnny Kinross fall in love with you, that is."

"Hmm?" Maggie was trying desperately to follow the conversation and fading fast.

"How do all the princesses get the princes to fall in love with them? They go to the ball, right?"

"Uh-huh."

"So tomorrow is the prom. You go to the prom, ask Johnny to dance, make him fall in love with you. Simple. So you can't leave yet."

The problem was that when the clock struck twelve, Maggie might not just turn back into Cinderella;

she may disappear altogether. With glass slippers and coaches that became pumpkins dancing through her head, Maggie succumbed to a slumber that would rival the Sleeping Beauty.

***

"Lizzie, how did your mother die?" Maggie looked at the girl beside her. "I don't think Irene ever told me." Maggie had awakened in the night to discover that she had not turned back into Cinderella after all. Lizzie had been true to her word, and her hand was tucked into Maggie's, her other arm wrapped around her elbow. Lizzie had awakened almost immediately, and now they lay in the dark, talking quietly.

"She got sick. She had cancer."

"I'm sorry, Lizzie." Maggie wanted to tell her that she understood how it felt to be a motherless child. But telling Lizzie would be wrong. After all, she would be telling her about her own daughter's death, a death that had occurred after Lizzie herself had succumbed to what had most likely killed Lizzie and Irene's mother.

"Why, Maggie?"

"Do you ever think about what life would have been like if she hadn't died, if she was still here?"

Lizzie lay quietly, not answering for several minutes. Only the tightening of her hand relayed that she hadn't drifted back to sleep. Maggie wondered if the topic was too much for the little girl, and cursed herself for letting her mind wander into the complexities of altering history, and then musing out loud. But when Lizzie finally spoke, her voice was troubled but not full of grief.

"Maybe if Momma were here, she would tell Irene to stay away from Roger. Daddy doesn't ever say anything. He thinks Roger's swell."

Maggie stiffened with the unexpected turn of the conversation. "And you don't think he's.....swell?" Maggie had never said the word "swell" in her life.

"No," Lizzie whispered. Maybe it was the dark room or the silence of the sleeping house, or even the distance she had traveled, but Maggie felt the hair rise on her neck and arms. When Lizzie didn't offer further explanation, Maggie asked the obvious, almost afraid to know the answer.

"Why, Lizzie?"

"You know how he called me Dizzy Lizzie?" Lizzie's voice was so hushed that Maggie shifted in the bed until her forehead rested against Lizzie's.

"Roger?"

"Yes. He and his friends call me Dizzy Lizzie."

"I just assumed it was because it rhymed -- just a silly nickname."

"Roger started calling me Dizzy Lizzie about six months ago when I fainted at a party for Irene's birthday."

Lizzie pressed her face into Maggie's shoulder, and her whisper was no longer audible.

"Lizzie? I can't hear you...."

"...It had been following Roger around all night..."

"Who had been following Roger around?" Maggie was only getting bits and pieces of the story at this point. Lizzie was pressed against her so tightly that Maggie feared she would fall off the bed if she moved an inch.

"It wasn't like other ghosts. It saw everything, watched everyone, but mostly it watched Roger. It stayed very close to him. I was afraid. I didn't want to say anything to Reney or Daddy because I didn't want to get in trouble."

"There was a ghost hanging around Roger?" Now Maggie's voice had dropped to the barest whisper.

"It wasn't a ghost. It was more like a...shadow....with eyes."

"What happened, Lizzie?" Maggie didn't want to talk about this anymore. She didn't worry about slipping back to the future any longer, but she worried about what their words would invite into Lizzie's bedroom. A room occupied by not one but two girls who shared a gift for seeing what others could not....and what others would rather not.

"I was so afraid, I forgot to breathe. I fainted right into my dinner. Nana came and helped me clean up, but I was still dizzy and felt sick, so I stayed up in my room for the rest of the night."

Maggie breathed out, slightly relieved that the story had ended rather anticlimactically. She had just started to relax when Lizzie spoke again.

"I think that shadow thing is inside Roger."

***

Morning came and with it the sunlight that cast the terrors of the night into a more manageable light. Lizzie hadn't wanted to talk anymore about the "shadow" inside Roger. She had clammed up and pretended to fall asleep when Maggie tried to coax her to explain what she meant. Maggie had lain in the dark for a long time after that, afraid that she was stuck in a whirlwind of events that she could only be harmed by, and uncertain as to where to proceed if given the chance for one more day in Johnny's world.

Lizzie had introduced her to Nana, claiming she was a cousin from McClintock, about two hours south, who had come to visit for the day while her mother spent time with a sick friend. Nana, who had the very unoriginal name of Mary Smith, said a polite hello but seemed very uninterested in Maggie or who she was, which was fortunate because she let the girls be. She was like an efficient shadow, cleaning and polishing, providing lunch and putting away laundry, never saying much, her neat self fitting into the neat corner the family had placed her in. She was unobtrusive to the point of being almost robotic, and Maggie wondered that Lizzie spent so much time in the company of someone who seemed so void of personality. It hadn't put a damper on Lizzie's personality, however. The girl was brimming with intelligence and life, and Maggie genuinely enjoyed being in her company. She had peppered Maggie with questions, and Maggie had tried her best to answer them, stopping altogether when she felt that strange tugging sensation inside that indicated she was nearing a line that should not or could not be broached.

The fatigue that had so consumed her the night before had left her, and Maggie wondered if it wasn't some form of cosmic jet lag that had left her system reeling rather then a signal she would soon be going home. With her returned energy, Maggie considered the idea of attending the prom after all. Johnny would be there as would so many others she had heard him talk about. She had even seen pictures. She could do it, couldn't she? Johnny would be there with Peggy, who was being pursued hotly by Carter, leaving Johnny somewhat free for a "chance encounter." She would have to go alone, but the more she thought about it, the more the idea appealed to her.

She bathed in the pink tiled bathroom with the perfectly square tub, brushing her teeth at the pink pedestal sink with handles to turn the water off and on rather than knobs. This bathroom had been redone sometime in the last fifty years. The pink was long gone in 2011.

She let her hair air dry, and then she and Lizzie rolled it into giant scratchy rollers with pink pins that stuck out every which way, making her look like a porcupine with pink quills. Lizzie thought they should go downtown and get her hair cut in the latest style, but Maggie declined. She was willing to go only so far to play the part of a '50s teenager. It was while they were rolling her hair in curlers that Lizzie made a horrifying discovery.

"You have holes in your ears!" Lizzie cried, her voice equal parts awe and horror.

"So?" Maggie raised her eyebrows, laughing at the shock on the little girl's face.

"Nobody has their ears pierced! Irene told me only girls who aren't very nice pierce their ears."

Maggie didn't know what to say. She stared at Lizzie for a moment, wondering if that were true of everyone in the fifties or just the Honeycutts. "No one wears earrings?"

"Girls wear earrings. See?" Lizzie grabbed a ornate jewelry box sitting atop the vanity table and riffled through it, pulling out two glittering bobs with screw like attachments on the back. She stared at the little loops in Maggie's ears, as if they were spiders hanging from her lobes.

"How do you get them off?" she whispered, poking at one of the loops.

Maggie popped the earrings out of one ear and then the other, showing Lizzie it wasn't that big of a deal.

"How do you put those on?" Maggie nodded toward the bobbles in Lizzie's palm. Lizzie eyed the holes in Maggie's now bare ears, her face wrinkled in revulsion.

"Good grief, Lizzie!" Maggie chuckled. "Where I come from, everyone has their ears pierced -- and sometimes their lips and eyebrows too!"

Lizzie backed away, horrified. Maggie could see that Lizzie was a little afraid of her now. Time to change the subject.

"Let me try these. Can't be too hard, can it?" Maggie stood and took the earrings from Lizzie's palm, giving Lizzie a comforting pat on her back before she moved away.

"Turn the back until it screws in tight," Lizzie supplied helpfully, her eyes never leaving Maggie's earlobes. Maggie sighed and shook her head. Ghosts and time travel didn't seem to bother the girl, but pierced ears had almost sent her over the edge. The earrings weren't very comfortable, and Maggie could see why women had eventually given in and put holes in their ears.

It seemed that Irene had more than enough make-up to spare, and Lizzie had spent a fair amount of time watching her big sister apply it. She showed Maggie how to wet the little brush and rub it across the black rectangular pan of mascara to coat it before combing it through her lashes. She then talked her through applying the foundation and powder "just the way Irene does, using the middle fingers only."

When they pulled out the curlers, though, Lizzie was horrified by the long drooping waves and curls. Maggie thought it looked kind of pretty, though, kind of like a movie star from the 1930s or '40s. She parted it on the left side and let the right side play peekaboo with her lined and mascaraed blue eyes. She thought she looked kind of sexy. Lizzie just sighed and let her shoulders droop dejectedly. Maggie was pretty sure

Lizzie thought she had blown it before she even set foot at the prom. Hopefully Johnny would think differently.

The wrinkles in the red dress had all but disappeared, and Maggie slipped it on over the half slip, the nylons and the garter belt (gasp!), and the strapless bra Lizzie had pilfered from Irene's drawer. The slip kept the net skirt from irritating her legs, and Maggie wondered why slips had ever gone out of style. She'd never worn a slip or hose. The garter belt dug into her skin, and the nylons were torturous, but they weren't so different from dance tights, so she endured them. The bullet shape of the bra still embarrassed her, but she had to give it props. The girls never looked better...or more deadly.

Lizzie tried to douse Maggie in Irene's perfume, but Maggie declined. If she got close enough to Johnny tonight for him to smell her perfume, she didn't want him to think of Irene. Instead, she dabbed the spot behind her ears, the inner crease at her elbows, and the barely visible valley between her breasts with a little rose water that Lizzie had been given for Christmas and never used.

When she was ready, she twirled for Lizzie and picked up the little silver purse that had still been wrapped around her wrist when she had awakened to find herself in a time long since past.

"You're so pretty....even with that old-fashioned hairstyle," Lizzie sighed, her smile slightly dreamy. "I wish I could come." Lizzie sat up suddenly. "Maggie? How are you going to get there?"

Maggie had thought of that already. She would walk, of course. It was only three blocks down and three blocks over. She would be fine and told Lizzie as much.

"You can't walk!" Lizzie said, horror-stricken. "You can take Nana's car. She'll never know."

"I can't take her car!" Maggie gasped, equally horrified. "What if she discovers it's gone and calls the police, and I get thrown in the slammer and have to try to explain who I am and where I came from."

"Let me take care of Nana!" Lizzie resisted the notion that Mary Smith would ever discover her car had been absconded by a teenager from the future, posing as her young charge's cousin.

"I will walk, Lizzie."

"Maggie!" Lizzie got all watery-eyed and serious immediately. "You can't walk in the dark, at night, completely alone."

Maggie tried to brush Lizzie's worries aside. "See these red shoes? I'll just click my heels three times and wish myself home." She thought Lizzie would laugh. But Lizzie just shook her head soberly.

"If you disappear, no one will ever know what happened to you. No one here will even know to look for you! And I will worry about you.....forever."

Maggie had no response, and Lizzie knew she'd won.

"I will get the keys and distract Nana. She always watches *Perry Mason* on Saturdays. I think she's in love with him. After that it's *Lawrence Welk*. When Daddy's gone, she doesn't budge from the couch all night long. I'll go down and tell her your mother is coming to pick you up, and then I'll sit with her and whine about wanting to watch *Dick Clark*, and I'll make sure the television is plenty loud. Go out to the garage, start the car, and before you go, give a loud toot on the horn. I'll run and call up the stairs that your mother is here and then talk for a moment like I'm saying goodbye. Then I will walk to the front door and open it. When I shut it, wait a few seconds, and drive away. She'll be fast asleep when you get back, but there is a key under the rocking chair on the porch just in case I fall asleep too, all right?"

"How old are you, Lizzie?" Maggie had to laugh at the devious mind of her young maternal grandmother. She had a sneaking suspicion she had inherited it. She gave the girl a fierce hug and suddenly felt close to tears.

"Lizzie, I don't know when or if all of this will end. If I don't come back tonight, then you'll know why, okay?"

"But I need to know what happens. I want to know if Johnny falls in love with you!"

"Well, I guess you'll just have to ask Johnny," Maggie winked, and Lizzie huffed, folding her arms.

"I will, you know!" Lizzie grinned impishly. Then she turned and ran out of the room. In seconds she was back with the key to Nana's car. She threw herself at Maggie, hugging her around her waist, and then without a word ran down the stairs again. Maggie took a deep breath and descended the stairs just enough to hear what was going on below. Sure enough, Lizzie commenced whining, and Mary Smith commenced sighing. Then the volume on the television was turned up, and Maggie sneaked the rest of the way down the stairs and out of the house.

She raced to the garage and found Nana's car parked in its stall. Very little had changed in the unattached building in fifty years. It even smelled the same. Maggie felt a sudden tugging, as if the smell of home had telegraphed a message to some far-off time and place and received an immediate response. Breathing through her mouth, she heaved the garage door upward, wincing as it refused to ascend quietly. She jumped behind the wheel and shoved the key into the ignition. Without turning on the lights, she backed out of the garage and halfway down the drive. Then she laid on the horn, causing her heart to bounce erratically, as if trying to escape its bony confines. She laid a hand across her chest, soothing it as she searched for the headlights. There they were; the beams hit the windows on the front of the house, and twenty seconds later the door swung open and then shut again almost immediately. Maggie counted slowly to ten and then backed out of the drive.

She didn't see the door open and Mary Smith rush out into the front yard seconds after she had pulled away.

~12~

A Time to Dance

The dance was already in full swing when she arrived. Maggie saw only one couple walking along the sidewalk towards the entrance of the school gymnasium. When she slid into an empty spot and turned off the engine, she could hear music pouring from the building. Fear and adrenaline shot through her in equal measures. What was she thinking going to a prom all by herself? What would she do once she got inside? Maggie considered turning the car around and high tailing it back to the relative familiarity of home, even though it wasn't currently her home.

And then Johnny's face appeared in her mind's eye. Johnny. He was inside, and she couldn't wait to see him. She checked her lipstick and bared her teeth in the rear view mirror, making sure none of the bold red had found its way onto a tooth. All clear. With a fortifying inhale, she stepped from the car and placed the key just under the gas pedal. She wasn't too worried. No one stole cars in Honeyville, certainly not in 1958.

The sidewalk leading up to the entrance was lined with lanterns and a thick red carpet, the kind that brought to mind movie premiers and Hollywood starlets. At the entrance to the gymnasium was a huge pirate's chest, spilling out all manner of treasures; golden goblets and plastic gold coins, beads and baubles littered the ground around the base of the trunk. Maggie peered through the open door and slowly walked into the highly decorated hall. The entrance had been made to look like a sunken ship, and for a moment she could not see the people beyond its gaping hull. Then she was inside, silhouetted in the doorway, staring out at the swirling dresses in a myriad of pastel shades; ruffles and sparkles and white sports coats were everywhere. She looked down at her own dress and back at the dresses of the girls being escorted to and from the dance floor. She stood out like a sore thumb.

She caught a few curious glances and felt the same fear that had gripped her in the car. And then she saw him. He was on the other side of the room, but her position on the gang plank elevated her enough to see him clearly. He had stopped and was staring at her, and then he was moving, not breaking eye contact, coming toward her. She watched him make his way through the milling crowd, until he stopped several feet in front of her. Her fear faded like yesterday's daylight, and the heat of his gaze sputtered and sparked something deep within her belly. She smiled at him.

Johnny smiled back. It was a slow, curving smile that lifted the corners of his well-shaped lips and marked his lean cheeks with deep grooves on either side of his mouth. For a minute, the world righted itself, and Maggie had the distinct sensation of time stopping, adjusting its track, and beginning again. The moment was so ripe with possibility, the flavor of forever so sweet upon her senses, that it was all Maggie could do to not walk right into Johnny's arms and lay her smiling lips on his, sealing him to her for eternity.

Instead she said, "Are you going to ask me to dance?" Her voice was amazingly steady, as if she traveled through time to dance with her lover on a regular basis.

Johnny held out his hand, and she closed the distance between them. She took it without hesitation, the contact making her catch her breath in wonder, and she knew he felt it too. He seemed to hesitate when they reached the dance floor, as if the song that had begun was not his preference. Oh, but it was hers. She had been waiting so long to dance with him again. Her skin was on fire, the music sending flames licking their way down her body. He looked down at her, and his eyes held a question. She raised her chin, urging him forward, and that was all it took. She was swinging in and out of his arms, flying in time with the drummer who knew his craft. She knew Johnny's body, the way he moved, the way he danced, and she reveled in the knowledge, matching him step for step and throwing herself into every move he asked of her.

People gathered around them, but her eyes were locked on him, and she didn't want to look away. The song ended and they were surrounded by applause, and someone hollered out, "I taught Johnny everything he knows."

Johnny seemed to recognize the voice and shook his head, laughing as he pulled her into his arms, wrapping his arms around her waist. She lifted her arms and settled them on his shoulders, a sloppy imitation of an embrace. The Bell Tones crooned out in harmony, and the couples around them turned away to dance or leave the floor. Johnny looked down into Maggie's face, and his arms tightened, pulling her closer.

His eyes were on her mouth, and Maggie lifted her chin, inviting him, and her eyes slid closed.

"Johnny," she whispered, and he froze above her.

"You know my name?"

Maggie nodded slowly, realizing her error. "Yes...I do."

"Should I know yours?" Johnny wasn't flirting. His brow was furrowed as if something niggled at him, as if somehow he had missed something vitally important, and had just realized it.

"No.....would you like to know mine?" Maggie *was* flirting, and she smiled a little to make the cheesy pick-up line a little less cheesy.

"I would very much like to know yours." Johnny's brow furrowed again, as if he wasn't used to playing the anxious admirer.

"My name is Maggie."

"Maggie....That's right," Johnny said, and then looked surprised. "Are you sure we haven't met?"

"Now that you mention it....I'm not so sure....I feel like I've known you for a long time." Maggie meant to continue the playful exchange, but her words rang too true, and she felt a sudden rise of nostalgia engulf her and her eyes sting with emotion.

Johnny had stopped dancing, and Maggie's arms dropped to her sides. His hands found hers, and the music whirled around them. "*Earth Angel, Earth Angel...*" The song echoed as if it came from somewhere far off, and Maggie gripped Johnny's hands, willing time to let her be.

Suddenly, from around them shouts rose up, and the singer at the mic was rather rudely pushed aside. The band ceased playing and a dull roar rose up from the dance floor. Johnny tore his gaze from hers and together they turned toward the bandstand.

A skinny man in an ill-fitting brown suit and thick black-rimmed spectacles stood testing the mic as if it hadn't just been used to serenade the people now staring up at it. The band's front man was looking at the interloper like he wouldn't mind shoving him off the stage. The man in the brown suit reminded Maggie of her chemistry teacher, Mr. Marshall, and she instantly disliked him. He was clearly the principal and seemed to relish the opportunity to hear his voice echo around the room   A policeman stood next to him, his arms akimbo, his stance wide, his face....familiar. Maggie wrinkled her nose in confusion. She knew him....

The answer came almost instantly, and Maggie almost jumped up and down in excitement. It was Clark Bailey -- Chief Bailey, she supposed she should call him. He was handsome in the way men are when they are solid and trustworthy. His shoulders were broad, and his big frame was well-proportioned and trim. Though his face was serious, his manner conveyed calm, and his tone was mild as he took over at the microphone.

"Students, we want to let you get back to the dance right away. We just need some information, and we would appreciate your cooperation." The man looked out across the upturned faces and waited for the excited chatter to cease.

"We got a report earlier tonight of a stolen car. We found that car here at the school just a few minutes ago, parked out in the back parking lot." Voices rose in question and wonder and Maggie felt her lungs seize and her breath hiss out in dismay. Johnny glanced down at her, his eyebrows raised in question. Maggie looked away, her mind racing to find a way out of the disaster that was hurtling towards her.

Chief Bailey continued. "The doors were unlocked, and we've recovered the key. No harm done. But we still need to know who is responsible."

Maggie moaned in abject horror and then bit her lip in censure and to keep more from escaping. Johnny was staring at her in wonder, and a small smile was playing around his mouth. He leaned in until his lips touched her ear, and in spite of her fear, she shivered at the brief caress.

"Why, Maggie....are you a car thief?"

Maggie shook her head adamantly, her blue eyes wide and beseeching. "It's not what you think," she mouthed, her voice so low only he could possibly hear.

"Maybe there's a reward for the apprehension of the little thief," he mouthed back, one eyebrow quirked. Maggie's eyes widened even further.

"Please help me get out of here, Johnny." Maggie gripped his hand and turned into him, her lips barely moving, her eyes trained on the officers now stationing themselves at every exit. "I promise I'll tell you everything. I'm really not a bad girl."

Johnny's eyes twinkled, and his lips twisted wryly. "Yeah, I was afraid of that." He gripped her arm and led her to where a tall blond kid stood with a glass of punch, hanging on every word spoken by the girl who swayed in front of him, her skirts swishing to and fro as she looked at him coyly from beneath her lashes. Peggy Wilkey was a very attractive girl, and Maggie held back a little, suddenly remembering that Peggy was Johnny's date for the evening.

Johnny leaned toward Carter, sliding an arm around his shoulder as he conveyed something neither Maggie nor Peggy could hear. Carter wasn't as discreet.

"Oh man, Johnny! You didn't! I shoulda known you had somethin' to do with it!" Carter groaned and then threw his head back and laughed. Johnny just shook his head indulgently and smacked Carter in the center of his forehead, stopping him mid-chortle.

"I need you to get Peggy home. Can you do that, Slick?" Johnny turned to Peggy and gave her a kiss on her cheek. "Carter will take good care of you, Peg. It looks like I've run into a little trouble, and with your daddy being who he is, I think it'd be better if I got out of here. Thanks for coming with me tonight; you look beautiful."

Peggy looked from Johnny to Maggie, and there was a fleeting wistfulness in her gaze. It disappeared when Carter raised his glass of punch and said happily,

"I'm taking Peggy Wilkey home! Thank you, Jesus!" Everyone within earshot started to laugh, and Peggy blushed prettily, her attention now riveted on the boy who was so obviously smitten by her.

Johnny grabbed Maggie's hand and began heading for the entrance doors like he didn't have a care in the world. Chief Bailey had parked himself in front of them, along with a young officer who barely looked older than the kids he was questioning. Maggie had thought Johnny would find a back entrance or devise a distraction. Nope. He was walking right up to Chief Bailey, easy as you please. Maggie looked around in panic, wondering if she should abandon Johnny and try to exit on her own, maybe hide in the ladies' bathroom until the prom was over so she could sneak out after the police had gone. Her eyes landed on a figure slouched against the back wall. He had watched her walk across the floor, her hand in Johnny's. He tipped his chin at her now and raised his hand in a jaunty wave. Maggie didn't wave back. She had no desire to encourage Roger Carlton in any way. She looked around for Irene, but the crowd was thick, and several couples were making their way to the exits, curious about the stolen car and wanting in on the action.

"Hiya, Chief Bailey," Johnny called out as he neared the policeman.

"Hi Johnny. You haven't been out stealing cars this fine evening, have you?" The police chief spoke without rancor, but his eyes were sharp, and Maggie figured he didn't miss a whole lot. Her gut twisted anxiously. Johnny's hand tightened briefly around hers. He pulled his car keys out of his pocket and handed them to Clark Bailey.

"You know what I drive, don't ya Chief? I can't very well drive two cars at once, now can I?"

"No, but I actually heard that it might have been a lady driving the getaway car. I'm afraid I don't know your date, Mr. Kinross."

Maggie froze, and her mind scrambled for something plausible to say. She almost blurted out that she was related to the Honeycutts when the thought entered her mind that maybe Nana had already put the newly arrived "cousin" together with the stolen car, and informed the police that she was a possible culprit.

"I'm Maggie. I'm related to the Russell girls," Maggie lied smoothly, extending her hand to Chief Bailey. "Nice to meet you, sir." The funny thing was, Maggie had been in trouble many times before. Foster kids were the first ones to get fingered if something went missing or somebody got hurt. This was the first time, though, that she was actually guilty of exactly what she was under suspicion for. She felt like her guilt was written in black Sharpie across her forehead.

"Nice girls, Cathy and Shirley. Now are you related on their father's or mother's side?"

Maggie smiled and prayed she wasn't walking right into a trap. "Their mother and my mother are first cousins. I'm just visiting." Not too close, but close enough for there to be a thin layer of protection. It would be just her luck if both Mr. and Mrs. Russell grew up in Honeyville, their siblings and family trees well known by all who grew up alongside them.

"Hey, Chief! You writin' a book? The girl didn't steal a car. She's been with me all night. Can we go, please? I promised I'd have her home early." Johnny started to move forward, and Chief Bailey stepped aside and let them pass. They were just about out the door when the chief called out after them.

"Say hello to your mother for me, Johnny."

Johnny stiffened, and Maggie glanced back in surprise. Clark Bailey must have realized after the words left his mouth how they might be perceived. His cheeks darkened briefly, and he turned away, launching into an immediate interrogation of the next couple in line.

Maggie looked up into Johnny's face, and his mouth was set in a hard line.

"Johnny?" He glanced down at her. "I know it's none of my business...but trust me on this. Clark Bailey genuinely likes your mother, and he meant no disrespect."

Johnny's eyebrows shot up, and he halted in his tracks. "Is that so?"

"Yes.....it is." Maggie struggled to find words and finally just sighed and said, "There are plenty of bad guys in the world. I just didn't want you misjudging one of the good guys."

"Pretty tight with Chief Bailey, are you? He sure didn't seem to know who you are. Come to think of it, that "good guy" you defend so readily wouldn't hesitate to throw your pretty tail in jail if he knew you stole that...." Johnny's voice faded off as he took note of the cop car, complete with flashing lights, parked beside Mary Smith's pilfered car. A police officer leaned against it, chewing his finger nails, clearly bored.

"You stole an Edsel?" Johnny's voice was filled with incredulous mirth, and he covered his mouth as if trying to hold in a belly laugh.

"A what?" Maggie was clueless.

"If you're going steal a car, baby, at least steal something classy. Shoot! The Edsel is the biggest waste of metal on the road. Mark my words, in a couple years that car isn't gonna be worth a damn dime." Johnny squeezed the bridge of his nose as if he were afraid he might start to howl and draw unwanted attention.

"What?" Maggie was baffled. She'd never even heard of an Edsel. "I didn't steal it to make a buck, silly!" she hissed at him, and whacked him with her little silver purse. She looked back at the car and at Johnny, who was still shaking his head and laughing, albeit silently. She couldn't help but smile at his enjoyment of the situation. Her smile quickly faded, however, as the gravity of the situation started to sink in. She couldn't go back to Lizzie's house. Surely the police would return the car, which solved that problem. But Lizzie was going to be frantic. And Maggie had no place to go. Maggie walked several steps and sank down on the curb, her legs suddenly too weak to stand.

"Hey....hey, Maggie. I'm sorry, Doll. Don't feel bad. I'm sure you'll make a better choice on your next heist." Johnny sank down next to her. "Hey....I'm teasing." He tipped her chin up with a long finger. "Are you okay?"

Maggie felt the sudden urge to cry and looked away. "I don't have anywhere to go....and I don't know what to do. I have no money....I don't have a set of wheels. Even an....an Ethel?"

"Edsel."

"Right. Even an Edsel is better than nothing."

"I see." Johnny was quiet for a moment, and then he looked at her, and his eyes were soft and his voice gentle. "Well. First things first. Let's grab something to eat. The Malt stays open late on Prom Night. We'll beat the rush. Then we'll find somewhere nice and quiet to have our picnic, and you'll tell me your story. And then we'll figure out what to do next."

Maggie gave him a wobbly smile and a small nod of her head. "Sounds like a plan. Thank you, Johnny."

He stood, brushing off the black trousers he wore with his white sports coat. He extended his hand and pulled her to her feet beside him. He didn't release her hand but kept it enveloped in his as he made his way to his car. He opened her door and waited until she was settled before he ran to his own, and without a backwards glance at the police car or the beleaguered Edsel, he spun out of the school parking lot and headed to The Malt.

~13~
A Time to Embrace

"She's going to be worried about me," Maggie murmured to herself.

"Who?"

"Lizzie Honeycutt. The car back there? It's their housekeeper's car. Lizzie and I thought she would never never notice it was gone. I was going to bring it back, really."

"You stole the Honeycutt's housekeeper's car? Oh, this is rich," Johnny sighed, a smile playing around his lips. He swung into The Malt's parking lot.

"Maybe you should stay in the car, Bonnie. We don't want any witnesses." Johnny stepped out of the car, shutting the door firmly behind him. Maggie decided to stay put. He was back about ten minutes later, a brown bag of food in one hand and two glass bottles of coke in the other.

A car pulled up beside them in front of the diner. For a brief moment, Irene Honeycutt's pale face was illuminated in the light pouring out of The Malt's windows. Irene looked right at Maggie, and Maggie stared back, transfixed. Then Roger opened his door and stepped out, obscuring Maggie's view, and Johnny backed out of the space and headed out of the lot. Maggie quickly rolled the window down, calling for Johnny to stop.

"Irene! Irene Honeycutt!" Maggie called. Irene stopped, confused, and looked around in surprise.

"Hold on, please!" Maggie implored Johnny.

"Maggie--"

Maggie jumped out of the car and hurried back to where Irene stood, Roger at her arm, watching her run across the lot toward them.

"Irene. Please tell Lizzie I'm just fine. Tell her not to worry; tell her I'm with Johnny," Maggie blurted out when she was within ten feet.

"Wh-what?" Irene stammered.

"Just tell her, please? She'll understand."

Irene looked at Roger and then back at Maggie. Roger smirked at Maggie and turned to go inside.

"Oh, and Irene?"

"Yes?" Irene looked extremely dubious, and she kept eyeing Maggie's dress suspiciously.

"You need to get a new boyfriend. That one's bad news." Maggie's voice was loud enough for several other couples entering the restaurant to hear. She tossed her head toward Roger, who had stopped in his tracks and was staring at her open-mouthed. Irene looked like she'd been slapped. Maggie didn't know if it would make a difference, but she had to try. "If you don't, you'll regret it for the rest of your life."

She couldn't say more. The insistent tugging from the pit of her stomach had started as soon as she had opened her mouth to warn Irene. Frantically, she turned and ran back to Johnny's car. He had stepped out of the still running Bel Air and stood framed in his open car door, hands in his pockets, waiting for her. She could tell by the expression on his face that he'd heard the entire exchange. She hustled to the passenger side and got in as he slid back in beside her.

"Will you hold my hand for a minute...please?" Maggie gasped. The pull had grown stronger. She was paying for her interference. NO! She couldn't leave now!

Johnny looked at her, his eyes serious and his head cocked to one side. Without a word, he stretched his hand out and she grasped it, clinging to it with both hands. It was big and calloused and warm. She focused on the ridges and grooves, the length of his fingers and the width of his palm. She rubbed slow circles into his skin with her thumbs, the back and forth motion soothing her and quieting the intense quickening within her.

Johnny let her be for a few minutes, but then pulled on his hand, silently asking her to let go. She did so immediately, but felt the loss acutely, as if he were a lifeline in a raging storm. He tossed the food onto the seat behind them and with one steady motion leaned over and pulled her up tight against his side. Oh, the advantages of a bench seat.

"I need my hand for a minute, but you hold onto me if you need to." His voice was gentle and without reproach, and Maggie thought, not for the first time, how unthreatened he seemed by her wild behavior. She had blown into his life less than an hour ago...and brought havoc in her wake. He hadn't even batted an eye.

"Where are we going?" Maggie asked, burrowing into his side. She really didn't care. For the moment she felt safe and exactly where she belonged.

"My favorite place to think and talk, or just be left alone, is the reservoir. There are some big trees, and a cool breeze comes up off the water. It's not too hot yet, but it will be in another month, and the place will be hoppin'. It should be quiet tonight, though."

In Maggie's time, the reservoir had been closed to the public. Some tiny fish with a funny name had been discovered in the reservoir and a wildlife organization had come in and claimed the guppy-like fish was at risk of extinction. The government had stepped in and made it a preserve. So now the only creatures to enjoy the reservoir were the four-legged kind or the itty bitty three-finned variety. Kind of sad, Maggie thought. The reservoir was manmade, but that hadn't mattered, apparently. As a result, she had never even seen the reservoir.

"I heard a story about you, this car, and the reservoir. It was a pretty cool story."

Johnny looked down at her in wonder. "You heard that story?"

"I did," Maggie smiled. "Your reputation preceeds you."

"Boy, I hope not," Johnny grinned. "And here I know nothing about you...well, other than you steal cars, you're beautiful, and you don't like Roger Carlton. Of course, I find all three of those attributes almost impossible to resist."

It was Maggie's turn to laugh, and laugh she did. "Is that why you called me Bonnie back there? Like Bonnie and Clyde?"

"Yes, ma'am. Bonnie was a beautiful woman, too. And she was also a famous thief. I'm not volunteering to be Clyde, though. Those two ended up getting shot to death in their vehicle, didn't they? I like my car too much to take that kind of a chance."

"I don't think there would have been a Bonnie without Clyde." Maggie flirted a little.

"Oh you don't, do ya? Well you might be right about that. Behind every bad man is a woman who can't resist him."

Maggie didn't respond. There was a story in that comment, though his voice suggested he was kidding.

Johnny drove the car up a long bumpy incline that finally leveled out at the top. Slowing to a stop, he put the car in park. The moonlight spilled softly onto the surface of the lake, and Johnny cranked his window down, letting the night air brush their cheeks and fill the interior of the car. Maggie scooted over and out the passenger side, and Johnny pulled their food from the back seat. He popped the trunk, pulled out a scratchy army blanket, and spread it out on a relatively flat area several yards from the car.

They made short work of the chicken, potato logs, and coleslaw. Maggie had thought she might not be able to eat, but the food actually steadied her, and the tugging eased and then ceased altogether as she ate her fill. Everything was delicious, and the Coke in a glass bottle was a treat. It tasted a little sharper than the Coca Cola of 2011, but she liked the difference.

Johnny finished before Maggie, and he removed his bow tie and pulled off his sports coat, setting it behind him on the blanket. He made short work of the cummerbund as well. Rolling up his sleeves and unbuttoning the top buttons of his white dress shirt, he lay back and sighed like he'd just been released from shackles and chains.

Maggie wished she could unclip her nylons from the garter belt and roll them off but thought it might create the wrong impression. She settled for slipping off her shoes and laying back beside him, a couple of feet between them, looking up into the firmament.

"So what was that all about -- the scene with Irene Honeycutt and Roger Carlton? I think you made an enemy out of Roger, maybe out of both of them."

"Irene is family. It's complicated," Maggie sighed, knowing that if she were going to stay beside Johnny under the moonlit sky, she would have to tread very carefully. "Her little sister is afraid of him, which is always a warning sign. Kids and dogs, right?"

"What do you mean?"

"You know, when kids or dogs don't like someone, it's usually a pretty a good indication of a person's trustworthiness."

"So you just decided to call him out and tell Irene he was no good based on that?"

"It was the truth," Maggie declared vehemently, and dared him to deny it.

"Hell, yes, it was," Johnny agreed, and laughed a little. "Remind me not to get on your bad side, Bonnie."

"I don't know how long I'll be here! I had to speak up when I had the chance," Maggie defended herself lightly.

"So you're new in town, and you don't know how long you'll be here. How did you find yourself at the prom, without a date, in a stolen car?"

"I had an amazing dress." Maggie stalled.

Johnny just turned his head and looked at her, his face patient, waiting.

Maggie decided to go all in. "I went to the dance to find you."

Johnny sat up slowly and looked down at her, laying with her hair spread around her, skin porcelain in the darkness.

"You better be careful, little girl," Johnny's voice was quiet, but his eyebrows were drawn together over his deep set eyes, eyes that were colorless in the white light of the moon. "You're all alone out here with someone you really don't know, saying some pretty serious things. You could give a boy the wrong idea."

Maggie felt frustration well up inside her and tears gather in her eyes. Gravity betrayed her, and several leaked out the corners and hurried straight down to pool in her ears.

Johnny reached out and wiped one damp trail with the pad of his thumb. "Don't cry. I didn't mean to scare you." Maggie just shook her head a little, and his hand fell away from her face, but he braced it next to her head and continued looking down at her.

"Have you ever been somewhere, doing something when all at once you swear you've done it all before? Everything feels like it's repeating itself all of a sudden?" Maggie asked hesitantly.

"Like Deja vu?" Johnny answered

"That's what some people call it. My friend Gus told me that his grandma said Deja vu is actually time changing its mind."

"What do you mean?"

"She described it as time making a shift from the way things were to the way things are, and sometimes we feel that shift, or briefly remember how things were....before."

"Before what, Maggie?" Johnny's voice was hushed, but he didn't sound frustrated or even confused. He was just listening.

"Before someone or something caused time to change."

They gazed at each other for several heartbeats, until the crickets started up softly and other night sounds wafted around them. Johnny seemed to be mulling over what she had said.

"Have you and I met before?" he asked finally.

"Yes....and no."

Johnny waited again.

"If time is sequential, then tonight is the first time we've ever met. But if time is just one eternal circle, it's hard to know when 'before' ends and 'after' begins."

Johnny stood up abruptly and walked down to the water's edge. He set his hands on his hips and stared out, facing away from her. He was silhouetted against the silver glass of the lake, youthful and strong, and still doomed by fate. Maggie knew she was talking in riddles, making absolutely no sense.

Maggie slid her feet into her shoes and made her way across the rocky shore and down to the hard packed sand, stepping gingerly in the high red heels to keep from twisting an ankle. She too stopped at the water's edge, just out of reach of the lapping tide.

"What do you call a smart blonde?" she blurted out awkwardly.

Johnny's head swiveled around in confusion.

"What do you call a smart blonde?" she repeated.

"I don't know," Johnny hedged, his eyebrows high, waiting.

"A golden retriever."

Johnny threw back his head and laughed. "What?!"

"Well, I thought the time space continuum might be a little heavy for the first date." Maggie wrinkled her nose at him sheepishly. "I thought I'd tell you a joke to lighten things up."

"I see." Johnny grinned down at her. He was quiet for a moment, his wheels turning. Then he offered a joke of his own.

"You heard about the blonde coyote that got caught in a trap, didn't you?" Johnny was pretty quick on the uptake. Blonde jokes were not a fifties phenomenon.

"No, I didn't hear about that," Maggie smiled, waiting.

"Yeah, it gnawed off three of its legs and it was still stuck."

Maggie's laughter peeled out over the water, and they were off, shooting jokes back and forth, the weighty conversation of minutes before long forgotten. They bantered like that for almost an hour with silly things and questions designed to get to know one another. Maggie recognized the Johnny she had come to know and love, but she also enjoyed the Johnny that was not yet weighed down or aged by the years he'd been imprisoned in Purgatory. She didn't return to the topic of her appearance at the prom or why she had no place to go. She lived in the moment with him and resolved to will herself home when and if the moment passed. And of course the thought niggled at the back of her brain...what if she could stay?

"All right, the question that everyone asks eventually...favorite color?" Maggie intoned.

"Pink," Johnny replied seriously,without pause.

"Really?" Maggie had asked him this question before....or after. She shook her head, her mind swimming. In Purgatory he'd told her his favorite color was white. He said white felt safe.

"Yep. Think about it. Everything that's pink is usually soft, pretty, and it tastes good." Johnny's voice was husky, and he drew his words out slowly. She knew he was flirting, that he had possibly used the line before, but it didn't matter. His words made her hot inside, and she wished for a second that she was the kind of girl who would take what she wanted and to hell with the consequences. But she wasn't. Life had taught her that consequences were ugly and painful, and seldom worth the pleasure they had been bartered for.

"It's your turn."

"Huh? Oh. Yellow," she supplied. "Yellow is happy."

"Put yellow and pink together, and it makes peach....soft, pretty, tastes really good, and makes you happy."

"Perfect. Then we're meant for each other." She sighed and batted her eyes, and Johnny laughed again.

It was his turn for a question. He asked her for her favorite movie. He'd just seen Hitchcock's *Vertigo* and liked it - Maggie had no idea what to say. So she offered *Rebel Without a Cause*.

Johnny groaned. "All the girls say that. James Dean isn't really that good looking, is he?

"I think he looks a little like you," Maggie grinned.

"Well, then. I guess he is pretty irresistible."

"I guess so," Maggie snickered.

Favorite song? Johnny liked too many to decide. Maggie scrambled to claim a favorite from his decade and blurted out "Smoke Gets in Your Eyes."

Johnny shook his head. "I don't know that one. Kinda funny title. Sing a little for me, and maybe I'll recognize it."

"It's an oldie, but it's probably still the best love song I've ever heard." Maggie grimaced. She didn't know when that song actually came out. She shouldn't have said it was an oldie. She tried to change the subject.

"I can't sing it to you because I sing like a frog. I'm a dancer, not a singer."

Johnny got a speculative look on his face and without warning, he loped back up the hilly incline to the car. He started it up and flipped on the lights and within seconds Ray Charles was groaning out "A Fool For You," the gritty longing pouring out of the windows and touching her like a caress. Shutting the doors, Johnny walked back down the hill, and just liked he'd done earlier in the evening, he held out a hand to Maggie.

"You only got to dance to two songs before the heat caught up to you." Johnny's lips turned up at the mention of 'heat.' "Would you like to dance?"

Maggie slid into his arms like she had never left, and he immediately spun her out again, and then pulled her close, locking her up tight against him. Maggie caught her breath. The song was sexy and sinuous, and Maggie closed her eyes and moved with him. Freed from the confines of a crowded gymnasium, neither of them seemed willing to maintain a respectful distance. But in spite of their proximity, the music was not an excuse to simply hold one another, and they danced, gliding around the hard-packed beach with the car lights creating a spotlight that blotted out the rest of the universe.

One song led to another. "In the Still of the Night," "You Send Me," "Stardust," and "Mona Lisa" echoed out across the glassy water. Maggie was grateful for the melancholy radio announcer spinning out love song after love song, mournful ballad after mournful ballad, giving them words when it was too soon to speak them.

"And here's to all the young lovers, wherever you are - so many people have sung this one...but I like the way Frank sings it best. Here's 'Where or When.'"

The opening bars of a song Maggie had never heard before rang out and wrapped around them in silky persuasion.

It seems we stood and talked like this before
We looked at each other in the same way then,
The clothes you're wearing are the clothes you wore
The smile you're smiling you smiled then
But I can't remember when.

Some things that happen for the first time
Seem to be happening again
And so it seems that we have met before
And laughed before
And loved before
But who knows where or when

Maggie tipped her head up to look at Johnny. He didn't break his gaze as his legs moved against hers, her skirts wrapping around him as they danced. His arm was firm on her waist, her hand tucked against his chest, his eyes on hers. The last notes rang across the distance, and Johnny dipped Maggie so low that her hair brushed the beach before he swung her back up against him.

The lights on the car flickered once and faded sickly. The climactic final note still echoed in her head, but no more music filled the air. Johnny stepped back slightly and dropped his hands to hers. The lights from the car no longer illuminated the dark, but Maggie could still see Johnny's face, though it was shadowed. He had an inscrutable expression in his eyes, like he was fighting an inner battle of sorts. Maggie stared, not willing to step away, but afraid to step forward. It could be too soon, but it might be all they had.

And then he closed the space and his mouth was poised above hers. His breath fanned against her face, tangling with her own in a heady mix of anticipation and desire. His hands released hers, sliding up the smooth skin of her arms, up her shoulders to cradle her face in his fingertips. He lifted her chin slightly and touched his lips to hers, leaving the barest whisper between their mouths.

"Maggie?" Her name was a question on his lips, and she whispered back the answer.

"Johnny."

Then the whisper was chased away by the roaring in her ears and the pounding of her heart. He kissed her madly, his hands leaving her face to wrap around her waist, and he lifted her off the ground as his mouth plundered hers in a kiss as thorough and complete as the solitude was around them. The world tilted, and Maggie felt herself go with it, unaligned with the natural order of things, but in complete harmony with the boy in her arms.

"There..." Johnny tore his lips away, gasping. "There...did you feel that?"

Maggie stared up at him, waiting, her chest heaving.

"Deja vu." They said the word in unison. Johnny shook his head, almost like he needed to clear it.

"Time changing its mind," he whispered.

"From what was to what is," Maggie finished, her voice as hushed as his.

***

The car battery had died but neither of them really cared. Johnny said there would be a park ranger at the ranger station on the north side of the reservoir first thing in the morning now that warmer weather had brought the Sunday crowds. He would run for cables and the attendant's car and they would be on their way first thing in the morning.

It had grown late, and the summer was still a little more than a month away. The night air suddenly felt cold on Maggie's bare arms and shoulders, and she was thankful for the nylons she had wished to be rid of only a couple of hours before.

Johnny pulled another scratchy blanket from the back seat of his car and wrapped her in his jacket. They lay side by side on one blanket, pulling the other over the top of them both. He pulled her into his arms, a solid presence at her back, his chin resting on her head, her head cushioned on his shoulder. The blankets smelled of a greasy mechanics shop, but Maggie was too happy to care. Her eyes slid closed, confident that she would be safe from time's pull in the circle of Johnny's arms.

"How do you keep a blonde in suspense?" Maggie yawned and let her heavy eyes rest.

"How?"

"I'll tell you tomorrow..."

Johnny laughed, and Maggie felt the rumble against her cheek.

"Well, Bonnie. It's official. You've left the straight and narrow. Car theft, evading the police, and spending the night in a stranger's arms. All in the space of a few hours."

"Well Clyde. I guess you're right...but you helped me evade the police, provided the getaway car, and you are now about to sleep next to a known criminal." Maggie felt his laughter flutter her hair. She smiled drowsily. She really couldn't keep her eyes open.

"I like it when you call me Bonnie," she mumbled.

"Why, Bonnie?"

"My dad used to call me bonny Maggie," she sighed. "It makes me think of him."

"Bonny means pretty, right?"

Maggie nodded, almost asleep.

"Maggie? Where are your parents?"

She didn't answer right away, and Johnny thought she must have fallen asleep. So it almost startled him when she answered softly, her voice heavy with impending slumber. "They haven't even been born...and when I return - they will already be dead." Maggie's voice drifted off as sleep overcame her, and she offered nothing more.

Johnny lay beside her and held her as she slept, his mind a jumble with the impossibility of the girl in his arms and the frightening way he felt about her. She was beautiful, but there were other beautiful girls. She was funny and zany and different from any girl he'd ever met. But even that couldn't account for the almost desperate attraction he felt after such a short time. Sleep evaded him until the first blush of dawn pinked the eastern horizon, and the birds kicked up their sunrise chatter. Then he fell into an exhausted sleep, where even dreams could not disturb him.

~14~
A Time to Keep Silent

Maggie didn't know what awakened her. Maybe it was the weight of Johnny's arm or the heat that his body produced. Most likely it was the pressing need of a very full bladder, but Maggie resisted movement for as along as she could, filled with an inexpressible joy that morning had come and Johnny lay beside her. Hope filled her chest like a yellow balloon, and Maggie felt a sudden urge to leap from the blankets and have a "Sound of Music" moment, complete with spread arms and joyful singing. But her body insisted that she find a bathroom or a grove of trees first. She eased out from Johnny's arm, trying not to disturb him. He slept deeply, not even stirring when she picked her way across the distance from the blankets to his car. With luck he would have a comb in his jockey box or some tic tacs or something. Did they make tic tacs in the '50s? Did they have jockey boxes? Maggie giggled softly and looked back at Johnny, hoping she hadn't awakened him. One arm was flung over his face, and the other lay against the blankets where she had slipped from his embrace.

Maggie eased the car door open and slid inside, looking for anything to make her morning self more attractive. The rear view mirror showed that her makeup hadn't really survived the campout. Her mascara was flaky, and her lipstick had been kissed off. Well and truly kissed off. Maggie flushed and grinned at her reflection. After a few moments, she still hadn't found a comb or a breath mint. She reached under the seat and felt around, hoping for a miracle.

"Ah hah!" She said triumphantly, pulling out the little silver purse that she'd taken with her to the prom. It had fallen to the floor and been kicked beyond her sight. She knew Aunt Irene had tucked a lipstick inside when they'd been playing dress-up. She popped it open and pulled out not only the lipstick but her black framed glasses.

"I forgot these were in here!" Out of habit, Maggie unfolded them and set them on her nose. She pulled the cap off the gold tube of lipstick and lifted her eyes up to the mirror to guide her application.

Something was wrong. Maggie reached out to touch the mirror, confused by the empty glass. She couldn't see her reflection. She tried to adjust the mirror, positioning herself directly in front of it, but her hands disappeared in front of her face as she stared at them through the lenses of the glasses she had not needed since slipping through time.

"No!" Maggie reached for the handle of the door, crying out for Johnny. What had been an insistent tugging previously was now a black hole -- a sucking, churning whirlpool. Maggie tried to remove the glasses from her eyes, but she had no power over her limbs. There was no sound and no air and then the world around her faded, and she was no longer in Johnny's car. Maggie clawed frantically for something to cling to but felt herself being pulled under. She couldn't breathe. She couldn't breathe! And then darkness engulfed her, and she fought no more.

***

Maggie wasn't lying next to him when he awoke. The sun had risen quite high in the sky, and Johnny sat up suddenly, astonished by the length of time he had slept. Maggie's red shoes lay next to his near the bottom of the blanket, so she couldn't have gone far. He rubbed his hands back and forth through his rumpled hair and ran his hands across his bristly jaw. He must look a sight. It was a good thing he was a handsome son of a bitch. He laughed at himself and realized that he felt almost euphoric. He was in love with a girl named Maggie. He'd never been in love before. He didn't even know her last name. He stood, stretching and looked around. Where was she?

"Maggie?" he called, combing the beach with his gaze. He swung around, calling her name. The driver's side door of the car was slightly ajar. He walked to it and opened the car door all the way, almost expecting her to be sleeping on the front seat, having gotten uncomfortable or cold in the night. She wasn't there. He slid in and felt around, hoping he had left a comb in the jockey box...or maybe a breath mint. Her little silver purse lay on the seat. He popped it open, but it was completely empty. What girl brings an empty purse to a dance? Don't they cram as many things as they can into their bags and purses? Apparently not Maggie. He stared into it, at a loss. He caught a glint of something gold and shiny out of the corner of his eye. He leaned down and picked up a cap off of the floor of the Bel Air. It looked like the cap from a tube of lipstick.

His rear view mirror was at the wrong angle, and he righted it, thinking Maggie must have checked her reflection for it to be so skewed. She must have walked down to the water. Maybe she had gone to find a bathroom. He didn't know why she'd left her shoes. Of course, her red heels couldn't be much more comfortable than walking barefoot, especially where the sand got deep. He stepped out of the car and slipped his own shoes on. He loped down to the water and proceeded to wet his hair, wash his face, and rinse his mouth with cold water. He would just wait until she came back, and then he would head over to the Ranger station to get help starting his car.

An hour later there was still no sign of her. Johnny had walked up and down the beach, calling her name. He had walked the quarter of a mile down to the Ranger station, where there also happened to be some nicer bathrooms, but no one had seen any sign of her. The beach had started filling up with cars and families, with their kids and their pets and their big brightly colored umbrellas.

Three hours after he'd awakened to find Maggie missing, Johnny had to admit to himself that she was long gone. He was angry, but more than that, he was afraid. Why wouldn't she take her shoes? The girl was a mystery, no doubt about it. She had said that she didn't know how long she would be around, and some of her comments of the night before now niggled at him. Maybe she was a little messed up in the head. It had all been so romantic and real, and she had been so intense and clear eyed that he had almost believed her when she had started saying things that he didn't understand and couldn't even fathom. But he couldn't stand the thought that she might be gone for good. What if he never saw her again? The answering ache that gripped his chest was almost as frightening as her disappearance.

He headed home, checking to make sure his momma had made it in the night before and that Billy was okay. Billy had made himself a big sandwich and was reading the business section of the *Texas Times* when Johnny walked in the front door. Johnny was good at math, and he could fix almost anything, but he had never sat down and read the newspaper like his little brother or poured over books at the library like they held the secrets of the universe. Billy was smart, and if Johnny looked out for him and made sure Momma stayed out of trouble, Billy could grow up to be somebody important one day. He could go to college, see the world, make something of himself. That's what Johnny wanted more than anything.

"Are you just getting home?" Billy's eyes were wide behind his thick glasses. "Peggy's old man is going to kill you!" Peggy's father was a deputy for the Honeyville Police Department, and he really didn't like Johnny very much. He also didn't like the fact that his daughter attracted boys like flies.

"Carter took Peggy home, so if anybody is going to die, it'll be him," Johnny smiled at his little brother as he took a swig straight out of the big glass bottle of orange juice on the top shelf of the fridge. He pulled out a couple of eggs and proceeded to scramble them up, his mind on the reason he hadn't taken Peggy home.

"Is Momma here?" he asked Billy after a while.

Billy glanced up, nodding his head. "Yep. I stayed up until she got in last night, though." Billy looked down at his paper as if trying to decide to tattle on his mother. "She was with the mayor again. It was his car she got out of, unless she and Mrs. Carlton have suddenly become friendly."

Johnny swore under his breath and shook his head in disgust. He didn't need this shit, not today of all days. Lord, save him from beautiful women and their shenanigans. He had one girl who couldn't stay put and another who just couldn't seem to stay away. Too bad it wasn't the other way around.

"Is she asleep?"

"No. I think she's hiding. She knows I saw her. I think she's hoping I don't tell you."

"Yeah, I just bet she does." Johnny and his momma had argued a time or two about her choice in men.

"So.....why are *you* just getting in?" Billy had abandoned the business section altogether and seemed anxious to change the subject. That was Billy, always the peace-maker. Johnny let the issue of Momma's men drop for now. He'd deal with it later.

"I went to the rez, turned on my music, ended up sleeping out there. It was nice." It had been more than nice. It had been the best damn night of his life. He felt the ache punch him low in the belly again, and reconsidered whether he could actually eat the omelet he was frying up. Where had that girl gone? He couldn't just assume she was all right.

Billy kept the conversation moving. "I went down to the corner store this morning, picked up my paper, and got Momma some coffee. We were all out. Mr. McNinch said somebody took the Honeycutts' housekeeper's car last night. He said the cops were everywhere. They found it, though. He said Mary Smith, the housekeeper, had come in just before me and was relieved to have it back."

Johnny froze, his spatula hanging in mid-air as he tuned into his little brother's account. A car theft in Honeyville was big news, and it didn't surprise him that everyone knew about it already. Mr. McNinch, owner of the little corner grocery, was as bad as an old woman when it came to gossip. If you wanted to know anything, all you had to do was engage him in a little conversation, and you knew who was doing what in a minute flat. But it was the mention of the Honeycutts that had reminded him of something. Maggie had mentioned Lizzie Honeycutt several times the night before. He finished his eggs without tasting them and was out of the house, showered and shaved, within a half hour. He was going to find Maggie.

Johnny didn't know how he was going to get an audience with Lizzie Honeycutt. The girl could only be ten or eleven at the most. He plotted and brooded, and finally just swung his car into the drive and figured he'd wing it. It turned out he'd stewed and worried for nothing. Lizzie Honeycutt sat on the front porch swing eating an ice cream bar like she didn't have a care in the world. There wasn't another soul in sight. Johnny hoped Mrs. Smith wasn't looking out the window, ready to chase him away with a broom. If she came out on the porch, he'd just ask her if Mr. Honeycutt wanted him to take his vehicle to Gene's for a tune-up. He'd picked up Jackson Honeycutt's Buick before, so it shouldn't make her too suspicious.

The girl was slumped down, lazily pushing the swing with the pink painted toes of one bare foot, her other leg folded beneath her. Her eyes widened, and she ceased licking and swinging as she watched him get out of his car and stride up to the porch.

"It's gonna drip if you don't get to it." Johnny smiled down at the little girl who bore an obvious resemblance to both Irene.....and Maggie. The wide, sky-blue eyes were something they all shared. Seems Maggie hadn't been fibbing when she had said they were family. Still, he would bet his life that Irene

Honeycutt had never met Maggie before the confrontation in the parking lot of The Malt the night before. She had looked at Maggie like she was a total stranger. And a crazy one at that.

"Can I sit?" Johnny asked politely. Lizzie Honeycutt scootched to her right, pulling her leg out from underneath her, leaving a space plenty wide for Johnny to sit comfortably beside her.

"I bought another. The Good Humor man let me have two for the price of one since I'm such a loyal customer. I actually think he was trying to get rid of me 'cause I couldn't make up my mind. Would you like it?" Lizzie Honeycutt raised her eyebrows expectantly.

"No, thanks," Johnny replied, although the ice cream looked pretty good. He didn't want Lizzie running back into the house and alerting the housekeeper that they had company.

"Thank goodness!" Lizzie sighed gratefully. "I was just tryin' to be polite, anyway. I didn't want to share." Her smile flashed, and her eyes twinkled, and Johnny saw Maggie all over again. They were firecrackers, both of them.

"So...." Lizzie said, after taking a long lick up the side of the shrinking chocolate wedge. "Are you in love with Maggie?"

Johnny choked a little, and she reached over and patted his back, dripping a little ice cream on his shirt as she did.

"Oops, sorry." Lizzie grimaced and started licking in earnest, ready to be done with the mess.

"I was wondering if you'd seen Maggie this morning."

Lizzie stopped licking once more and eyed Johnny with indecision.

"I'm a little worried about her, you see." Johnny didn't think it was appropriate to tell the little girl that he and Maggie had slept on a blanket under the stars, and his voice faded off awkwardly, trying to think of a way to word his question without giving too much away.

"Is she gone, then?" Lizzie asked, her mouth turned down in a slight frown.

"I don't know," Johnny answered carefully. "We had a picnic out at the reservoir after the dance. I fell asleep, and when I woke up, she was gone. But her shoes were still there."

"Oh." Lizzie nodded, as if her question had been satisfied. She finished off her ice cream and proceeded to lick her fingers clean.

"So do you know where she is?" Johnny was really trying not to get impatient, but so far he had gotten exactly nowhere. He wondered if Lizzie Honeycutt was good at chess.

"She probably went back," Lizzie dutifully protected her queen.

"Back where?" Johnny leaned toward the little girl and stared hard until she turned her head and caught him looking. She blushed a little, and her hands dropped to her lap.

"It's hard to explain," Lizzie mumbled. She licked at a spot she had apparently missed. She offered nothing more.

Johnny tried again. "I need to know if she's okay, Lizzie. If you know something, I would appreciate you telling me. Obviously you know something, or you wouldn't have known why I was here."

"I thought maybe she sent you....so I wouldn't worry about her," Lizzie answered softly. "I knew she couldn't come home because the police brought the car back. Nana is very suspicious of her now, too."

"Wait...Irene didn't tell you Maggie was with me?" Johnny's head began to spin. "Then how did you know?"

"Irene didn't come home last night. She slept over at the Russell's with Cathy and Shirley. I didn't know, not until you got here. I was hoping, though. After all, you're the reason Maggie went to the dance in the first place."

Johnny felt the hairs stand up on his arms and neck, and his face must have conveyed his astonishment, because Lizzie began speaking again without any prodding.

"She said she was in love with you." Lizzie searched his expression, worry stamped across her small face.

Maggie had told Johnny she had come to the dance for him. But he had assumed she was coming on strong, letting him know she wanted him. But when he'd challenged her, her eyes had filled with tears, contradicting her forward display. He hadn't known what to make of it then. He didn't know what to make of it now.

"Do you know where I can find her, Lizzie? No more games, little girl."

Lizzie Honeycutt folded her arms defensively, and Johnny thought maybe he'd been too blunt. She was obviously uncomfortable and had moved as far from him as she could. She answered his question with a finality that said she had said all she was going to say.

"No. She just kinda showed up, and I helped her. She couldn't tell me some things. She tried, but it made her really dizzy and tired. She's been here before. If she comes back, I'll tell her you're looking for her. I promise."

Johnny thought of the way Maggie had clung to him after she had warned Irene to stay away from Roger Carlton, when she had asked him so sweetly if she could hold his hand. She had been shaking like a leaf, and she had held his hand like he was the only thing between her and hell's fiery furnace.

Johnny got up off the swing and was about to walk down the front steps when Lizzie stopped him.

"Do you have her shoes with you?" she questioned hopefully.

Johnny nodded briefly.

"Can I have them, please? They're Irene's. She's not gonna be too happy when she finds out her dress is gone. If I put back the shoes, maybe she won't be so mad."

Johnny laughed right out loud and shook his head in wonder. Maggie had had the gumption to walk right up to Irene Honeycutt and tell her to get a new guy while wearing her dress. He might just be a little in love after all, damn it.

"I've got 'em." He smiled at the little girl and turned again to walk to his car. At that moment, Irene Honeycutt decided to come home. She slid into the drive and flew past Johnny's car, with barely an inch to spare between the two vehicles, making him flinch and cry out. She jerked to an uneven stop, and she and the two Russell sisters tumbled out of the pink Cadillac as if they couldn't believe their eyes. Shirley, the youngest of the three, was the first to recover, and she smiled brightly and waggled her fingers at him.

"Hiya, Johnny," she cooed. Cathy looked at her sharply and took a couple steps, shifting herself to a position in front of her younger sister.

"Yeah, hi Johnny!" Cathy offered, even more brightly. Shirley elbowed her sister out of the way and hurried to Johnny's side.

"Did you have fun last night?" Shirley chirped, looping her arm through his. Johnny sidestepped the pretty brunette, gently extricating his arm.

Cathy tapped him on the shoulder. "We saw you dancing with that new girl. We were all just *sooo* surprised because she was wearing a dress just like the dress Irene was going to wear."

"Oh, Irene, wouldn't that have been awful if you'd both come in the same dress!" Shirley moaned, looking at her friend.

Irene tossed her head, as if the memory of the girl just made her angry. "She was so rude to me, Johnny Kinross!" Irene stomped her foot and crossed her arms, looking at Johnny like she blamed him for Maggie's behavior. "Roger was so mad. He said he's going to find her and put her in her place! Why the nerve! My dress looked nothing like hers. Hers was just a cheap imitation. I just hope she gets what's coming to her!"

"Roger Carlton is a first-class jerk, Irene, and you would do well to heed the warning you were given. And if your precious Roger touches so much as a hair on that girl's head, he'll answer to me." Johnny turned and strode to his car, the three girls huddled together in stunned silence. When he reached the Bel Air, he leaned inside and pulled out the red shoes Maggie had left behind.

"I think these belong to you, Irene." He walked to where the girl stood, her mouth gaping, her arms hanging loosely at her sides. "In my mind, they're pretty big shoes to fill. I don't know if they'll fit anymore." Johnny turned on his heel, walked back to his car, and drove away.

~15~
A Time to Speak

Two hours later, Johnny was still driving around, trying to decide what to do. He had been back out to the reservoir and asked around, but no one had anything to offer. No one had seen a girl in a red prom dress wandering around the area, and everyone he talked to looked at him like maybe he was a little bit nuts when he had suggested it.

It was a perfect Sunday afternoon in May, and people were out and about enjoying the day. He saw people walking out of church, all dressed up, the women in hats, the kids done up in hair bows and bow ties. Two little boys raced down the street, loosening their ties as they ran, anxious to stretch their legs and be free of church for one more week. It reminded Johnny a little of him and Billy racing home the few times Momma had made them go. It had been a long time ago, when they weren't much bigger than the little boys he'd just seen.

Momma had been a very faithful church goer for a while, until the young preacher at the church she had chosen up and married someone else. She had quit going right after that and they had never been back. When Johnny had asked her about it, she'd seemed sad and said God didn't need people like her in his church. Johnny hadn't known what she meant then, but he had thought about it since. Momma just never could get past her own pretty face. She always believed it was all she had to offer, and seemed lost when it wasn't what some men wanted. He wondered if she had been born an ugly woman if it would have served her better in the end.

He drove past the police station and thought of Chief Bailey telling him to say hello to his Momma for him. Momma would never look twice at Chief Bailey, and if Bailey were a smart man, he wouldn't spend any time looking at Momma. Johnny slowed and pulled into the station. Nobody should be here on a Sunday - so he was a little surprised to see a black and white in the empty parking lot. Well, speak of the devil. Chief Bailey pushed through the double doors on the front of the building and headed for his car at the same moment Johnny decided he had nothing to lose.

When Clark Bailey saw Johnny Kinross step out of his low-riding Bel Air, his step slowed and his eyes narrowed the slightest bit. Johnny Kinross was the last person Chief Bailey expected to see anywhere near the police station -- and on a Sunday afternoon to boot.

Johnny leaned back against his car and watched the Police Chief walk toward him.

"Mr. Kinross. What can I do for you, son?" Chief Bailey said cordially, extending his hand toward the young man as if he were an equal and didn't have a reputation for being a hood.

"Chief." Johnny clasped his hand and straightened up, looking the man in the eyes, taking his measure for a half a second. He hoped he didn't regret this.

"I wanted to file a report, I guess. I'm not sure the person's even missing, but if she is, and I don't do anything about it, well....I'd feel terrible if she was in trouble."

"How long's your momma been gone?" Chief Bailey replied, concern flitting across his amiable face.

"No, um....Momma's fine. It's not her I'm here for." Johnny shook his head.

"I see. Come on inside then, Johnny, and we'll see what we can do. It's too damn hot out already. By August this whole town's gonna be a big puddle; we'll all have melted away. It's way too hot too soon."

Johnny followed Chief Bailey inside and felt a little of the relief the chief had promised, but he was too knotted up inside to be reassured by a little shade and a whirring fan.

"All right." The chief sank down into his office chair and took out a pen and an official looking form. "Tell me who's missing."

"Her name is Maggie," Johnny started, "and I'm gonna tell you some things that you aren't gonna write on that paper there." Johnny nodded his head toward the paper Chief Bailey's pen was poised above. He stared at him until Chief Bailey sighed, threw the pen down, and sat back in his chair, tossing one leg up on the corner of his desk.

"How about we just talk for a minute, and then we'll decide whether we need to fill out a form at all. Deal?" Chief Bailey offered, folding his hands in his lap. Johnny nodded his head in response and sat back in his own chair, slightly more comfortable.

"Her name's Maggie." Chief Bailey prodded him.

"Her name's Maggie. I don't have a last name. I know she's related to the Honeycutts. She was with me last night at the dance. Do you remember her?"

Chief Bailey nodded and brought his linked hands up to rest them on his head. "I remember. Real pretty gal, dressed in red, right? I thought you were going to the dance with Wilkey's daughter, so I was a little surprised to see you leave with someone else."

Johnny didn't come to gossip like the ladies gathered in front of the church a few blocks down, and he slowly raised one eyebrow at Chief Bailey. The chief smiled a little bit and liked the kid just that much more for his unwillingness to kiss and tell.

"All right, then. Keep going. You left the dance together. Then what?"

"We ended up at the reservoir. We danced and talked. The battery died in my car, so we couldn't get help until the morning. We ended up falling asleep. When I woke up, she was gone, but her shoes were still there. I looked for her all morning, and I went back this afternoon. Nobody's seen her, and I don't know enough about her to know where else to look."

The chief screwed up his face in concentration, looking off for several moments, his hands still resting on his head.

"Did she leave anything else behind?"

"She had a little silver purse, and it was laying on the seat of my car where she'd left it. I looked inside thinking maybe she'd left some i.d.. It was empty, though. I found a gold cap on the floor that looked like it was from a lipstick," Johnny added. His stomach tightened even further. Talking about it made it seem all the more bizarre. None of this made any sense. Why would a girl empty out her purse, leave it behind, and leave her shoes behind as well?

"And you didn't hear anything that woke you up, maybe alerted you that she was gone, huh?"

"No. I woke up because the sun was beating down on me, and I was hot. I couldn't believe how long and deeply I'd slept. I saw Maggie's shoes and thought she'd probably taken a walk along the beach, waiting for me to wake up. I could see that she had been in the car because the driver's side door was ajar."

"I'll want to see the shoes and the purse, as well as the lipstick cap."

"Aw, shit," Johnny thought to himself and ran aggravated hands through his hair. Why hadn't he held onto the shoes? He hadn't been thinking, that's why. Now he was going to have to explain to Chief Bailey all about the connection to the Honeycutts. And how was he supposed to do that without getting Maggie in a whole heap of trouble?

"Is there anything that happened at the dance or before you got to the reservoir that was out of the ordinary -- that makes you suspicious now?" Chief Bailey's voice had become softer, and he was zeroed in on Johnny's face, watching him, as if he knew Johnny was trying to determine what and what not to tell him.

Hell, what hadn't happened? Johnny thought. "The whole night was out of the ordinary." Johnny leaned forward, his arms resting on the chief's messy desk. "Here comes the part where you and I are just gonna talk," Johnny suggested.

Chief brought his hands down from his head and set his feet on the floor. Then he leaned forward too and leveled his eyes at Johnny.

"She took that car last night, didn't she?"

Johnny sighed and dropped his head in defeat. Chief Bailey was no dummy. If Johnny was going to help Maggie, he couldn't lie now.

"She did. She and Lizzie Honeycutt seem to be friendly. Lizzie helped her devise a plan to borrow the housekeeper's car. They didn't think Mrs. Smith would even notice it was gone, and Maggie was just going to bring it back when the dance was over."

"Lizzie Honeycutt? Don't you mean Irene?" The Chief of Police was a little perplexed.

"No, I mean Lizzie. Lizzie and Maggie both say they are related, but neither of them would tell me more than that. Lizzie seems to think she went home...or, in her words, 'back where she came from.' But she doesn't seem to know where that is."

"So you've talked to Lizzie since Maggie disappeared?"

"I went there earlier today. She hadn't seen Maggie either, and honestly, she didn't tell me much. She asked for the shoes -- and Maggie's dress for that matter. Apparently Lizzie helped Maggie 'borrow' a dress from Irene. I handed over the shoes. I didn't think....I'm sorry."

Clark Bailey had resumed the position, hands on head, eyes trained on the ceiling, thinking.

"You shouldn't have helped her leave the dance, you know." Chief Bailey dropped his eyes and pinned a look on Johnny. "Technically, I could charge you as an accessory to a crime."

Johnny sighed and folded his arms, a little of the hoodlum resurfacing to smirk at the chief's bluff. "You're not gonna do that, Chief. The car is back in the garage, no harm done, and I didn't take it. Plus, if you're ever gonna have a chance with my mother, you'd better not throw me in jail on a two-bit charge like that."

Chief Bailey actually blushed a little and started moving papers around on his desk. Johnny laughed out loud.

"Chief, take it from me, it's gonna take a catastrophic event to make my momma wake up and come to her senses. She's a good lady, and Lord knows she's a pretty one, but she is downright stupid when it comes to men, and you're not her type. I actually wish you were 'cause I think Maggie was right. I think you're one of the good guys, and my momma could definitely use one of those."

Chief Bailey stared at the mouthy teen for a minute, wishing he didn't like him so much, but recognizing a bit of the young Clark Bailey's attitude and guts in Johnny Kinross. Damn if the kid wasn't right. Clark Bailey knew he would never get Dolly Kinross to turn her head long enough to discover that he could take care of her if she would let him.

"Well, it seems we're both a little blind when it comes to certain women, now doesn't it, son?" Chief Bailey had recovered from his discomfort and was back in the driver's seat once more.

Johnny grinned at that. "Yes, sir. I guess so. But in my defense, Maggie seemed pretty gone on me too."

"I'm sure she was, son. I'm sure she was." Clark Bailey shook his head and laughed. He'd had to listen to his deputy, Brad Wilkey, complain for two weeks about Johnny Kinross. He had been sure his daughter was going to be ruined after attending the prom with someone like him. It seemed to Clark that Brad should spend a little more time worrying about the reputation his daughter had acquired *before* she'd been asked out by the young Kinross.

"Tell you what, Johnny. I will make some calls and see if there are any missing persons reports for a girl matching Maggie's description in the surrounding areas. I will also have my men be on the lookout around here. I will go see the Honeycutt's housekeeper this evening, just as a courtesy call, and I will ask to speak to the little girl as well -- see if I can get some information about the girl she told Mrs. Smith was her cousin. Beyond that, I don't know that I can do much more. But if I find anything, I'll let you know."

Johnny stood and held out his hand. "Thank you, sir. I'd appreciate that."

He turned to go, and then stopped, looking back at Clark Bailey. "She said you were one of the good guys, Chief. How do you think she knew that? You didn't recognize her did you?"

"No, son. I didn't. I don't know why she'd say something like that, although I'm grateful she did."

Johnny nodded again. "Just ask my momma out, Chief. All she can say is no, right? You can't be afraid of a little rejection, not a big, tough, Police Chief like yourself?"

"Go on now, kid." Clark Bailey shook his head and proceeded to fill out the form on his desk. Johnny laughed and left without another word, but thoughts of missing girls and missed opportunities nagged at Clark Bailey for the rest of the day.

~16~
A Time to Gather Stones Together

The end of the school year was three weeks away,
and Johnny was failing English. He'd flirted with Miss
Barker all year -- just enough so she cut him some slack
here and there. But she had decided to get some
backbone and was insisting he read some book and take
a test on it in order to get a final grade. He had never
read an entire book in his life, and he didn't plan to now.
He was smart enough that he usually managed to listen
in class and get the gist of whatever they were reading
and studying, and he had always squeaked by. But he
had missed class a time too many, missed one too many
assignments, and was now between a rock and a hard
spot. He knew if Miss Barker gave him a test on *A Tale
of Two Cities* by Charles Dickens, he would never pass.
Cheating was beneath him. Sweet persuasion wasn't,
but looking on another kid's paper or stealing the
answers just wasn't in him. It rankled when others did
it, and he wouldn't do it himself. Maybe because it was
what people expected of Johnny Kinross, or maybe it

was his own warped moral code, but he did have one, and he didn't cheat.

So here he was, sitting in Miss Barker's class after school, watching the poor little brown bird, as he secretly called her, blush and flutter and hating school and himself with a passion. He felt a little sick as he smiled at her, giving her a full taste of "the devil's charm" as his momma liked to call his dimpled grin.   She stuttered and seemed to forget what she was saying. Johnny stood and walked to where she was standing by her desk. She bowed her head a little, almost shyly, and he looked down at the surprisingly crooked part that divided the sides of her head into almost equal halves. She always parted her hair in the middle, pulled it back severely, and secured it at her nape. She wore it like this every day. Johnny always wondered why. It was as if she tried to be as unattractive as possible. If he could mix his momma with Miss Barker, he would probably get a good balance - as it was, each woman could probably benefit by spending some time with the other.

He crowded her a little, knowing that he made her nervous in a very non-teacher/student way.

"What if you just tell me about this book, and I'll listen very attentively, take the test, and we'll call it good," Johnny suggested oh-so-helpfully.

Miss Barker looked as if she might give in, and her eyes fell for a moment on his lips. Then her gaze shot up to his, and there was a look in her eyes that caused him to take a step back. There was hope in her eyes. The expression on her face reminded him of the way Maggie had looked at him when he'd kissed her on the beach -- the moment he'd felt the very thing she had been trying to explain to him. That kiss had rocked his world. Her sweet mouth, her arms locked around his neck, her slim form pushed up against his, the love that he had felt as soon as his lips touched hers.

For a moment he forgot where he was, the memory hung around him like he was there all over again, and Maggie was looking at him like maybe they had a chance. Then Miss Barker spoke, her voice an unwelcome reminder that he hadn't seen Maggie in two weeks, and would likely never see her again. He steeled himself against the memory. He'd had fun before her, he'd have fun after. He looked down into Miss Barker's expectant face, and his heart tripped up again. Damn.

He could do it! It would take one little kiss on that sad little mouth, and she'd talk him right through the book, and he'd be home free. He could do it. Just don't think about it, Johnny, he told himself. Miss Barker was a very nice lady-- maybe only four years older than he was himself. And she wanted him to! He could see it written all over her homely face. Damn! He could do this!

He couldn't do it. The thought of Maggie, her face shining with hope, filled him with a self-disgust that he couldn't swallow and he didn't want to live with. Maggie wouldn't like him kissing other girls, as if her kisses had meant nothing to him. She wouldn't want him to treat Miss Barker that way, either. Hell, *he* didn't want to treat Miss Barker that way. Damn it! He pushed away from the teacher's desk and walked several steps away.

"Give me the book," he said curtly, holding out his hand before he changed his mind. "I'll do the best I can. Will you give me a week?"

Miss Barker's mouth had dropped open, and she seemed at a loss for a minute. Then she closed her mouth, squared her shoulders, and nodded primly. She walked to where he stood, hand outstretched, and placed the book in his open palm.

"Absolutely. You'll do fine. It really is a wonderful book," She didn't even stutter or blush when she spoke, and Johnny wondered for the first time if she had really wanted him to kiss her after all. Maybe she was afraid of him. Maybe that had been it all along -- not attraction, but intimidation. The thought made him uncomfortable, and he resolved to read the book and do well on the test as a sort of penance. His own words to Maggie rang in his head. "Behind every bad man is a woman who can't resist him." He didn't want to be a bad man. He would read the book. The thought that Maggie would be proud lingered somewhere in the back of his mind. He shoved it away and walked out of the room, letting poor Miss Barker be.

***

The book wasn't half bad. In fact, he actually even liked it. By the end he was riveted on the tale of the underdog who became the hero. He even imagined himself in the shoes of Sydney Carton, the character who gave his life to save another man, a man he knew was a better man that he. He had willingly gone to the guillotine. Man, that would be a scary way to go, Johnny shuddered, contemplating it. But it would be quick -- and probably painless. Could he do it? Could he give up his life for someone else?

Johnny thought about it long and hard when he finished the book, gripping the novel between his hands, the final pages long since read. He had always been the man of the house, and men protected their families. The original John Kinross -- his father -- had long since gone. No one knew where, and Johnny could barely remember him, so he didn't ever miss him. In fact, he'd wondered before if Billy was John Kinross's son at all.

Dolly called both her sons by the Kinross name, the name she kept herself, and it was good enough for Johnny. Billy was his, whether or not their fathers were the same. Yeah, he'd die for Billy if he had to.

And for Maggie? A little voice inside of him questioned, much to his disgust. He growled in frustration, making Billy stir in his sleep, lying in the narrow bed alongside his. He threw the book across the room and watched as it collided with the wall hard enough to break the binding of the book. Billy sat up like he'd been slapped and then lay back down as if nothing had happened, falling carelessly back into sleep. Johnny had to smile at the rumpled hair and sleepy face of his younger brother. When Billy had his glasses off he reminded Johnny of the way he had looked when he was really little. It made Johnny hurt a little inside, the way a parent does when they realize the child they loved has morphed into a whole new creature.

Johnny felt a helplessness descend on him, and it wasn't just the melancholy of time passing. It was Maggie. Maggie who had disappeared without a trace. Maggie with no phone number and no address. Maggie, who he had been unable to get out of his head. He dreamed about her, laughing up at him, her long dark hair swinging around her, her movements confident and smooth, matching his as they danced around the gymnasium, into the starlit night, and out onto the beach, where his dream always ended short of kissing her again.

Chief Bailey had talked to Lizzie Honeycutt. She had been vague in the way that kids are vague -- telling him something seemingly helpful, only to contradict it in the next sentence. The only thing that was clear was that she did know Maggie, she had helped her take the car, and she didn't know where she was now.

Chief Bailey had also talked to Mr. Andrew Russell and his wife, as well as their daughters Cathy and Shirley. They had not had any family visiting recently, nor were they related to anyone by the name of Maggie. It appeared that Maggie had concocted the story on the spot. The discovery almost made Johnny feel better. The mystery of her disappearance was equalled by the mystery of her identity, making him believe she had vanished deliberately and was not the victim of something nefarious.

There were no missing person alerts for young girls in the whole state of Texas, not to mention girls matching her description. Texas was apparently a great place for young ladies ages 15-20, because every one of them had stayed put in the time frame Maggie went missing. Chief Bailey said he had filed a report and tucked it away, but there wasn't anything else he could do. He had said it was like looking for a ghost.

***

Graduation came and went. He made it. Johnny got his diploma, and he had actually earned it...well, mostly. He had flirted his way through some of it, but he scored an A on the final test for *A Tale of Two Cities*, which should count for something. And in so many ways it was "the best of times and the worst of times." He was free. No more school, no more teachers, no more Principal Marshall breathing down his neck. He could work full time at Gene's shop, spending time doing what he loved most. "Fixing cars and hitting bars," Carter had said when they'd done the man-hug thing after graduation. Carter was whoopin' and hollerin'-- and for a minute, Johnny saw himself doing just that, fixing cars and going to bars and getting old. And he panicked.

Johnny wasn't sure that was all he wanted anymore. He definitely had to hang around until Billy was out of school. He needed to make sure Momma didn't fall in love with the wrong guy and get herself in trouble, too. But then what? Maybe there was a much bigger world out there. A world where Maggie existed somewhere beyond the confines of his own little life. He had felt desolate all of a sudden and ended up leaving the after-graduation party early, heading out to the reservoir to skip rocks and sleep on the sand. He'd spent many a summer night out at the rez. Now here it was, halfway through the summer, with August breathing down on him with her hot breath and her short temper, and he found himself there again. He had driven out after he got off work, threw off his shoes and jumped fully clothed into the drink just to escape her. Then he had laid out on the beach and wished like hell he was dancing with Maggie.

He had his car radio cranked up just like he'd done the night of the prom. He listened as the same old announcer spun out some of the very same songs, and he laughed at himself for being such an old woman. Here he was, Johnny Kinross, who could have any girl he wanted, sitting by himself, mooning over a girl he had met only once.

"And here's a brand new one coming out to you across the airwaves, folks. It's a beauty...tell your friends you heard it here first. The Platters singing 'Smoke Gets in Your Eyes.'" The announcer's practiced voice introduced the next song with all the enthusiasm and vigor of a true music lover, and Johnny sat up abruptly as the opening bars bled out across the sand. He listened, growing more and more baffled. He had never heard this song before - he would have remembered it for the title alone.

It was her song. The song Maggie told him was her favorite. How could it be her favorite song when it hadn't even been released yet? She'd said it was an oldie but still the best love song she'd ever heard. An oldie? The announcer said it was brand new....

"What the hell, Maggie?" Johnny yelled out, his voice echoing angrily across the water, only to yell right back. "None of it makes any damn sense! Where are you?!" He stood and chucked the rock in his hand as hard as he could throw it. He felt like crying and was suddenly mad as hell and clueless as heaven, and done sitting at the rez, talking to the water. He grabbed his boots and shoved his feet inside and marched to his car, flipping the radio off and gunning the engine. He spun out and headed back into town, the hot summer air whooshing through the windows and merging with the frustrated heat inside his chest.

Johnny pulled in to The Malt and sighed. He wasn't fit for company, and he wasn't dressed for it either. His clothes had dried in the August night, but they were stiff and sandy, and his hair was probably a mess. He ran his hands through it, tugging his comb from his back pocked to put it to rights. He may not be fit for company, but he needed it, and The Malt was as good a place as any to find it, plus he could check on his momma.

His mother had told him it was over with the mayor. Mayor Carlton, Roger's dad, was as slick and handsome as his son, without the mean streak. Dolly Kinross said he was nice to her, and she said he was lonely and miserable, and "it really wasn't like that, Johnny!" She had huffed at him, her hands on her hips in mock outrage.

"Good, Momma. Then you won't mind tellin' Mayor Carlton that he can solve his loneliness problem by gettin' off his ass and doing the job the people of Honeyville elected him to do. You end it, Momma, or I will!" Johnny had said. "Billy isn't complaining, but I think Roger Carlton's been making his life difficult. I wouldn't be surprised if it has something to do with his daddy spending time with you."

"Roger?" Dolly Kinross had squeaked out, and she got a funny look on her face. "He's been giving Billy a hard time?"

Johnny just looked at her hard, folding his arms and waiting.

"I'll tell the mayor we can't be friends anymore, Johnny. I promise," Dolly looked sincere. "Roger scares me a little. I didn't know he was bothering Billy."

That was a week ago, and so far so good. Momma had been coming home right after work, and Billy even saw her talking to Chief Bailey yesterday on her lunch shift.

Johnny walked inside The Malt, and a few friends called out his name. Carter and Peggy had been inseparable since the prom, and they sat at a table in the back, a few other friends surrounding them. Carter had his arm slung around Peggy's shoulders, and she kept looking at him like he wasn't a tall, skinny, yellow-haired scarecrow but something special. She was too pretty for him, but they looked good together, and they complemented each other in a way that surprised Johnny. He chatted with them for a minute and looked around, expecting to see his mother waiting tables.

"Hey Carter, you see my momma tonight? Was she here?"

"She was, but she hustled on outta here just before you came." Carter lowered his voice and leaned in to his friend, speaking directly in to his ear. "Roger Carlton was in here. He got a little hot under the collar. He was being a complete nosebleed, if you ask me. Anyway, she dumped a drink over his head to cool him down some, I guess. She apologized, but Val sent her home."

Roger Carlton again. He was really gonna have to do something about the kid. He had let things go so far because he'd felt like maybe his mother had been the cause, but Roger just wouldn't go away. Johnny grabbed a burger and a Coke and headed for the door.

Momma wasn't home, though. Neither was Billy.
Johnny sat and waited for a while. He showered the
reservoir sand and grit off his skin and got ready for bed,
revisiting some of his favorite parts in his now favorite
book. He was just dozing off when Billy came in. His
face was flushed, and he was wearing a pair of sweats
and a tee shirt and sneakers. The kid wasn't exactly an
athlete, and he avoided sweating at all costs, but it
looked like he was taking up running or something. Billy
was always neat as a pin and careful about his
appearance. He didn't look at Johnny as he started to
undress, and then he paused, gathered up his clothes
and went into the bathroom. Johnny raised his
eyebrows at his brother's retreating back and decided it
must be a puberty thing. Billy getting shy about
changing in front of him almost made him laugh out
loud.

It was 2 a.m. before his mother came in. Johnny
jerked awake and listened, hearing her walk down the
narrow hallway between the bedrooms. She flipped on
her light and shut her door softly. Johnny eased out
from under the covers and opened his bedroom door,
wincing as it squeaked loudly. Billy didn't stir. Johnny
tapped on his mother's door to warn her he was coming
in, but didn't wait for her to give permission. He didn't
want to give her any time to compose herself. Two a.m.

meant she had been up to no good, and he was tired of worrying about her.

She screamed a little and tried to say she was undressing, not to come in, but Johnny didn't listen. She was fully dressed and sitting on her bed, hands in her lap. She stood and turned quickly, hiding her face from him, but not quickly enough.

"Ah, shit! Momma!" Johnny flew across the room and spun his mother to face him, sucking in his breath as his eyes landed on her bruised and swollen right eye. Her bottom lip was puffy too, and it was split down the center.

"Who did this!" he roared, not caring anymore about being gentle or quiet.

"It was a misunderstanding," his mother started, folding her arms against his anger.

"Bullshit, Momma!" he groaned, turning from her and locking his hands behind his head in frustration. "No one smacks a woman in the face, more than once by the looks of it, without understanding exactly what he's doing."

"Johnny Kinross!" his mother hissed, grabbing his arm and turning him to face her once more. "I am a grown woman, and you are my son, and you will watch your mouth around me. I may make mistakes, but you won't talk to me that way!" Her lips trembled, and her eyes fought against the tears that she had probably been holding in for a while.

"Momma," Johnny sighed, more softly now. "Me respecting you is not the problem here. You don't respect yourself."

"That's not it!" Dolly Kinross started up, but Johnny wouldn't let her continue.

"Yeah, Momma. It is. You think you deserve to be slapped around and treated like garbage, so you do things you know you shouldn't do so that when you *are* mistreated you can justify it. But if you think I'm gonna stand by and allow someone -- the mayor or anyone else -- to put a mark on my mother, then you don't know me very well."

"It's over, Johnny. It's done. I'm not seeing the mayor anymore. I promise," his mother called out behind him as he turned to leave her room. "Please don't do anything! Just let it go!"

Billy stood in the hallway between the bedrooms. He wasn't wearing his glasses, and his face was creased with sleep. He didn't just look tired. He looked weary, and Johnny paused a moment, looking into his younger brother's face.

"Is she okay?" Billy blurted out before Johnny could say a word.

"She's fine," Johnny soothed instinctively. "She's just been hanging around the wrong kinds of people in the wrong places, and it caught up with her." Johnny put his arm around his brother's shoulders and led him back into their room. "I don't want you to worry, Billy. I'll take care of you, and Momma too, if she'll let me."

"She said for you not to do anything, Johnny! What are you going to do?" Billy grabbed Johnny's arm. "You're not going anywhere are you? The mayor could throw you in jail if you go after him, Johnny! I don't want anything to happen to you!" Billy looked as if he were going to burst into tears, and Johnny pushed the anger away temporarily, for the sake of his younger brother who could obviously tell Johnny had revenge on his mind.

"I'm not going anywhere tonight. Let's go back to bed. Come on." Johnny pushed his brother gently back to his narrow bed and then climbed into his own, pulling the thin blanket around his shoulders and closing his eyes to Billy's worried gaze.

"You promise you aren't just waiting until I fall asleep?" Billy's voice wavered, unconvinced.

"I promise I will be here all night long, and I'll still be here when you wake up," Johnny said calmly, fighting the impulse that wanted to send him raging through town, throwing bricks through the windows of certain distinguished citizens' homes. He lay there silently, perfectly still, until Billy finally fell asleep and the tiny, dumpy house on Julian Street was hushed and still.

Johnny would be true to his word; he would be there when Billy woke up, but he hadn't abandoned his need for revenge, and the mayor was going to pay.

~17~
A Time to Cast Away Stones

"Maggie! Maggie! Wake up, Johnny's here!" Irene was shaking her and Maggie winced, not knowing where she was or frankly WHEN she was. She lifted her weighty lids and peered at her aunt. Aunt Irene's neat grey chignon and eyes lined with years met her bleary gaze and she readjusted herself to 2011.

"Wh-what?" Maggie moaned, pushing her hair from her face. Her glasses hung from one ear, sliding down her nose lopsidedly before she pushed them into place. She was still wearing Johnny's white sports coat.

"Why are you in here?" Irene wondered out loud. "When I woke up this morning you were gone. I thought you were at school. Did you come in here and lay down after I got up?" She halted and gasped, looking at the rumpled red formal Maggie was wearing under Johnny's sport coat.

"Where did you get that dress? It looks just like a dress I used to have. I looked everywhere for that dress...." Irene fussed at Maggie, and Maggie just stared down at the red formal and then around the room in wonder. Irene was acting like they hadn't played dress up and fallen asleep in a tumble of tulle and old memories. Had they? Reality was a bitter old lady with a switch in her hands, waiting for you to turn your back. Maggie closed her eyes and flung herself mournfully back across the bed. She wanted to howl and kick her legs, and she fought the urge to shriek in frustration.

"Maggie?" Irene questioned, worry tinging her voice. She reached out and rested her hand on Maggie's brow. "Are you sick? You feel a little warm."

"Yes. I think I must be." Maggie's voice wobbled, and she pulled a pillow over her face, hiding her despair from Irene. How many times would she have to lose him? The hole was widening and her sorrow was sucking her under. She needed Irene to leave her alone for a while. Maggie didn't want her to see the messy display that was threatening to boil over.

"He's downstairs. He's seems very agitated, but I'll just tell him you're not feeling well, all right?" Irene turned to leave.

"Wait! Who's agitated? Who's downstairs?" Maggie had missed an essential part of the conversation, it seemed.

"Why, Johnny, dear. I told him you weren't here -- that you were at school. But he said you weren't at school, that he had already been there this morning looking for you!" Irene's voice dropped to a girlish whisper. "I told him I would come see if you were here after all."

Maggie shot upright, flinging the pillow to the side. "I want to see him. Stall him, please?"

"Are you sure you feel well enough, dear? He scares me a little. He's so intense! It's like he looks right through me and doesn't like what he sees." Irene's voice had faded a little at the end, and Maggie looked back at her aunt, remembering the girl in her peach prom dress, standing in the parking lot in front of The Malt with her whole life in front of her. A pang of loss surged through Maggie, and she turned and wrapped her aunt in her arms.

"Aunt Irene? I don't want Johnny to leave. Will you please just tell him to wait. I want to see him, Aunt Irene. I need to see him. Okay?" Maggie released her aunt and stepped back, slipping the white coat from her shoulders. Surprisingly, Irene made no comment about the jacket, she seemed too stunned by the red dress.

"Irene?" Maggie waved a hand in front of her aunt's face, jolting her from her reverie.

"Oh! Okay then. I'll go....Maggie, you've got....something....is that sand? Do you have sand in your hair, Maggie!" Irene's face wrinkled in confusion.

"Of course I don't, Irene!" Maggie lied, and then she laughed,and then she wanted to dissolve into messy, futile tears, remembering how the sand got there. Irene shrugged, turned, and left the room. Maggie brought the jacket to her face and inhaled deeply. Johnny's face rose up before her, wrapped in his scent. Her knees buckled, and she thought she might not be able to face the boy who waited downstairs. But her need to see him was greater than her dread that nothing had changed.

She ran up the stairs to her own room and laid the precious white jacket on her bed, shimmying out of the red dress and pulling a brush through her curls as she raced around the room. Oh yeah, that was definitely sand. She yanked on a pair of jeans and her favorite pink shirt, ran back to the bathroom and brushed her teeth twice. Did her hair smell like the reservoir? She sniffed, trying to detect anything fishy. Nothing. Good. She didn't have time to shower. Her hair still bore some curl from the prom, but her face needed make up. Time travel had left her haggard. Maggie stared at her reflection and tried to get her bearings. She dabbed on a little of this and a little of that and tried to bring her face back to the present. She tried to keep her mind from dwelling on Johnny, just two floors below. She would see him soon enough.

$$***$$

He paced from one side of the room to the other, and when she came into the room he stopped, his jean clad legs spread in a belligerent stance, his arms clenched at his sides. He clasped Roger's scrapbook in his right hand. But the expression on his face wasn't belligerent; it was undecipherable. He walked toward Maggie and stopped a few feet in front of her. He took the book from under his arm and opened it, skipping through the pages until he found what he was looking for.

"Can you explain this to me?" His voice was so low Maggie couldn't tell whether he was angry or not. His face was carefully blank, and Maggie reached out to take the book from his hands.

She looked down at the page he had opened to, looking into the laughing visages of Irene and her friends. She had seen that picture before. There was the picture of Johnny and Peggy. A hard lump formed in her throat as her eyes lingered on Johnny's smiling face. Just last night, just hours before, she has kissed that mouth and danced in those arms, and here he was again with the great stone face.

And then her eyes fell on a picture that she hadn't seen before. It was a shot of the dance floor. Couples danced in close proximity, and the effect was slightly blurred as if the cameraman had caught everyone in differing degrees of motion, everyone but the couple in the center of the shot. Maggie gasped as she recognized what she was seeing.

It was a picture of Johnny and her. They stood motionless, their hands clasped between them. Johnny was staring down at her, and her chin was lifted toward him, her eyes locked on his. Maggie couldn't pull her eyes away from the picture, and for several hushed seconds the sounds around the room magnified tenfold: the ticking of the clock on the mantle, the chirping of birds outside, the far off sound of a passing car. And her own heart, pounding in her chest.

"I remember you, Maggie," Johnny whispered, close to her ear, his breath tickling the hair that hung near her cheek. She raised her eyes to his and the blank, harsh expression was no longer there.

"I still don't remember anything after the night of the rumble, but I remember you. I remember this!" He pointed at the picture of the two of them, captured forever in the image on the page. "I don't know what to think, or how to feel...but I remember you."

"You remember me?" Maggie held her breath, not daring to hope.

Johnny clenched his jaw, and he nodded once and then again, confirming her question. "I remember the prom and the way I felt when you walked in. How we danced and how you stole that damn Edsel. It was so funny, and I was trying not to laugh because you were scared to death." Johnny laughed harshly, and then the laughter broke off, almost in a sob.

Maggie dropped the book and reached for his hands, mirroring the way they stood in the picture. His breath was harsh like he struggled to control his emotions, but he let her take his hands. He wouldn't look at her though, dropping his chin into his chest as if the weight of his memories made his head too heavy to hold upright. She stared at his bowed head and struggled to keep from touching his golden hair.

"I didn't remember anything yesterday. This morning it was all there. The memories, the dance, the feelings...everything....all of it in my head, and I don't know what to make of it. That picture wasn't here before."

Maggie held onto his hands, gripping them and wishing she could explain everything and not knowing how - and not really understanding it herself.

"Maybe...maybe you didn't remember because it hadn't happened yet," she pondered out loud.

"What the hell does that mean, Maggie?" His voice wasn't angry, but pleading, almost begging her to explain.

"Do you remember what I tried to tell you?" Maggie rushed ahead, trying to make him understand. "You asked me if we had ever met before. You hadn't met me, but I already knew you." She forced his chin up, looking into his eyes, pleading with him to listen. His eyes roved over her face, searching.

"You said time could change its mind. Is that what this is?" Johnny looked away and grabbed the book again, flipping the pages as if his life depended on it. He found the page and slammed his hand down on it. "This is the report I filed with the police! You just disappeared! I thought of you every day, Maggie. I looked for you. Why did you leave like that?"

Maggie stared down at the missing persons report with her name on it. Her first name but no last name. This hadn't been in the scrapbook before either. Why did Roger have a copy of this? History had been altered and here was the proof. Quickly her horror was replaced with the realization that Johnny had tried to find her. He had tried to find her! She felt suddenly euphoric and short of breath, and her head spun trying to comprehend the incomprehensible. It had been only hours since she'd fallen asleep in Johnny's arms, and yet here she stood, decades later, staring down at a police record with her name on it.

Maggie collapsed into a chair as the room around her tipped dizzily. She felt, rather than saw, Johnny letting the book slide to the floor as he knelt beside her. This time, he was the one who forced her to look at him, bracing her face with his hands.

"You didn't disappear, did you? You came back here. It's the only thing that makes sense."

Maggie nodded, her eyes filling with tears, unable to speak.

Johnny looked like he might cry right along with her, and his jaw tightened again, holding back the emotion she could see mirrored in his blue eyes. "It's the only thing that makes sense, and it makes no sense at all," he whispered.

Maggie reached up and locked her hands around his wrists where he still held her face in his hands. He was right. None of it made sense, but it didn't make it any less true.

"Did I remember you in....Purgatory?" he asked, his eyes still on hers, his voice still laced with feeling.

"No," Maggie whispered. "You said I was familiar, that you felt like you knew me. But I thought it was because I looked like Irene."

"How can that be? Purgatory came *after* I met you. You said I knew who I was, and I knew my family, my story, right? So why didn't I remember you? I wouldn't have forgotten you, Maggie. After that night, you were all I thought about. I was obsessed with you." Johnny shook his head, incredulous.

Maggie smiled at that, a hint of pleasure tinging her cheeks at his frank confession, but her smile faded quickly as she struggled to suspend his disbelief. "You and I met in Purgatory, Johnny. That's all I know. For you and me, Purgatory came first....1958 came after. I can't explain it. But maybe there's someone who can."

~18~
A Time to Heal

They arrived at the school when classes were dismissing for the day. Maggie hoped she wouldn't run into any of her teachers and have to explain where she'd been during class. Mr. Marshall, her chemistry teacher, had become more bold and more brutal since Johnny had tried to teach him a lesson. It had scared him off for a while, but he'd slid back into his old ways before too long. She would have to tell Johnny about that day he'd put the nasty old man in his place; she thought he would probably enjoy the story. She just hoped she wouldn't have to deal with Mr. Marshall today.

She and Johnny walked through the front doors and veered down a long flight of stairs in search of Gus. Maggie had folded her arms only to have Johnny reach down and snag her hand as they walked by a group of guys who seemed more than a little interested in the way Maggie looked in her snug jeans. He quirked one eyebrow as he looked down at her.

"I think I prefer girls in skirts," Johnny said dryly, and tightened his hand around hers. He tossed a black look over his shoulder at the group of boys, and Maggie's heart sang a hopeful tune. A possessive Johnny was a very good sign.

Johnny received his fair share of interested looks as well as they navigated the crowded halls to the gymnasium where the janitor's closet was located. Jillian had kept the explanation of his presence in the small town very vague, and Johnny had kept an extremely low profile. But it was a small town after all, and he was a very good looking guy. Word spread and people, especially teen-aged girls, were curious, to say the least. This was the second time he had been seen in a very public place, and both times in Maggie's company. There would be talk.

Shad was at the janitor's closet with his grandfather when they arrived, and Maggie tried not to groan out loud when Shad folded his arms and stuck out his chest like a peacock. His lower lip jutted out too, and his eyebrows lowered in displeasure. He opened his mouth to say something, most likely something that would make Maggie groan even louder, but his grandpa shoved him lightly in the middle of his back and gently told him to "Get a move on, Shadrach. You know what needs to be done."

When Shad walked away, after looking back and glowering several times, Maggie entreated Gus for a private place where they could talk. Gus led them into the gymnasium and, using the rickety railing, eased himself down onto the lowest bench of the old bleachers. Maggie and Johnny climbed up a few rows and sat above him. Johnny had kept her hand clasped in his, and Maggie was pretty sure Gus had not missed the significance of his grip. He released her when they were seated, and moved away, shifting slightly so he could look at both her and Gus as they talked.

"How are you, boy?" Gus said gently, looking at Johnny with something very akin to affection in his chocolate brown eyes.

Johnny rested with his elbows propped on his knees, his hands loosely clasped, looking down at Gus from two rows up. "I'm okay, sir," he answered quietly.

"Ah, call me Gus." Gus waved a hand in the air, shooing away the deferential "sir."

Johnny nodded his head, but didn't comment further. Gus looked at Maggie questioningly, and Maggie dove in.

"Remember what you told me about your grandmother, Gus?"

Gus nodded, his gaze sharpening immediately.

"It happened, Gus. I fell asleep in Irene's room last night. Irene had been digging through some of her old things and I was wearing her prom dress when I fell asleep. When I woke up, I was still in Irene's room, wearing the same dress, but it was 1958. We'd been talking about the prom when we'd fallen asleep, about....Johnny and....regrets," Maggie didn't want to air Irene's personal sorrow so she tiptoed through her explanation, still wanting to give Gus enough information to understand what might have triggered the time travel. "Irene's room has all of her old things from when she was a girl. Her bed, her furniture, almost all of it is the same, and she has arranged it to look like it used to look too."

"Last night?" Johnny interrupted, his expression one of shock. "This happened last night?"

Maggie nodded her head, entreating him with her eyes. He just stared at her, trying to make the details fit. "Is that why I woke up this morning and suddenly remembered everything? Because it just happened?"

"What happened, Miss Margaret?" Gus chimed in, clearly a little lost. "When you realized you were somewhere else, what happened?"

"My grandmother, Lizzie, she remembered me, Gus! She remembered me from the time before. She helped me. She's just a little girl, but she's funny and smart, and she reminds me a little of ...well, me! I was there for a day and a half, and I saw so many things. I saw Billy Kinross, and I saw Johnny's mother," Maggie shot a look at Johnny's face, gauging his ability to hear what she had to say. His hand shot out and grabbed hers.

"You saw them?" he cried.

"Yes...and I saw Roger and Irene, and so much more!"

"What else, Margaret? How did you get back home?" Gus laid his hand on her leg, pulling her attention back to him.

"I couldn't talk about the future. Every time I did, I felt like I was being pulled away, like any minute I would be wrenched back to the present. I fought it, and Lizzie seemed to accept what I could tell her." Maggie proceeded to tell Gus about the prom, about meeting Johnny, spending the evening with him, and then how she had been pulled forward in time once again.

"I didn't need these." Maggie pulled her glasses off her nose and looked at them accusingly. "I put them on and it was as if I'd flipped a switch. I called for Johnny, but it was too late. And then I woke up, back in Irene's bed. Irene was trying to wake me up. It was as if I'd just been dreaming."

"But it wasn't a dream," Johnny added softly. "She was there. I never knew what happened to her. She just disappeared. I spent the next three months wondering where she was." Johnny opened the scrapbook they had brought along and showed Gus the picture and the missing persons report.

Gus placed a little pair of wire-rimmed spectacles on his nose and stared at the picture and then carefully read the report Clark Bailey had penned fifty-three years before.

"You say this wasn't here before?" Gus tapped the plastic covered page.

"No," Johnny replied swiftly. Maggie nodded in agreement. "I've been through that book over and over. The picture of the two of us wasn't there either."

"You goin' back changed things, Miss Margaret," Gus spoke carefully, thoughtfully.

"Not enough, Gus. Billy still died, and Johnny still lost everything, and Irene married that jerk..."

"Margaret!" Gus spoke sharply, cutting her off. "You gotta leave well enough alone. You can't be goin' in and tryin' to fix things. You don't understand the harm you could do!"

Maggie bit her lip, surprised by Gus's vehemence.

"None of what happened to Johnny or Billy or Irene is your fault. Johnny bein' here now ain't got nothin' to do with you!"

"How is it that Irene remembered a girl who danced with Johnny at the prom...a girl who looked like me...before I ever went back?"

"I dreamed about the prom, about Maggie, right after I met her the first time in the hospital. The dream was so real, down to the smallest details...and it felt like a memory, yet I knew it wasn't. I remembered the prom, and she wasn't there," Johnny broke in, contributing to Maggie's argument.

"That which has been is now; and that which is to be has already been," Gus quoted quietly.

Maggie and Johnny stared at him, their eyes wide, not understanding.

"Wh- what?" Maggie stuttered.

"It's scripture. In Ecclesiastes. See, nobody knows that verse. Everybody quotes the parts about there being a time to be born and a time to die, a time to dance and a time to mourn. But if you keep reading, you'll find that verse. My grandma used to quote it. I think it helped her understand her ability. And you have the same ability, Miss Margaret. You gotta listen to me, child. Listen good. You're tryin' to put everything in a tidy little box and wrap it up tight, but I'm tellin' you, you have the ability to change lives and alter destinies. I don't know why or how Johnny is here, but be thankful for it, and don't go tryin' to unravel mysteries that can't be unraveled without unraveling people's lives."

"I'm not *trying* to do anything, Gus! I didn't *try* to go back in time. I just did!"

"I don't want to scare you, Miss Margaret, but you gotta understand. My grandma was deathly afraid of slipping into another time. And after that first time, when she'd seen the slaves trying to escape, she felt the layers were especially thin. She said it almost got to the point where she feared sleeping alone or being alone in any place where the history of her family was the strongest. She made my grandpa hold her while she slept, to make sure she didn't slip away."

Johnny and Maggie shared a glance, remembering how she had clung to him in the car, holding onto his hand for dear life.

"My grandma worked in a big old house in Birmingham owned by some rich white folk. Her mother, and her mother's mother had both worked in that house as well, along with various cousins and aunts and uncles going back several generations. That was how she got the job. Originally, our family had been slaves, and after emancipation, we just kept on working for the same family, 'cept we got paid a little. It wasn't really much different than it had been before. After my grandmother had her experience with the dogs and the slave trackers, she said working in that big house became a nightmare. It was as if the floodgates had opened. The blood connection, along with the house that had been standing for more than a century, filled with the history of her family, became like one of them houses of mirrors at the circus. You ever been in one of those? There's a million of you in all different shapes and sizes, and you don't know which one is real - which one is actually you.

"One day my grandma was at work in the big house, and she started feelin' poorly. The lady of the house told her to rest herself in the parlor in a big rocking chair. My grandma fell asleep, rocking back and forth in that chair. She woke up to find a young white girl strugglin' to fight off an older man who was makin' improper advances." Gus looked uncomfortable but soldiered on. "My grandma didn't think twice and started poundin' on the man's back, tryin' to pull him off the girl. The man ran from the room, and the girl cried in my grandmother's arms, begging her not tell what she'd seen.

"The girl was dressed in the style popular around the turn of the century, and my grandma realized she had woken up in the same room, but not the same decade. She was afraid, both for herself and the girl. The girl was about eighteen or nineteen and was apparently engaged to be married. The man who had attacked her was the girl's uncle, and the girl knew it would destroy her mother, embarrass her fiance and his family, and probably cost her her engagement. The girl was more afraid of losing her fiance than she was of her uncle, and she promised my grandma that she would 'be more careful' in the future.

"A black woman, a servant, walked into the room while my grandma was trying to calm the young woman. She apparently worked in the house; my grandma said she was certain it was a young version of her grandmother. Of course the woman who walked in didn't recognize my grandma and demanded her name and who she was, tellin' her to leave at once, puttin' her arm around the young woman, who protested in defense of my grandma. The servant hurried the young lady out of the room, telling my grandma she was sending for the authorities. My grandma got in the rocking chair and pulled her Saint Christopher necklace out, and started rubbing it and rocking in the chair, holdin' my grandfather's face in her mind. She said she came abruptly awake, back where she'd been when she'd fallen asleep, thankfully back in her own time."

"She saved the girl, Gus! How could that be a bad thing?" Maggie interrupted.

Gus looked at her for a long moment, his eyes grave. "My grandma was shaken up and didn't want to be alone. She wanted to go home and went lookin' for her employer." Gus reached for his hat and pulled it off his head, rubbing the brim and twisting it between his long fingers. Maggie didn't like the way he'd paused in the story, as if trying to find the courage to continue.

"What's wrong Gus?" Johnny asked softly. "What aren't you saying?"

"When she found the lady of the house....she didn't recognize her," Gus whispered. "Her voice was almost the same, but the woman was tall where her previous employer had been short - her hair dark where the lady of the house had been blonde."

"I don't understand. What changed?" Johnny questioned.

"Was the house owned by a new family - did that event cause some kind of rift that changed the history of the house?" Maggie asked.

"Nope. The woman had the same name," Gus answered. "She was married to the same man. Nothing had changed but her appearance."

Maggie and Johnny stared at him, dumbfounded.

"The woman had a different father," Gus said flatly.

"The girl your grandma helped didn't marry her fiance after all?" Maggie guessed.

"No..that ain't it," Gus retorted. "She married him and she had a daughter...the lady of the house was her daughter."

"Your grandmother prevented a rape that resulted in the girl becoming pregnant by her uncle." Johnny's face was grim as he supplied the correct answer. He looked at Maggie and then back at Gus. Gus nodded, and Maggie breathed a whispered exclamation. The three of them sat in contemplative silence.

"But Gus...your grandma helped the girl," Maggie repeated, insistent.

"Yes she did, Miss Margaret - and in that moment she altered circumstances dramatically enough to make one woman completely disappear and another take her place. Do you understand what I'm tellin' you?"

Johnny reached out and touched Maggie's hand again, almost as if he was suddenly afraid to lose her. Maggie clasped his fingers and wrapped her hand around his.

"You might have the very best of intentions, Miss Margaret, but this is life we're talkin' about, and you can't play with it. What was and what is can be changed in an instant. Sometimes people's memories are a little slow in keepin' up. All those things you don't understand? That's just time changing its mind, like I told ya. Time is shifty...like those fun house mirrors, but it ain't a game, girl. It's for real. "

***

Johnny helped Maggie with her janitorial duties that day, and it was almost like the old days when he was invisible to everyone but her, the imaginary friend only she could see. She told him how he had been able to accomplish things that took her hours, simply by wishing it so. He just shook his head in amazement and tried to make the floor clean itself, only to have the floppy mop fall to the floor in a wet heap.

"So Purgatory had its advantages," he sighed, and Maggie laughed at his glum expression.

"It did - but I don't think you'd go back - not for all the power in the universe. You were like a genie in a bottle - completely trapped."

"Would you have me go back?" he queried softly.

"To Purgatory?" she squeaked, incredulous.

"Yeah. I get the feeling you're in love with the ghost, and the real guy is a bit of a disappointment."

Maggie stared at him and then looked away guiltily. She mopped silently for a moment, trying to put her thoughts in order before she spoke them.

"No. I wouldn't. But I....miss you. I miss the Johnny that read to me and made me laugh and thought I was....something special. I miss your affection and your touch. I miss being able to touch you in return, to dance when I know you're watching. I miss my friend."

Johnny felt her yearning, and it echoed painfully in his chest. He had tasted what loving her could be like. He'd only had the one perfect night under the stars, with her in his arms, but it had given him a glimpse of the love affair that was possible, and it had been enough to keep him looking for her when he thought she had run out on him.

Maggie tried to smile at him, a wobbly turn of her pink mouth, but he could see her unhappiness. "I miss you, Johnny. But I've lost a lot in my life, and I will survive losing you too if it comes in exchange for your happiness or your freedom. But I really hope..." she broke off then and stared at her Converse sneakers. "I really hope I don't have to," she finished in a rush, and her cheeks flushed, spreading the stain down her slim neck and into the V of her pink tee shirt.

"Can we start over, Maggie?" Johnny took the mop from her hand and pushed her glasses up on her little nose. They suited her, somehow, and he liked her all the more for the way they camouflaged her sexiness, making any guy have to look twice to see the obvious.

Maggie smiled at him like he'd hung the moon -- a slow spreading grin that lit her face like a sunrise. "I'd like that, Johnny."

He leaned in and touched his lips to hers ever so softly, feeling his stomach flip over and his knees go weak at the contact. Her mouth was silky and her breath sweet, and the relief that coursed through him made him want to cry like a baby and bury his face in her hair. Maybe everything would be all right. He had Maggie, and for the first time he believed he would survive life after Purgatory. He had Maggie, and maybe that was enough.

~19~
A Time to Hate

Roger Carlton parked his car across the street from The Malt and waited until he saw her come out. His lights were off, and the businesses around him were closed for the night. There weren't any cars in the lot in front of the diner, and he had seen very few automobiles pass on the quiet street that crossed in front of the popular hangout. Val rode a bike to and from work; Dolly and the other waitress, the little fat one, usually walked. It wasn't far for either of them. Roger knew Val would watch as Dolly made her way down the street. He didn't like the ladies walking home at that hour. Ten o'clock was still early on a summer night, but Val was protective. Roger eased his car out of the parking lot and circled around the block in the other direction. He would intercept her before she reached her house.

Roger was alone; he'd gotten rid of his friends when he went home to change. They had all thought it was a little too funny when Dolly Kinross poured that glass of lemonade over his head. Val had told her to go home, but apparently she stayed in the kitchen for the remainder of the evening, washing dishes and keeping a low profile. Val should have fired her. Irene's daddy owned the place. Maybe he would have to put the idea in his head that Val was letting the place go downhill. The guy was a Commie anyway. Anybody could see it.

Roger had watched her house for a while, but it hadn't taken him long to figure out no one was home. He had come back to the diner looking for her and had seen her through the front windows, sitting at the bar, having a cup of coffee while Val mopped the floor.

But now she was walking home, and his was the only car in sight. There she was. His headlights picked her up, walking along the right side of the road, heading straight for home like the good little mommy she wasn't. His passenger window was down. He had made sure of it. He pulled alongside her and slowed as he matched her swift pace.

"Hey Doll. You like it when I call you Doll, don't you? I heard my daddy on the phone with you a while back. Seems that's what he calls you too. Like father like son, huh?"

Dolly Kinross folded her arms and kept walking as quickly as her legs would carry her. She didn't look at him, but sighed and shook her head.

"Roger Carlton, it's way past your bedtime, and I am not interested in babysitting. Obviously you didn't get the message I was trying to send with that glass of lemonade. Go home before I tell your daddy that you've been bothering me. I heard you've been bothering Billy too, Roger. I won't have it. You leave my boys alone, you hear?"

Roger felt a hot, pulsing anger radiate from behind his eyeballs. He swerved wildly in front of Dolly Kinross, almost hitting her in the process, and came to a screeching halt in front of her, blocking her way. He threw himself across the seat and out the passenger door, grabbing the stunned woman by her upper arms, pushing her into the car. He leaned in and pressed her back onto the seat of his daddy's Lincoln, pressing his forehead into hers, holding her arms at her sides. He screamed in her face, his spittle landing on her cheeks.

"You will not talk to me that way, you whore! You think I want my daddy's sloppy seconds! I'm not here because I want you! I'm here because I hate you!"

Dolly Kinross lay frozen, shocked at the violence and vehemence of the young man who, despite his claims to not want her, was practically laying on her, his body pushing into hers, his arms pinning hers between them.

"You need to get off of me, Roger. Someone will come along, and you will get in trouble. You don't want that, do you?" Her voice was calm and serene, like she was talking to a naughty two-year-old, and Roger became even more incensed.

"You need to shut your mouth, whore! If someone comes along, what are they gonna see? You seducing the mayor's son, that's what! You think it's gonna hurt my reputation any? You're the one who needs to be worried.

Dolly didn't respond but held herself very still as Roger seemed to momentarily get a grip on his anger. The truth of his words lay heavy on her chest, almost as heavy as Roger himself. People wouldn't believe her. He was right about that. Car lights swung across the front window, and Roger stiffened. Apparently, he wasn't completely ambivalent about getting caught.

"Now I'm gonna get out and walk around the car, all easy like, and you are gonna lay here until that car passes. Then you're gonna sit up, and you and I are gonna take a little drive. I've got a few things to say to you, and I'm not done saying them. If you run or try to get away, you'll make a scene, and you and little Billy will pay. Now you don't want that do, you?" He smiled as he mocked her with her own words. No, Dolly Kinross didn't want that. Roger slid off of her and pushed at her legs so he could close the passenger door behind him. Then he walked around the car, waving at the car as it passed, and slid in behind the wheel like he hadn't a care in the world.

He started the car and pulled gently away from the curb. "That was my friend Darrell. He smiled and waved to me. Guess he won't be coming to your rescue, now will he?" Roger giggled, and Dolly Kinross realized that she was in serious trouble.

Roger picked up speed as he headed out of town, both hands on the wheel, a slight smile around his lips. He was a handsome boy, but there was something wrong with his eyes. They were a strange color -- a flat green -- and Dolly knew it was probably her terror that was playing tricks on her, but they seemed to glow a little in the dim light of the car's interior.

"Where are we goin'?" Dolly kept her voice relaxed and calm, her hands folded primly in her lap, but her mind was scrambling.

"Far enough away that no one can hear you scream and beg," he said jubilantly, as if he'd just revealed the A+ he got on his report card.

"What is it you need to tell me? I think this is far enough. My boys will be wonderin' where I am." Dolly wondered if Roger would believe her. He probably knew she'd kept some late hours with his father.

"They'll just think you're with my daddy," he answered, immediately confirming her fears.

"I'm not seeing your daddy anymore. Did he tell you that?" Dolly prayed he had. "I told him last week it wasn't gonna work out. He's got you and your mother to take care of, and I've got my boys. We decided to go our separate ways."

She was telling Roger the truth. And they'd never slept together. Dolly had been holding out in hopes of making the bigger score. If the mayor would leave his wife and marry her, her life would be so much easier. But that had been before Roger had started sniffing around her, before she'd become afraid of him. Then last week, Johnny had told her Roger was bothering Billy. That had been the last straw, and Dolly gave up her dream of becoming a mayor's wife, just like she'd given up on being a preacher's wife, and then an actor's wife when Johnny's father's big dreams of movie-stardom hadn't included a wife and a baby.

"Ahhh, really?" Roger cooed sarcastically. "Boy, that is just swell! Well then, you and I are free to be together now, aren't we?" He swung his right hand off the wheel and pawed at the opening of her dress, popping a button as he shoved his hand downward. Dolly gasped and pushed his hand away, lashing out with her feet and arms. She caught the wheel with her left foot, and the car swerved wildly.

Roger cried out, cursing and yelling, but quickly regained control of the wobbling car. He turned on her, viciously backhanding her across the face. Dolly's head spun, and she lashed out again, yanking on the steering wheel and pressing both of her feet into the gas. The car swung in a wide circle, and Roger instinctively bore down on the brakes as the car continued to spin, its back fender on the passenger side colliding with a fencepost that managed to slow them down just enough to abbreviate the spinning. The car came to a dramatic rest facing exactly the same direction they had been heading.

Roger sat half-dazed from the turbulent and terrifying ride, and Dolly Kinross threw herself out of the passenger door. Roger reacted a smidgeon too late, and Dolly Kinross was free and running, veering erratically as if the adrenaline coursing through her had messed with her equilibrium.

"You whore! You filthy tease!" Roger staggered out of the car, shouting and cursing, giving chase immediately.

A pair of lights turned off of the reservoir road and sliced through the field of the waist high weeds and prairie grass through which Dolly Kinross ran for her life. The lights continued toward Mayor Carlton's abandoned car, and Roger halted abruptly, caught between his desire to hunt down his prey or return to the car. The driver's side door hung wide open, and the lights were blazing. In fact, the car was still running. The dent on the rear passenger side was telling, though it wouldn't be immediately visible to the oncoming car. Whoever was approaching would almost certainly stop to investigate. He had to go back.

He sprinted to the car and then waited casually by the open driver's side door as an ancient truck approached the damaged Lincoln. The driver of the truck slowed and stopped, and the rusty heap shuddered for a full ten seconds after the driver turned it off. Roger's blood turned to ice. He recognized the old truck. Clark Bailey rarely drove it; it usually sat in front of his little bungalow and collected bird droppings, but a fishing pole was leaning over the tailgate and the police chief wore a floppy hat with various homemade flies and lures stuck in the brim. He had apparently spent the day out at the reservoir, though everyone knew there wasn't much to catch worth eating.

"What's the problem, son? You havin' car trouble?" Chief Bailey stepped out of the truck and had to slam the rickety door twice to get it to stay shut.

"No, sir. Not exactly," Roger smiled sheepishly. "I saw a deer and swerved to miss it, but ended up hitting the fencepost instead." Roger inwardly preened at his own genius. "It still runs, but my daddy's gonna be none too happy when he sees the dent."

"A deer, huh?" Clark Bailey's eyes swept out over the fields, trying to catch the movement he had spotted when he'd stopped. "What you doin' out here at this time a night?"

"Just driving, sir. I thought maybe I'd take a late night dip in the rez. I have to be home at midnight, so it woulda been quick, but it sure woulda felt good. It's been so hot I can't stand to sit still; even now it's probably 90 degrees!" Roger jabbered conversationally as he opened his car door and slid back behind the wheel. He put the car into gear, crossing his fingers that it would still drive. He wasn't afraid of his father; the man would yell and threaten and then give Roger whatever he wanted just like he always did. But Roger *was* a little afraid of Clark Bailey. That man wasn't a fool, and he didn't miss much. Roger would be lucky to drive away without alerting his suspicions. He hoped Dolly Kinross was still running.

"That's true enough, but you shouldn't be swimming at night, especially by yourself. You head on home now. I'll be right behind you in case you did more damage than you think." Chief Bailey climbed into his truck, turned on the tired beast, and waited for it to roar its discontent before backing up twenty feet to allow Roger space to swing a U-turn and head back toward town.

Dolly watched as the old truck rumbled after the glossy blue Lincoln. She remained crouched in a shallow ravine, her blonde head peeking up over the edge, until the headlights disappeared into the dark. It was Clark Bailey. He had saved her without even knowing it. She had heard his voice carry over the distance she had run. Recognition had brought sudden relief, along with an onslaught of hot ears streaming from her eyes -- one of them black and swollen-- and down to her bleeding mouth. Her jaw felt funny, too. It caught a little when she opened her mouth. That was an old injury, rearing its head. She had been hit in the face before, though her momma usually hit with an open palm and was careful not to bruise her daughter's pretty face. Her mother had made sure Dolly knew how important that face was to her survival.

She could have run to Clark, crying for help, pointing the finger at the demonic Roger Carlton. She could have. She should have. But she didn't. She had stayed huddled and fearful, not wanting him to see her with her face swollen and her hair a mess. She liked Clark Bailey. She had always liked him; he was the kind of man she never pursued because he deserved so much more. She didn't want him to see her this way; what if he thought she wasn't pretty anymore? And what if he thought she had been the one to pursue Roger Carlton? What if he didn't believe her? No, she had done the right thing. She was okay. She had been in worse situations than this. Town was only about five or six miles away, definitely no more than seven. She had on her flat shoes, so she could walk home just fine. Straightening her hair and using her apron to dry her eyes and tidy her makeup, she set out for town, her face throbbing with every step.

She watched fearfully for car lights, worried that Roger would return as soon as he was no longer under Chief Bailey's watchful eye. But no one came. A little more than two-and-a-half hours later she reached Julian Street. It had to be close to two a.m.. Johnny's car was parked in the pockmarked drive of her two bedroom home, and the lights were all off. Dolly sighed gratefully. She was good with makeup. If she could just get through the night and steer clear of her boys until tomorrow, with a little foundation and paint she could make this whole dreadful episode go away. She just needed to make it into her room.

She had made it down the hallway and into her room before remembering that she had told Val she would cover the breakfast shift in the morning, only four hours from now. And then Johnny burst through her bedroom door.

***

Chief Bailey was angrier than he had been in a long time. He'd dropped in for a coffee and a big man's breakfast at The Malt that morning and discovered someone had marked up Dolly Kinross's pretty face. Oh, she'd done a good job of applying the goop and arranging her hair just so, but Chief Bailey knew a black eye and a split lip when he saw it, and she definitely had both. And she was dead on her feet, and her smile looked like it hurt to show teeth.

He normally didn't stop in for breakfast, but Dorothy had told him that Dolly would be covering her morning shift today. He had decided he was going to take the kid's advice and just go for it. He was gonna ask Dolly Kinross on a real date. What was the worst thing that could happen? But when he saw her face he decided romance would have to wait; she was in no condition to be hit on. He pretended he didn't notice her injuries, because he knew that was what she wanted. But he'd finished his breakfast without tasting it and burnt his tongue when he'd gulped his coffee before it was sufficiently cool. When he paid for his meal, he pulled Val aside and asked the manager if he knew the story. Val shrugged and sighed.

"She's been havin' trouble lately here at work. She's been jumpy and jittery. She even spilled a glass of lemonade over the head of a kid last night. I know she and her oldest son had words a week ago. She told me he thinks that he's the parent. The kid has a temper, I know that much. I've heard he knows how to fight and won't take anything from anyone. Maybe it was him that roughed her up. Like father like son, you know?"

Chief Bailey didn't know, and he really didn't want to know, either. Johnny Kinross hadn't struck him as the kind of guy to hit his mother. He liked the kid. Still, it wouldn't hurt to have a word with him. If there were some domestic problems at the Kinross house, it would help everyone involved, including the police, if he could head them off right now.

***

Johnny lifted the hood of the jalopy and tried to hold back the anger that wanted to spill over like the oil that was leaking from the jalopy onto the shop floor. He had come to work that morning just as angry as he had been when he went to bed. Momma had been up and out the door at the crack of dawn, supposedly to work at the diner, though Johnny had stopped in to make sure she was there before heading to the shop. She had covered up the damage pretty well. But she hadn't made eye contact with him, even when she handed him two pieces of buttered toast with an egg and a few slices of bacon sandwiched between them.

"You're gonna be late for work if you don't hustle," was all she said. He'd left the diner with no appetite, but he was sure hungry for a fight.

Then not ten minutes after getting to work, Mayor Carlton and that little creep Roger had shown up at Gene's. Apparently, young Roger had swerved to miss a deer and wrapped the tail end of his daddy's Lincoln around a fencepost. Mayor Carlton was not a happy man. Roger seemed unconcerned by the damage he had caused but had the sense not to say much. He smirked over at Johnny a few times, leering a little at his soiled coveralls. Johnny wished the dipstick in his hand was a sword that he could use to wipe the self-satisfied smile off of Rogers face. He wondered how Mayor Carlton would react to having his son's face marked up. He sure as hell didn't like the mayor marking up his mother. Let him see how he liked it.

Johnny finished checking the oil and moved to the back of the jalopy, opening the trunk to remove the spare that the owner had said needed replacing. When Johnny pulled the tire free he uncovered something else. The nose of a gun peeked out from beneath an old blanket that had been partially caught beneath the spare. Johnny glanced around almost guiltily. It was as if his wish for a weapon had materialized into an actual gun. He leaned into the trunk and slid the revolver out, running his hand along the smooth barrel, wondering if it was loaded. It was small and light weight. It would fit inside Momma's purse just fine. He could teach her to use it. Then nobody would ever hit her again.

"Johnny?"

Johnny jerked, cracking his head on the trunk as he swept the blanket back over the little gun and stood at attention. Gene was walking toward him with Chief Bailey in tow. The morning just kept getting better and better.

"Hey, Johnny. Take five kid. The Chief here wants to chat with you a minute. You ain't in trouble, are ya?" Gene winked at Johnny and relieved him of the tire he'd removed from the jalopy. He rolled the wheel expertly across the floor and returned to visit with the mayor about the likely cost of repairs to his shiny automobile.

"What can I do for you, Chief?" Johnny asked, and his mind raced, wondering if he had done anything recently that might encourage a visit from Honeyville's finest. Nope. He was clean, he decided. Maybe the chief had news about Maggie. Maybe he'd found her. Johnny's eyes swept over the policeman's face, and he felt a flash of fear at the grim look in the man's eyes.

"I just need a minute, Johnny. Let's get some sunshine while we talk," Clark Bailey said mildly, and Johnny followed him out of the garage without a backward glance at the Carlton's, all thoughts of the gun in the jalopy's trunk completely replaced with thoughts of a girl he barely knew but couldn't forget. Please, please, let her be all right, he prayed silently as he settled himself down on the bench that Gene had placed in front of the shop.

"Is she okay?" Johnny blurted out without preamble, and Clark Bailey's eyebrows lowered dramatically over his steel grey eyes. He leaned toward Johnny, anger flitting across his face before he schooled his features into a frown.

"Well, I don't know, kid. She sure as hell didn't look okay when I saw her about fifteen minutes ago." Chief Bailey's voice dripped sarcasm, and his hands curled at his sides as he glowered at Johnny.

"You saw her fifteen minutes ago?" Johnny's heart galloped wildly, and he was back on his feet immediately. "Where is she? I want to see her."

"Whaddaya mean where is she? She's at work. Or didn't you know she had to face the crowd at Val's this morning with a black eye and a fat lip?"

"Huh?" Johnny stuttered, his face wrinkled in confusion. "The diner? Are you talking about...my mother?" His voice rose awkwardly, and his brain shifted gears from what he thought to what he now knew.

"Who did you think I was talking about?" Clark Bailey growled in disbelief.

"I thought you were here....to give me news about...about Maggie." Johnny was tripping over his words, which rarely happened, and he collapsed back onto the bench, running his hands through his hair in both dejection and relief. No news wasn't good news...but it wasn't the worst news.

"Maggie? Oh! Oh..Maggie." The chief was caught completely off guard, and it was his turn to play mental catch up. "No. I don't have any information on the girl...."

Johnny sighed and dropped his hands into his lap. Then the conversation sunk in. Johnny scowled at the Chief of Police. "So you came here thinking that I what? Slapped my momma around last night? That's real nice, Chief. Real nice opinion you have of me." Johnny shook his head in disgust.

"So what did happen?" Chief Bailey ignored Johnny's impudence; he figured he kinda deserved it.

"Momma drug in around 2 a.m. last night looking like she'd been through a battle with Custer and all the angry Indians at Little Bighorn. When I demanded she tell me who hit her, she just told me it was a misunderstanding and clammed up like she didn't speak English."

"You got any ideas?" Clark Bailey asked quietly.

"I got no proof....but I wouldn't be surprised if the mayor knew something about it."

Chief Bailey's face got cold and blank in less than a heartbeat. "You mean to tell me that your momma has been hangin' out with that sleazeball?"

Johnny didn't reply; he wasn't going to go saying ugly things about his mother, whether they were true or not. He just stared at the chief for several long seconds, letting the silence tell Clark Bailey all he needed to know.

"Why?" Clark Bailey's tone was so incredulous and befuddled that Johnny almost forgot the seriousness of the situation and laughed right out loud. Suddenly, he really liked the Police Chief.

"Ah, hell, Chief. Do you really need me to explain it to you? I'm nineteen and you're forty. You should be explaining it to me!"

Clark Bailey snorted and lightly cuffed Johnny on the back of the head. "You're kind of a smart aleck, aren't you?"

"I am," Johnny agreed without rancor. "But if you talk to the mayor, tell him if he ever touches my mother again I'm gonna find him."

"Don't do that, kid. Let us handle it." Clark Bailey stood as if to end the conversation, but his face was wrinkled in thought, and he scratched his clean-shaven jaw for a minute, looking off at nothing at all.

"Roger Carlton had the mayor's car last night. I saw him after he met up with that fencepost. So unless the good mayor and your momma were at his place, which I doubt Mrs. Carlton would have tolerated, it doesn't seem likely that they were together. Your momma doesn't have wheels, does she?"

"No sir, she doesn't. When she needs something or to go somewhere, she uses mine."

"Well, then. I guess your momma has some explaining to do, and the mayor looks like he's in the clear. I'll still have a word with him, though. You best be gettin' back to work."

*** *** ***

     It wasn't until much later that Johnny remembered the gun in the back of the rusty grey jalopy. He waited until closing time, when it was time to sweep out the garage and put the place to bed. Gene was up front, running numbers and closing up the office. Johnny popped the trunk and felt around for the gun. It was gone. He pulled the blanket free and patted his hands all around the floor of the trunk. The spare had been changed out. He heaved it up and out. Still no gun. Maybe Gene had seen it and removed it until the owner could come back and claim his car. That was probably it. After all, you never knew who could get a crazy idea -- a crazy idea like stealing it. Johnny shook his head ruefully and silently thanked God for granting the tender mercy of a couple of hours and a cooler head. He would use his fists, thank you Lord. He didn't need a gun to speak for him. Slamming the trunk, he finished up and headed out for the night.

~20~
A Time to Love

2011

A few nights later when Johnny dropped her off, Maggie asked if he would come inside, just for a minute. She had something she wanted to show him.

"Won't...Irene...uh, your aunt mind if I'm in your room?"

"It's just for a second. Don't worry."

Johnny looked unconvinced but followed behind her as she climbed the stairs to her room. She walked straight to her closet and pulled the red prom dress from its hanger and held it in front of her.

"Recognize this?" she asked shyly.

Johnny reached out and fingered the tulle of the skirt. "Yeah."

"And here's your sports coat." Maggie reached for the white sports coat and handed it to a stunned Johnny. "I didn't mean to steal it. Hmm, I seem to be saying that a lot lately."

Johnny shrugged the jacket on and looked at himself in the mirror. "Momma was so mad at me when I told her I'd lost this. She'd rented it for me, and we ended up having to pay for it. She asked me how I could lose a sports coat. I couldn't really explain." His eyes met Maggie's in the mirror. Maggie realized this was the first time she'd ever seen Johnny's reflection.

"I couldn't tell her a pretty car thief had disappeared with it." Johnny shrugged out of the jacket and seemed uncertain what to do with it.

"Johnny? I know girls don't usually ask guys...but Saturday night is the Prom. My prom. I would really like to go with you. I already have a dress." She held up the fluffy red confection. "And you now have a sports coat." She winked. "I'll be driving a Cadillac this time."

Johnny's response was interrupted by Irene calling up the stairs.

"Maggie? Are you home dear?"

Johnny looked at the door, and Maggie opened it wide and called down to her aunt.

"I'm here, Aunt Irene. Johnny's here with me. We'll be down in a second."

The silence that answered her was telling, and Maggie wondered how Irene and Johnny would ever be comfortable in each other's presence.

Maggie shut the door and turned back to Johnny. He stood with his hands shoved in his back pockets, his head tipped to the side. He looked quite delicious standing in her room, and she had to swallow her heart once, then twice, as it threatened to tumble from her chest. He was here. And she was here. Finally together - no Purgatory, no anger, and at this moment, no regrets. Once he had told her that every moment with her had made the fifty years in Purgatory worth it. Now she had reason to hope that he would feel that way again. The intense gratitude that suddenly consumed her rose up and spilled onto her cheeks.

"Hey? Are you okay?" Johnny asked softly, taking a slow step toward her, his head tilted to one side.

"I'm better than okay," Maggie whispered, and her chin wobbled the slightest bit. She yanked off her glasses and cleaned them on the bottom of her T-shirt to create a diversion from the sudden weight of her emotions.

"Maggie?" He took her glasses from her hand and set them on her nightstand.

"Hmmm?"

"Look at me, Maggie."

Maggie felt him close the final steps, but she didn't dare look up. "Don't cry, baby. I'll go to the prom with you," he teased quietly.

Maggie giggled, but the giggle broke into a sob, and she stepped into him, holding onto his shirt and rubbing her face across the familiar planes of his chest, breathing him in and letting him comfort her like he had many times before.

"Shhhh," Johnny soothed, sliding his hands up and down her back, nuzzling her hair. "Car thieves don't cry, baby. You gotta toughen up if you're gonna have a future with good old Clyde here."

"I like it when you do that."

"What?"

"Call me baby," Maggie whispered.

"You liked it when I called you Bonnie too," he replied with a smile in his voice. "Why?"

"You used to call me baby all the time. It makes me believe you can love me again."

Johnny wrapped his arms tightly around her waist and lifted her to him, kissing her tear-streaked cheeks before he touched his lips to hers.

"I'm already there Maggie. I fell in love when you begged me to help you escape the cops. I fell in love when we danced to Nat King Cole singing 'Stardust' on a moonlit beach. Hell, I fell in love when you told me how blondes spell farm."

"E-I-E-I-O," Maggie quipped wetly.

Johnny laughed and held her even tighter.

"There's something I want to give you," Johnny whispered into her hair. "It used to be the thing to do-- though I never did, 'cause I didn't ever have anyone I cared about in that way."

Maggie pulled back so she could look into Johnny's face.

Johnny reached into his front pocket and pulled out a silver pendant hanging from a long chain.

"When I was in high school, guys would give these to their girls. I've been thinking about it since Gus told us about his grandma and the Saint Christopher medal she always wore. I want you to wear it. Maybe it will help keep you safe." Johnny held the pendant in his palm. It was silver and dainty, a weary traveler with a walking stick and a child on his back engraved in fine detail on the surface. Circling the edge were the words 'Saint Christopher Protect Us.'

"Does this mean I'm *finally* your girl?" Maggie tried to be glib, but her voice was reverent as she fingered the pretty little pendant.

Johnny laughed and gently fastened the long chain around Maggie's neck. Smoothing her hair back over her shoulders, he touched his lips to hers again.

"Thank you, Johnny." Maggie cradled his face in her hands and brushed her lips up and then down, answering his questioning kisses with her own. Then she touched her tongue lightly to his fuller bottom lip. He stilled, and her breath caught. He returned the caress lightly, tasting the salt of her tears and the warmth and silkiness of her mouth. And then the restraint was gone. Her hands slid into his hair as he wrapped hers around his fists, pulling her head back to give him a better angle on her lips. The door met her back as he pushed her against it, using it as leverage to bring her closer. She rained kisses along his jaw until he growled and pulled her mouth back to his. One hand flexed at her waist while the other palm flattened on the door above her. And then the other hand joined it as he tried to push himself from her while still keeping his lips locked on hers. She moved to follow, but his hands slid to her shoulders and gently kept her pressed against the door. He kissed her once more, and then again, as if he couldn't pull himself from her. With a groan, he broke away, his hands holding her still, his eyes locked on hers, as he tried to master his desire.

"Irene is downstairs. Or upstairs...or...right outside...who knows. I have to go right now or I'll end up dragging you out the door and having my way with you in the Bel Air, which isn't what good guys do, and though I've never pretended to be one of the good guys, I want to be one with you."

Maggie didn't respond. She wished he weren't such a good guy at the moment. She wished that she wasn't tempted to run to the Bel Air like the bad girl she had never been. Her eyes dropped to his mouth, and she pushed against the hands still keeping her from him.

"Maggie..." he groaned again, and her eyes snapped back to his.

"You better go," she giggled, biting her lip. "I can't promise that Bonnie won't attack Clyde."

He laughed but grabbed at the doorknob desperately, releasing her as he did. She let him go but followed close behind him as he walked down the stairs. He reached back and grabbed her hand, and the gesture almost had her in tears again. Life had suddenly become so impossibly sweet she couldn't keep the joy from overflowing.

At the door he didn't kiss her again, which was probably wise, but he did press his lips to her hand. "In case you missed it before, I'd love to go to the prom with you, although I don't think I can dance to your music." He grimaced.

"We'll think of something." Maggie smiled. "After all, you had to teach me to dance to your music."

"'Night, my Bonnie," he murmured and let himself out the door.

"Goodnight, Johnny," she sighed, and watched him leave.

When Maggie shut the front door, Irene was nowhere in sight. Maggie hoped she wouldn't find her in the attic, madly trying to recapture her lost youth. Instead, Maggie found her in her little yellow sitting room, Lizzie's old bedroom, holding a book as if she were reading, but staring off as if her mind were full of other things.

"Irene?"

"Is Johnny gone?" Irene looked almost fearful.

"Yes." Maggie sat down on the little sofa next to her aunt, and reached out to touch her papery soft cheek.

"I love you, Irene. I don't think I tell you that enough."

Irene's book fell to her lap, and her hand reached up to cover Maggie's.

"I love you too, sweetest girl," Irene murmured, patting the hand that Johnny had recently kissed. She looked away almost immediately, as if something troubled her but she didn't want to unburden herself.

The joy that had been flooding Maggie only minutes before receded dramatically as she observed her aunt's obvious distress.

"I love him too, Irene," Maggie rarely called her aunt by her name but felt compelled to do so now, to drive home the importance of her words.

"Yes....yes...I know," Irene stammered. "I know Maggie. It's not that...."

"What then?"

"I had a dream. I thought it was a dream..." Irene's voice tapered off, and Maggie felt a cold dread seep through her.

"When I saw you in that dress the other morning, I was almost too stunned to speak....but, I've been thinking about it since then."

"About the dream?" Maggie whispered.

"It wasn't a dream!" Irene lashed out, dropping Maggie's hand and covering her face with her own. Maggie trembled at the sudden change in her aunt and was afraid to touch her again, afraid her touch might be rebuffed.

Irene was breathing heavily behind her hands, the harsh sounds making Maggie's hair stand up on her neck.

"It was you!" Irene cried in a horrified whisper. "You were the girl at the dance with Johnny, the girl who told me to get rid of Roger." She moaned into her hands. "I don't know how it was you. But it was! I saw your face in my dream. You were wearing my dress! How did you get my dress? I remember it now, so clearly -- as if it just happened today and not fifty- three years ago."

Maggie couldn't breath. Her heart was a pounding, and she wanted to wail like a wrongly imprisoned man who knew he was a dead man walking.

"Roger was so angry!" Irene rushed on. "He ranted and raged about you for weeks, saying you'd insulted and embarrassed him. Like a fool, I thought I needed to prove my loyalty all the more. I gave him my virginity that night, thinking it was the only thing I could do to show him I wasn't going anywhere. I told Nana I was staying at the Russell's again, and Cathy and Shirley covered for me....but I was with Roger."

Maggie grimaced and felt sorrow leaking from her eyes and sliding down her nose. Gus had told her there would be unintended consequences, things she could never predict, lives she would unknowingly alter....or shatter.

"By the time August rolled around, I had come to my senses. Roger had been unbearable, and I was quite afraid of him. When Billy Kinross died and Johnny disappeared, I was horrified, knowing that it was all Roger's fault. Billy had been so sweet to me, and he was gone -- at Roger's hand! I believed that, but it was too late. I was pregnant."

"No, no, no!" Maggie wanted to scream. This wasn't the way it happened! Irene had married several years after high school. She'd seen the wedding announcement in the old newspapers at the library.

"The baby was stillborn. Did I ever tell you that?" Irene's voice was almost trance-like as she remembered the child she almost had. "He was perfect. A beautiful, full-term little boy with lots of dark hair. But he was dead," she whispered. "I had hoped and prayed for a way to be free of Roger. Suddenly, I had it....and it had come at the price of my child's life. So I stayed. It was penance, my own slow dance in purgatory."

"Can you forgive me?" Maggie's agonized whisper filled the room, and Irene shook herself, abandoning the trance-like state she had hovered in. She stared at Maggie, her blue eyes wide and filled with anguish.

"There is nothing to forgive, Maggie," she said softly, reaching out and touching Maggie's stricken face.

"You're afraid of me," Maggie mourned, her voice barely audible.

"I understand what happened....at least I think I do," Irene replied quietly. "You slipped back....just like Gus said you would. You tried to help me. I know that..."

"But..."

"Maggie! You tried to help me. Now," she said tiredly, rising to her feet, her back bent and her head bowed in exhaustion. "We need to get you out of this house."

***

Maggie had slept restlessly ever since coming home from the hospital after the fire. Dreams of Johnny and burning hallways made sleep a minefield, and though she had longed desperately for the relief unconsciousness would supply, she found that she no longer felt safe in her bedroom.

Maybe it was because she had been awakened twice in the last few weeks to see Roger Carlton, the aged and overweight Uncle Roger, sitting on the benchseat pouring over his old pictures. Both times, she had reached for her glasses on her nightstand, pushed them on her nose, and forced herself to concentrate on the details of the room she knew existed in present day, which did not include a ghostly fat man. Both times, Roger had flickered out almost immediately without even raising his head.

That night, the drain from the conversation with Irene had Maggie stumbling to her room and falling into a deathlike slumber. Irene had wanted to leave and check into a hotel. She was afraid that Maggie would slip away if she slept in the house again. Maggie thought of the tongues that would wag in the small town if she and her aunt suddenly checked into the Honeyville Suites right on Honeyville's Main Street. Plus, Irene didn't have the funds to waste on a hotel room when there were four perfectly good bedrooms right here.

Maggie was convinced it was the talk of 1958, combined with the furnishings in Irene's old room and the dress Maggie had donned, that had precipitated the shift. She had practically stepped back in time before she even fell asleep that night, and she told Irene as much.

"We have to get you out of this house," Irene said again, wringing her hands desperately, but she had gone to bed after a little coaxing and reassuring. Irene looked as if she were ready to collapse. Both of them needed rest before making any rash decisions.

Maggie had been pulled from sleep suddenly. She became completely and fully awake as if ice water had been poured over her, bringing her instantly and alarmingly from the depths of unconsciousness. She sat up and reached for her glasses on her bedside table, but the space was empty. She felt up and down, trying to connect with the surface of the table in the darkness of the room, knowing that she should be feeling the little knob on the drawer and the pointed edges of the table top. She felt a shift, a sense of falling, and then her legs folded and the surface beneath her changed. She was sitting upright in a chair. The chair was hard and the rungs dug into her shoulder blades. Goose flesh rose on her arms as she felt the cool against her bare feet which curled disbelievingly against the flat surface of her bedroom floor. It was still so dark. She looked toward where she knew the window should be and watched as they sky beyond lightened instantly by several shades, as if she were watching a time lapse on the news where the weather of the entire day is captured in seconds.

Roger sat at the window, his head bent over his scrapbook. The light beyond him was dusky, as if dawn had ascended while he read. He was younger, his hair thick and dark, his body still lean and his clothes reminiscent of a different decade. Maggie longed for her glasses. She didn't dare move or even breath, knowing that she was no longer observing him in her room. She was with him.

She must have exhaled too loudly, though she hadn't felt the release. Or maybe it was simply the sense of being watched, but Roger's head jerked up suddenly, and he screamed, a strange, high pitched cry that had Maggie flying up and out of the chair to cower in the corner.

"It's you!" Roger hugged the wall like a jumper on a ledge, easing around the room toward her. She had to get out of there, but could she run screaming through the house? She didn't know why she was here or what year it was. If Irene and Roger were living in the house it was after Irene's father had passed, after Billy had died and Johnny became trapped in Purgatory. She felt for something to shield herself with as Roger crept steadily closer.

"Are you some kind of a witch?" he breathed, his green eyes wide with fear and fascination. He poked at her with his foot. His shoe was pointed, and he shoved it into her as if she were an animal on the side of the road. She curled her legs into her chest and wrapped her arms around them, closing her eyes and willing herself home. She pictured Johnny in this very room, as she had seen him only hours earlier. The kiss that they'd shared, and the heat of his hands.

Roger kicked her. And then again. She cried out but kept her eyes squeezed shut and prayed for deliverance. She pictured her room, the pictures on her walls, the blanket on her bed, the fat yellow rug on her floor.

"I'm talking to you, witch! What are you doing in my house?" She felt his hands on her throat. He was pushing her back into the wall, forcing her head up. Her eyes popped open as he bore down on her, choking her, his eyes crazed yet eerily flat. The green was all one shade, without the striations of color and the golden flecks that made up the human eye. It was as if a child had taken a light green crayon and colored them in. Little spots of white started to flicker at the edges of Maggie's vision. He was going to kill her.

Then she remembered the pendant around her neck. She released Roger's hands and felt for the medal. She rubbed at it desperately.

"Johnny!" she gurgled, gripping the necklace Johnny had given her for protection. And then she recognized the sensation, almost like a carnival ride, of being pressed by centrifugal force into the wall behind her. Then she was falling away from Roger's hands as the air was forced out of her lungs and the pressure built inside her until she was no longer conscious.

~21~
A Time of War

1958

Irene Honeycutt slid onto the high stool and leaned on the bar, pressing her hot face into her hands. She had felt nauseous all day, and though her stomach rumbled hungrily, she was afraid to eat. She'd been careful to stay away from anything that might make her gain weight too fast, although her clothes were already starting to pull across the chest and her fitted skirts showed the slight swell at her hips and lower belly. She hadn't told anyone about the mess she was in -- not her daddy or Nana. She hadn't even told Roger. But she was so hungry, and the smell of the grill was more than she could take.

She had pled sick when Roger had suggested a day at the reservoir with all their friends. It was just so hot -- and swimsuits were too revealing. She had tried to sleep in this morning, tried to pamper herself and listen to her favorite records to keep her mind from dwelling on her troubles. Nana had taken Lizzie for some shopping. Lizzie was growing like a weed, and school would be starting up soon. Irene's senior year was approaching, yet she wouldn't be attending school. Girls who got pregnant got married. She would be getting married too. The thought should cheer her. She had always dreamed of her wedding day. She knew Daddy would give her a big wedding, regardless of her condition. She would buy a beautiful dress, and they would have the wedding in the yard at home. The backyard flower garden would be the perfect back drop. Roger would look handsome in his black tuxedo. Everything would be fine. Daddy would make sure of that.

So why did Irene feel like her life was ending, like her whole world was crumbling around her feet? She mopped at her forehead and tried to ignore her rumbling stomach as she requested a glass of water and a chicken sandwich with no mayo, cheese or bread.

"You want a chicken sandwich without the bread?" Val asked, his tone incredulous.

"Yes, please," Irene spoke primly, not making eye contact. "Just chicken, lettuce, and tomato." He grumbled under his breath about skinny girls getting skinnier.

"And a side of fries!" Irene burst out, succumbing to the mouth-watering smell of salty grease. Her stomach rejoiced, and her pulse quickened in anticipation of the treat.

Val chuckled but inclined his head, acknowledging that he had heard her. Irene sneaked a look at the other customers sitting at the bar, hoping they hadn't noticed her moment of weakness.

Billy Kinross sat a few seats down, but no one sat between them, and he shot a curious look down the bar before looking away shyly.

"The fries aren't for me," Irene offered, as if he cared. She could kick herself! Now she wouldn't be able to eat them! She felt like bursting into tears. Val slid a cardboard sleeve of fries in front of her, and Irene stared at them remorsefully. She shot another look at Billy, who she discovered was watching her.

Billy Kinross smiled at her and looked away again. He was cute, Irene noted with surprise. His hair was short and dark, his skin brown with his summer tan. His eyes behind his glasses were chocolaty with the thick lashes that were wasted on boys. He had a smattering of freckles on his nose and a hint of a dimple in his chin that was identical to Johnny's. She had never really looked at him before. Johnny had such a presence that when he was around nobody spared a glance at his younger brother. And Billy was young...only fourteen or fifteen. She was probably three years older than he was, and that was light years when you were a teen-aged girl.

"You should probably eat them," Billy offered suddenly, turning back toward her as if he had dared himself to do it.

"Why?" Irene countered, flirting in spite of herself.

"They'll get cold while you eat your sandwich, and then they won't be any good anyway."

Irene looked around her again, just as she had done moments before, checking who was in the diner. Nobody who ran in her crowd was there. They were all still at the lake.

"I can't eat them all myself," Irene lied prettily. "Do you want some?"

Billy looked stunned, but wasted no time sliding down the bar and onto the stool that was empty beside her. Irene slid the hot fries between them and shot Val a smile as he delivered her chicken "sandwich." She dug in without a word, trying to eat like a lady, but hungry in a way she hadn't been hungry before. The first three months she had had little appetite; everything had made her stomach roil. But in the last week or so, her appetite had returned with a vengeance, and hunger had become almost painful.

It took her a minute to realize Billy wasn't eating, and she glanced at him, shamefaced. "Aren't you hungry?"

"Not really," he smiled sheepishly. "I already ate. I just wanted to sit by you." His cheeks grew rosy under his tan.

Irene beamed at him, and warmth flooded her chest. He was so sweet. Then she remembered. The smile faded from her lips, and her appetite fled. What was she doing? In only a matter of weeks, she would be planning her wedding. In only weeks, everyone would know...and she was acting like a fool. Tears filled her eyes, and her stomach rebelled against the food she had filled it with.

Billy saw her distress and reached out tentatively, touching her arm. "Are you okay, Irene?"

Irene mumbled something about being perfectly fine when a voice rang out behind them.

"She's a little old for you, Billy Boy." Roger Carlton stood in the doorway of the diner, his brown hair slightly rumpled, his skin brown and his nose slightly burnt from the day he had spent in the sun. Irene saw the whole gang spilling out of cars in the parking lot. She had been caught faking sick. She shrugged, unable to muster the energy to care.

"I'm talking to you, Billy Boy," Roger repeated. "I don't like you putting your greasy paws on my girl." He strolled up to the bar and slung his heavy arm around Irene's shoulders, pulling her tight against him. She immediately slid off the school and tried to steer him away from the unfortunate Billy.

"He was just asking me if I was okay. I came here to get something to eat, but I shouldn't have. I started feeling sick right away," Irene explained, trying to soothe Roger's ruffled feathers. She was good at it. When were his feathers not ruffled?

Roger shrugged her off and grabbed Billy by the back of his collar, pulling him from his stool roughly.

"Take it outside, boys!" Val bellowed, and Roger shoved Billy toward the door.

"You heard him, Billy boy. We're taking this outside."

"Roger." Irene laid her hand on his shoulder, trying desperately to be cajoling and sweet, trying to distract him from his clear intention to pummel the younger, smaller boy.

Roger slapped at her hand, and Billy Kinross grabbed Roger's shirt, pushing him out of the diner in a way that surprised both Irene and Roger. It seemed the kid had learned a thing or two from his older brother.

Roger stumbled out of the door, Billy Kinross hot on his heels. The group of kids preparing to enter the popular hangout all stopped and stared.

Roger recovered instantly. His swing caught the younger boy full in the mouth, and he followed that with a hard slug to his midsection.

Billy went down with a grunt. Roger grabbed him, pulling him to his feet. Roger had about 20 pounds and several inches on Billy, as well as a streak of mean that wasn't natural, and he laid into the boy with a fervor that had the circle of kids shifting nervously. Billy had fallen to the ground again and was mostly just trying to protect himself as Roger fell on top of him, raining blows wherever he could connect.

Then startled cries and shouts rose up as a figure pushed his way through the crowd, shoving the nervous bystanders this way and that in an effort to reach his brother. Johnny Kinross grabbed the back of Roger Carlton's shirt with both hands and swung him up and off of his brother, tossing him to the side. He knelt by his brother without sparing the raging bully a second glance. A few of Johnny's friends stepped in and held the outraged Roger by the arms, waiting until Johnny was assured Billy hadn't been seriously hurt. Billy's mouth and nose were bleeding, but he waved off Johnny's concern and rose shakily to his feet. Johnny pulled off his shirt to stem the bloody flow, and checked his brother surreptitiously for more serious injury. When he was satisfied that his brother wasn't seriously hurt, he turned, his stance wide, his arms hanging loosely at his sides. His face wore the fury of a man who has been pushed as far as he will go.

"Let him go."

"Johnny?"

"Let him go," Johnny demanded again, raising his voice. His friends obeyed immediately, freeing Roger and stepping away from him.

Johnny strode forward and without pause or hesitation, plowed his fist into Roger's jaw. Roger dropped like a sack of potatoes, his head rolling to the side as his legs and arms flopped comically in a dead faint. The crowd grew quiet as Johnny leaned over the inert form. Johnny patted Roger's cheeks roughly until Roger responded, groaning and tossing his head from side to side. He would live.

Johnny straightened and leveled his gaze at Roger's cowering friends.

"Tonight, at the new school. We're gonna finish this. Just Roger and me and whoever else has a problem with the Kinross boys. You make sure he's there or I'll find him and I'll find all of you, and it won't be pretty. You got that?"

***

2011

There were marks on her neck the next morning. Maggie tried to convince herself it had all been a dream, but the bruises proved otherwise. And as afraid as she was of slipping back into a time and space that Roger occupied, she was more afraid of upsetting the new possibilities that loomed on the horizon. Johnny was hers again, Saturday was the prom, and the future stretched out before her like a golden sunrise. Maggie knew she had to get out of Irene's house. The episodes were getting worse. She only hoped that she couldn't die in another time, that her mortality would yank her back to where she belonged. But hope was a very weak lifeline, and she knew how foolish she was being.

Still, she didn't tell Irene what had happened. She didn't tell Johnny either. She told herself she would. She told herself she would come clean after the dance, and then she and Irene and Johnny would make a plan. Maybe she could stay with Johnny and Jillian Bailey. Graduation was three weeks away, and then she would be free to live or do whatever she pleased. She resumed wearing her glasses to bed and slept with her iPod programmed to play only current songs. With the music of her own time pounding in her ears, she managed to sleep and live without incident the following night and then the next.

~22~
A Time to Lose

Maggie picked Johnny up at eight o'clock in the pink Cadillac. She had resisted all his efforts to be the "man" and pick her up in his Bel Air. She remembered how, in Purgatory, he had wanted to drive the Cadillac, how he said he had coveted the car when spoiled Irene Honeycutt had received it on her seventeenth birthday. Now he would have his turn behind the wheel. Plus this way they could avoid Irene and any awkwardness. Irene had helped Maggie get ready, even getting a little teary when Maggie had donned the red dress. Maggie hadn't been able to explain that the reason Irene had never found the dress in 1958 was because Maggie had worn it back to 2011, skipping all the years in between. After all, there were never two red dresses. It made Maggie's head spin just thinking about it, and she and Irene didn't dwell on the tangled ball of yarn that time had become.

Maggie knocked at Jillian Bailey's door and waited on the top step, the traditional roles on Prom Night reversed. Johnny answered almost immediately, and they stared at each other in awe, memories of another prom fresh in their minds.

"That's my girl," Johnny breathed. "How is it possible that you look even more beautiful than you did that night?"

"Modern make up and no nylons." Maggie grinned and stuck out one of her smooth, bare legs in her new red pumps. The original shoes had stayed behind in 1958, and Irene hadn't kept them the second time around.

Maggie beamed and straightened Johnny's lapels. "No pink carnation this time, Mister. You and I need to match." She pulled the red rose from behind her back and proceeded to pin it on.

"Let me get a picture." Jillian Bailey stood just beyond Johnny's right shoulder and ushered Maggie inside where the light was considerably better. Dusk had descended, and night was crawling into the sky.

Maggie and Johnny looped their arms around each other, and instead of smiling into the camera, they ended up looking at each other.

"Hey, you two," Jillian smiled. "Yoo hoo! Can you look right here?" She snapped away, but in the end the best shot was the first one, where they couldn't seem to tear their eyes away from each other. Jillian promised Maggie that she would send the pics to her phone.

Maggie tossed Johnny the keys as they headed for the car. Johnny smiled and opened the passenger door, helping her in.

"The old girl looks almost as good as she used to. Maybe just a little rusty around the edges," he commented as he pulled away from Jillian's house. "The transmission feels nice and tight."

"It should. You just repaired it a few months ago."

"I did?!"

"Yes, you did. I sorta helped. Well...not really. But I kept you company. Told you blonde jokes and stuff."

"Now that I can believe." He grinned.

The prom was being held in the parking lot of the burned out Honeyville High School. The Ladies Historical Society had held their auction the night before the big dance, trying to raise money for the new school that would be built on the very same site, and giving the community a chance to rally around the seniors who had lost not only their school a few months before graduation but all the decorations and supplies they had painstakingly gathered. Irene had found the record player she was looking for and donated it as well as several other things that she claimed it was time to let go of. The auction had been a huge success, and the townsfolk then helped to set up the space for "Beneath the Stars - Prom 2011."

It worked out that the prom was actually held "Beneath the Stars," which seemed fitting. Maggie couldn't help but notice the similarity of the prom themes in 1958 and 2011, but was grateful she would be dancing with Johnny in the fresh air, where she would be safe from the pull of the past. Hundreds of silk trees lined the perimeter of the parking lot, and each had been densely strung with white twinkle lights, creating an enclosed dance floor. A popular band from Galveston had volunteered to play at the ravaged high school free of charge. Huge generators were brought in to power the band and the lighting, and several local businesses had donated tables and chairs, refreshments, and flowers to the senior class.

There is something very sexy about a guy who can dance, and apparently Johnny had been practicing some modern moves in the three days since Maggie had popped the question. It's amazing what someone can learn from satellite TV. Maggie was stunned and thrilled in equal measure. But the slow songs were the best, and Johnny held her like there wasn't another girl in the vicinity, which of course, there was. And the girls were all aware of him. Maggie caught several of them gawking and pointing and practically drooling when Johnny let loose on the dance floor. The boys seemed to be increasingly angry over the attention Johnny was getting from their dates; there was even a bit of a dust up at one of the tables. Derek and Dara were arguing quite publicly about the looks she was giving Johnny, and Derek ended up pushing away from the table, knocking over his chair, and storming out of the circle of lit trees to where all the cars were parked. Several of his friends seemed unsure of what to do, and Trevor ended up being the only one who followed him out. Maggie shrugged. She really didn't care about Derek or Dara.

Unlike most of the couples who made an appearance at the dance to see and be seen, get their pictures taken, and quickly leave, Johnny and Maggie lapped up every song and every second. Nobody else existed, and nobody else mattered for one night. If Maggie could stay in a moment forever, this one would have been a contender; purgatory had become paradise, and Maggie happily lost herself in it. Even the blackened remains of the high school, foreboding in the velvet moonlight, cast little shadow over her bliss.

Unfortunately, it appeared that Derek's jealousy got the best of him, and when the last song ended and Maggie and Johnny left the prom hand in hand, they discovered all of the tires on Irene's car had been slashed. The car sat in an embarrassed slump, and Maggie cried out and Johnny swore, closing the distance at a run, squatting down beside the right front tire, which was completely flat, the gash puckered and gaping.

Maggie bit her lip to keep from screaming out in vexation. She wished suddenly and fervently that she and Johnny could just run away together. She was so done with Honeyville and high school. But just as quickly, she stopped herself, quelling the thought. On this night especially, she was mindful of her blessings and grateful that for the first time, maybe even since her parents died, that she had hope for a future with someone she loved.

"I'm guessing you've got a spare in the trunk, but one spare isn't gonna do us much good," Johnny sighed. "Who would do something like this?"

"Did you notice all the looks you were getting from the ladies?"

"Absolutely." Johnny smiled laciviously, his eyebrows waggling.

"Yeah, well so did all the other guys. I'm guessing one of them - and his name starts with 'D' and end with 'erek' - was a little jealous of your hot moves and decided to take it out on our cool ride."

Maggie hunched down beside him and sighed. "How many blondes does it take to change a tire?"

"Only one, sweetheart, but this blonde can't work a miracle."

Gus's portentous words echoed in Maggie's mind. *Don't forget your miracle so quickly.* "This blonde IS a miracle," Maggie said quietly, sliding her hand into his.

Johnny's eyes softened, and he leaned in and kissed her slowly. Then he stood, pulling her up beside him.

"We aren't taking this old girl home tonight. You got any friends who could give us a lift?"

Maggie looked around at the mostly deserted car lot and then back toward the tree-lined dance floor. The band was disassembling and moving gear into the back of an old Ford pick-up overflowing with speakers and equipment. They weren't going to be able to squish in there, and Maggie didn't know any of the band members. Her eyes roved past the few remaining couples all walking out to their cars. One car pulled away as she watched, and another couple she knew only vaguely climbed onto a Harley Davidson Motorcyle, the girl hiking up her skirt and pulling on a helmet. The hog rumbled and belched, and they pulled away without a backward glance at the marooned Cadillac.

"Maggie! Do you guys need some help?"

Maggie swung around to see Jody Evans turn off the twinkle lights at the perimeter of the dance floor and head towards them. Jody was on her dance team, and she had always been nice to Maggie, helping her out with her make-up the night of the fateful winter formal and never letting Dara's opinions sway her.

"Jody!" Maggie called, relieved that someone she knew still remained at the dance. The place was now almost deserted. "We've got a little car trouble here. We need a lift. Could we catch one with you?"

"Sure! My boyfriend manages the band. We're just helping them load up, and then we'll drive back to the lead singer's place to unload. The committee will come back tomorrow to take down all this other stuff. It's way too late tonight to mess with it, and I don't think anyone's gonna run off with silk trees or twinkle lights. 'Course, judging by your car tires, there are some definite jerks out there. Geez! Who did that?" Jody's eyes widened at the damage done to the Caddie's tires.

Maggie let the question slide by, not wanting to point fingers when she wasn't absolutely sure of the offender. "Are you sure we could squeeze in? The truck looks pretty full."

"Oh sure. We'll figure it out."

But Jody's optimism was short lived. The lead singer, the drummer, Jody, and her band manager boyfriend were all going to cram into the front seat of the truck. There was no way Johnny and Maggie were going to fit.

"We might be able to get one of you in the back if you hold one of those speakers in your lap, but it ain't gonna be comfortable man," the drummer volunteered hesitantly, addressing Johnny.

"I'm not leaving Maggie here alone."

"Johnny, I'll get in the car, turn on the radio, and rest my feet." Maggie shrugged. "Plus, it'll only take you ten minutes to get to Jillian's house and be back here with your car. I'll be fine. I used to ride my bike to and from this very school by myself, day in and day out."

Johnny shook his head again, "No. We'll walk. It isn't that far."

"In those shoes?" Jody laughed, looking at Maggie's high red heels.

"I'll carry her," Johnny offered, as if he thought he really could carry her for three miles.

"In that dress?" Jody laughed even harder. "I'll stay with Maggie. You jump in the cab with the guys, Johnny, and you and Maggie can take me home when you get your car," Jody suggested cheerfully.

"Uh, Jody?" Jody's boyfriend definitely did not like that idea. He obviously didn't want Prom Night to end so soon, especially without even taking his date home.

"This is crazy," Maggie sighed. "I can't hold a speaker on my lap. It's bigger than I am, and I sure as heck can't walk home. Jody, we've already kept you guys long enough. Just let Johnny jump in the back, and I'll wait here for ten minutes for him to come back with his car."

Johnny scowled. He didn't like her suggestion, not at all. Unfortunately, it seemed the only solution, so after some growling and some worrying, he wedged himself into the crowded bed of the truck, straddling a speaker and keeping the cymbals from crashing together while he kept the snare from toppling over on top of him. The others piled in front as planned, and Maggie walked to the pink Caddie, now alone in the completely deserted lot. She waved and climbed into the car. She turned the key and lit up the console, flipping on the radio to keep her company until Johnny returned.

Her phone bleeped. It was going dead. Maggie clicked on the picture messages Jillian had sent, hoping she had enough power to open them. The first picture that opened was the first one Jillian had taken. She and Johnny were standing close, and her head was tilted up to his. They were gazing at each other, smiles of pleasure curling their lips. Maggie caught her breath and felt her eyes swim. It was perfect. Finally, a happy ending. Her phone bleeped again. She turned it off and sat back, smiling, with the picture filling her vision behind her eyes.

Johnny still had the radio tuned into the oldies station. A song Maggie faintly knew trickled out of the slightly tinny speakers and into the car. Maggie's smile broadened and her feet jived a little in time with the rhythm. She had heard this song somewhere before, but she couldn't place it. *"And we'll be rocking and a'reelin..."*

Lights flashed from behind her closed lids, and Maggie blinked in surprise. Johnny couldn't be back already.

The lights slid past the Caddie, and Maggie's view was suddenly obscured by the people that were sitting on the hood of Irene's car. She screeched and jerked upright, her eyes swinging wildly to the right. A mint green car, similar to Irene's in year and make, was parked next to her. Another pair of lights slid past and then another. A black truck with rounded edges and ancient curves jerked to a stop to the left of Irene's Cadillac, and Maggie cried out and then bit back the sound when the driver of the truck tossed a startled look her way. The driver's side window was down. The song that had been on the radio was now inside and outside of the car, as if the vehicles surrounding her were tuned into the same station.

"That's Chuck Berry, folks..." An announcer's voice bounced glibly over the tail end of the song, reading a commercial for Crest toothpaste: *"Look Ma, no cavities!"* Nobody on the radio spoke that way anymore. Maggie groaned in growing horror. How had this happened? She was in the car! This wasn't possible! Maggie's ever-accommodating brain supplied an answer almost immediately. She was wearing clothing from the 1950's, listening to oldies in a car that had been in her

family for decades. She groaned again and slammed her hand against the dash in frustration.

She wasn't wearing her Saint Christopher medal. It hadn't gone with her dress. She cursed herself and fumbled for her phone desperately, hoping for something to pull her back to the present. It was gone. Her purse, which had been sitting on the seat beside her only moments before, had disappeared as well. She had slipped her right foot out of her shoe when she had climbed into the car. The shoes were new, and she'd formed a small blister on her little toe while dancing. Her right shoe was missing. She looked down at her left foot, still wearing the high red heel and then at her bare right one and back out at the crowd that was forming beyond the car. Trying not to panic, she turned the radio off and rolled down her window a few inches, hoping to ascertain where -- and when -- she was.

"He's here!" a girl squealed, and the voices beyond the Caddie's windows rose and fell in excitement.

"Kinross is here!" The shout went out across the parking lot.

"Paula, don't say anything!" It was Irene's voice. She and her friends must be the girls sitting on the hood of the car.

"Yeah, Paula!" someone chimed in. Was that Shirley or Cathy? Maggie knew she had heard that voice before. "You always spill the beans!"

"Roger is up to something!" Irene said in a low, firm voice, and her friends quieted down. "He wants us to send Johnny inside the school, but don't any of you do it!! Do you hear me?"

"But Irene!" Paula wailed. "He'll be mad! He is still your guy, isn't he?"

Irene didn't respond. Maggie began to shake. She knew where she was. Oh, heaven help her! She knew where she was.

***

2011

The truck full of drums, speakers, lights, and equipment rumbled to a stop at the blinking red light. Johnny shifted his weight, trying to keep the cymbal from dinging him in the head. He had a bad feeling and wished he'd never agreed to leave Maggie behind, even for ten minutes. And he'd left her at that God-forsaken school. Just looking at the burnt out remains made him break out in a cold sweat.

Johnny felt sick and head-achy, and if he didn't get out of the bouncing truck soon he was going to be sick all over the equipment. This was not the way he had envisioned the night ending. He needed to get back to Maggie.

Jody Evans called out to him through her open window, verifying the directions to Jillian's. She was perched on her boyfriend's lap, her head almost touching the roof of the overcrowded cab. The light turned green, and Johnny tried to answer, but his throat was suddenly so tight he couldn't breathe.

"Johnny?" Jody peered through the back window, craning her head this way and that.

"Who are you talking to, Jody?" Her boyfriend laughed.

"Yeah, Jod. Most guys don't like it when their girls call them by the wrong name," the lead singer drawled.

"What did I call you?" Jody laughed, addressing her boyfriend.

"You called him Johnny," the drummer teased. "His name is Jeremie. And mine's Craig....in case you're thinking about replacing Jeremie."

"Shut it, Craig," Jeremie threatened cheerfully.

"I wasn't talking to you, Jer. I was just thinking we needed to....to..." Jody's voice broke off, and a puzzled look marked her pretty features. "Weird. I just totally forgot what I was going to say. And I feel like it was important. It's almost like Deja vu...or something."

Something crashed in the bed of the truck, Craig swore, and then Trey, the lead singer, threatened randomly, "Whoever didn't tie down that cymbal is going to buy it if it's busted." He slowed to a stop at the side of the road, and he and Craig spilled out of the driver's side door.

"Shit!" they heard Craig shriek. "The speaker tipped over, and the cymbal is shoved through the snare drum!"

Jody and Jeremie joined the melee and commenced rearranging the equipment so they could make it home without further incident.

No one seemed to remember that there had been someone in the back of the truck...someone they had agreed to help, someone who had been holding the cymbal that had skewered the drum. Reduced to a vague and fleeting sense of something forgotten, it was as if he had never been there at all.

~23~
A Time to Die

1958

Johnny slowed and then swung into the spot left open just for him. He opened the heavy door of the Bel Air and stepped out of his pride and joy. The sound of his black boot hitting the ground met with silence. He lit a cigarette like he had all the time in the world and no one was watching.

He was dressed like some of the other guys – jeans, boots, white tee and black leather jacket, but he seemed suited to his choice where the others looked posed. His dark blonde hair swooped high off his forehead, and his blue eyes swept over the kids standing by, or sitting atop, somebody's Studebaker or someone else's Lincoln or any one of the various cars and trucks arranged in two lines. Johnny noticed that Irene Honeycutt's pink Cadillac took up two spaces. It was a miracle she hadn't dented a tailfin yet. That baby was so long it could drive in two counties at once. Irene was the only girl in Honeyville who had her very own spankin' new wheels. He wouldn't mind taking that car for a ride, although he had lost a lot of respect for the girl. Irene glanced away uncomfortably, and thoughts of Maggie rose in his mind. Damn it all. He was too old for this schoolyard shit.

Donnie had put new wheels on his truck, and it looked like Carter's dad had come through on the new carburetor for his old Ford. The last he had seen, it was up on blocks. He would have helped him put it in if he'd known. Johnny let the cars distract him; the cataloging of parts and paint jobs calmed him down and made him forget for just a moment that he was here to bloody a few noses, break a few tail lights, and generally raise Cain.

But someone had alerted the ladies. Who the hell brought chicks to a rumble? Johnny sighed and tossed his cigarette. Eyeing the school, he thanked his stars that he had graduated, and he would never have to attend the shiny new edifice the whole town was talking about. He would be more than happy if he never had to set foot inside the new Honeyville High.

The passenger door on his black hot rod opened, and Billy stepped out. He didn't try to imitate Johnny. It would have been laughable if he had. Johnny didn't want Billy to be like him. Billy wasn't cool, but he was nice. He didn't have an attitude, but he had a brain. He might not have girls hanging on him, but he would be able to hang onto a classy lady someday. Johnny was sure of it. Billy was worth two of Johnny, and Johnny was proud of it.

Billy wore his thick, black-rimmed glasses, and peered through them nervously at the crowd that had collected in the brand new parking lot. His nose and lip were swollen from the altercation earlier in the evening. He wore a button-up, collared shirt and slacks, though it was sweltering out. Of course, Johnny had his jacket on, but that was all for the intimidation factor. Billy had insisted on coming along, knowing that Johnny was more likely to remain calm if his little brother was with him. Johnny had told him to stay home and had expected Billy to give in to his stern command, but for once Billy had been adamant, knowing that Johnny was set on picking a fight all because of him.

"You lookin' for Roger, Johnny?" someone called out. Johnny didn't bother to answer. They all knew he was. Johnny strolled down the line of cars and stopped in front of Irene Honeycutt's pink ride. Irene didn't smile, but her girlfriends giggled and elbowed each other. If he wanted to, he could crook his little finger at any one of the twittering females perched on Irene's car and be hot and heavy in five minutes flat. But he wasn't interested in Irene's friends; none of them could hold a candle to Maggie.

Irene looked different. She had always been a beautiful girl, but there was a stiffness and a strain in her eyes that had never been there before. She looked afraid. From what he'd seen, Johnny wasn't so sure the blue-eyed brunette was that into Roger, but who was he to question it? Roger was smart, rich, and popular, and Irene's daddy sure seemed to have plans for him. Johnny had plans for him, too. He was going to beat the hell out of Roger and all his boys and swear that it would be ten times worse the next time anyone messed with Billy Kinross.

"He isn't here, Johnny!" a plump redhead named Paula called out, and Irene leveled a look at her that Johnny couldn't decipher. The redhead squirmed nervously and ducked her head when another girl poked her in the ribs.

Johnny zoned in and moved close to the nervous little carrot-top. Tipping her chin up with a long finger, Johnny spoke loud and clear.

"Then where is he, Pidge?"

Paula stammered a little, and her cheeks flamed as bright as her hair. "I, um, I'm not sure...he just wanted us to tell you he had better things to do...or something...I think. Um...didn't he say that, Irene?"

"Then what are all of you doing here?" Johnny jerked his head, indicating the crowd, his eyes meeting Irene's, demanding an answer.

She didn't respond, but her blue eyes were wide, and the expression on her face had him smelling a rat.

The crowd shifted uncomfortably, and someone cleared his throat. A few of the guys that Johnny called friends started asking questions and calling out, and everyone seemed to chime in at once-

"We haven't seen him Johnny..."

"Somebody said they thought he was here!"

"Tommy swears he saw his wheels parked here an hour ago!"

"Go home, Johnny!" someone else called out. "No one wants trash like you or your brother hangin' around here!"

The voice came from back in the crowd and Carter and Jimbo were on it immediately, a scuffle breaking out before Johnny could even see who it was. Like it had been carefully orchestrated, Roger Carlton's friends were suddenly swarming out of the backs of trucks and cars. Fists were pumping and insults flying as Carter and Jimbo were swallowed up in the fracas. Donnie and Luke were in there somewhere, too. Luke's bright hair and superior height made him visible for a moment before someone pulled him down.

"Hey! Hey!" Johnny shouted out as girls screamed, and a few random horns bellowed as people scrambled to jump into their cars or out of their cars, depending on whether or not they wanted in or out of the trouble that had erupted.

Turning to Billy, Johnny swung his arm out fiercely, grabbing him by the shirt and pulling him in close. "Stay in the car, little brother. These guys don't fight fair, and it's gonna get ugly. I can't worry about you getting the crap beat out of you while I'm wailing on Carlton."

"Just let it go, Johnny," Billy pleaded. "We shouldn't have come here at all. I have the willies about all of this, like cooties marching up my spine or somethin'."

"Just stay out of it, Billy!" Johnny insisted again, releasing Billy's shirt and shoving his brother back toward his car. "Take my car and head down the road a ways. I'll meet you in an hour at The Malt."

"What if I get caught? You know I ain't got proof! And what if I wreck your car?"

"You'll be fine! Just go!" Screams and shouts pulled Johnny's attention from his little brother, and he shrugged out of his leather jacket, threw it at Billy, and took off at a run, barely intercepting an attempt to brain Carter with a piece of a two-by-four someone had snagged from the construction debris. Alarm sounds were jangling through Johnny's head as he realized these guys weren't playing around. In his periphery, he noticed cars peeling out as the ladies apparently realized this was not a place they wanted to be. Good. One less thing he had to worry about. And there was plenty to be concerned about because Johnny and his friends were sorely out numbered.

***

Maggie huddled in the front seat of Irene's car, hiding behind the people that perched and stood around the car, shielding her from anyone looking in, namely anyone who might recognize her.

Her heart had slammed into her chest when she had heard Johnny speak. She tried to imagine him, jeans and boots and slicked back hair, demanding to know where Roger Carlton was. The girls had giggled when he had come close, and she could almost feel their tension as he had tried to coax a little help from the redhead, who had gone on to lie to him. At least she hadn't sent him into the school. If Maggie could just keep Johnny and Billy out of the school. Then what? She chided herself. She didn't know what would happen. She might make things worse. And if events didn't transpire exactly as they had originally, Maggie would never meet Johnny Kinross. He would be lost to her.

Screams broke out, and Maggie watched as people started to scramble to their cars. She had to get out of Irene's Cadillac. She couldn't very well be sitting there when Irene and her friends piled back in. She pushed open the passenger door and hobbled out of the car on one red heel, not knowing where she was going but knowing her conduit was about to be invaded. She turned in circles, looking for a place to shield herself.

Maggie's gaze fell on Johnny's Bel Air. It sat serenely while cars and trucks peeled out around it, screeches and horns blaring the excitement of raging youth. Maggie seemed to have found the best hiding place of all. She was bumped and jostled as people scurried here and there, and nobody really stopped to take a good look, though she was wearing a bright red dress and only one shoe. She watched as Billy Kinross yanked open the door to his brother's car and slid behind the wheel, a look of pure horror stamped on his young face. He seemed unsure of what to do first and sat with his hands on the wheel, looking around for his first clue. He didn't have time to figure it out. Glass and metal complained mightily as Roger Carlton attacked Johnny's car with a baseball bat. He swung again and then again, battering the shiny black showpiece. The front window exploded, and Billy dove out of sight.

Maggie screamed, the sound high pitched and afraid, carrying across the distance to Johnny's car, causing Roger to pause mid-swing. His eyes lit on her like a rabid wolf, and Maggie froze in her tracks. He instantly dropped the bat and strode toward her, pulling a little gun out of the back of his waistband. He pointed it at her, and his hand didn't shake.

"Lizzie says your name is Maggie, and she doesn't know anything more." He said this in a high pitched soprano, mimicking the little girl. "She said I would never find you." Roger smiled, that slow creepy smile that didn't reveal any teeth. "How nice of you to find me."

Maggie couldn't take her eyes from the gun. She should scream or run, but deep down she believed Roger would shoot anyway. And he was close enough to make missing unlikely. The parking lot was still half full of kids who had decided to participate in or be spectators to the battle that raged beyond her right shoulder. If Roger did miss, someone else could very easily be hit. None of this was supposed to happen! Billy had been the one with the gun...hadn't he?

* * *

Johnny forced his way through the swinging arms, landing a few shots and taking more than a couple on his way out of the writhing mass of fists and feet. Just as he thought he would break free, someone flew into him, knocking him down and wrapping him up in the thrashing legs and arms of several people. By the time Johnny had fought his way back out, his friends had the fight well in hand, and Johnny knew it was only a matter of minutes before the whole thing was over. But Carlton still hadn't shown. Johnny had something to communicate to the bastard, and he wasn't leaving until his message had been delivered loud and clear.

Johnny's eyes swung left and right, and then swung right again and stopped cold. His car was still parked where he'd left her, but the driver's side door was hanging open as if Billy had suddenly changed his mind about leaving and bailed out in a hurry. The doors were dented and the front headlights were broken in. It looked as if someone had taken a bat to the windows, too. Rage pounded in Johnny's temples. He had no doubt who had inflicted the damage.

He was going to hurt Roger Carlton when he found him. And where the hell had Billy gone?! He was supposed to take the car and go! Then Johnny saw him. The walkway to the entrance of the school was lit up, and Billy Kinross was running toward the front doors at full speed.

"Billy," Johnny roared, yelling at the top of his lungs. Billy didn't even turn, but slipped through the double doors like the late bell had already chimed and he was tardy for class; the doors had been left unlocked. Something cold and desperate slithered down Johnny's spine. He knew that what waited beyond those doors was something he wanted no part of -- and he had no choice but to head for them at a run.

The double-doored entrance opened into a large three story rotunda with gleaming tiles and a great staircase that swept upward to twin balconies that edged the second and third floors.

"Billy!' Johnny called out, suddenly uncertain as to where to go. The school seemed silent and untouched, and all at once he doubted the wisdom in coming through the doors. If the cops caught him in here he would have more than a few bruises and a black eye to explain. Breaking and entering maybe, even though the doors had been open...

A gunshot rang out, interrupting his second thoughts. Johnny ran forward, taking the stairs three at a time, hurling himself up their wide expanse. Oh God, please no....no... no....the words pounded through his head as he cleared the stairs and skidded to a stop on the third floor, eyes searching both ways down a long wide hallway that ran beyond the balcony to corridors and distant rooms. Suddenly, Billy was running toward him, his shirt untucked, his glasses gone, his face a mask of terror.

"He's got a gun, Johnny. He's got a gun!" Billy looked over his shoulder and then past Johnny, as if expecting a full on attack from every direction.

"Who's got a gun?" Johnny was looking for blood and bullet holes. Billy seemed unharmed, but he was clearly terrified. "Billy!" Johnny reached out and grabbed onto his frantic brother, detaining him, trying to muscle him back toward the stairs. He needed to get him out of the school.

"Roger Carlton has a gun! He shot out a window back there! A bunch of his friends were in here, and when they saw the gun they ran! It made him mad, I guess. He shot out one of the windows, and he's got a girl, Johnny! I don't think he saw me, but I just can't leave her there. I heard him tell her he's going to shoot her!"

"What girl? Who?" Call him cold-hearted, but Johnny decided he would worry about the girl after Billy was out of danger. Again he tried to steer Billy back toward the stairs.

"I don't know her. I saw her once with Lizzie Honeycutt." Billy rubbed his head in distress. Johnny's stomach fell to his knees, and his breath caught in his throat. He knew what Billy was going to say next. "Roger called her Maggie."

***

Roger had taken her into the school. Maggie had walked alongside him demurely. She hadn't fought or even protested. If she walked quietly, without drawing attention, she could save Billy and Johnny. Billy didn't have a gun. He was still in the car. He had no reason to follow Roger. She could save him. She would save him. Roger held her arm roughly and walked like he had big plans.

Roger's friends had been alarmed by the gun and scattered every which way, running down the unfamiliar halls and away from the madman they had aided. Roger shouted, shooting wildly, and the glass on a new window pane exploded into the classroom he had taken her to. The police would be coming now. She just needed to find a way to keep herself alive until then. Roger had other plans.

"I think I'm going to kill you, Maggie," he sneered. "It's perfect really. I know Kinross has a thing for you. It'll upset him that you're dead. I'll tell the police he was the one who took the gun. I got it out of the trunk of a car he was working on. They'll believe me. And he'll go to jail, and his mother will suffer -- maybe worse than if I shot him, which was what I intended. And of course, there's the bonus of actually watching you die. You ruined everything. Irene says she loves me....but she lies. She wants to get away from me. And it's all your fault!"

"Johnny doesn't even know we're in here," Maggie replied softly. "Your friends saw YOU with the gun. You're here, he's not. Chief Bailey won't have a hard time putting two and two together. You will be the one to go to jail. You're eighteen, aren't you?" Maggie's mind raced to find something that might scare him. "You might even get the electric chair." It was Texas in 1958. She was pretty sure that was the method they used for the death penalty.

"Billy followed us in. Didn't you see him?" Roger snickered. "Johnny won't be far behind. He's rather protective of the little guy." The hand that wasn't holding the gun touched his bruised jaw gingerly, as if remembering just how protective.

Maggie didn't know Billy had followed them in. She had drawn him there, and he would draw Johnny. Fear slammed through her. No! She wouldn't let Roger have Johnny. She whirled on Roger, pushing him with such rage and aggression that he stumbled back, the gun falling awkwardly from his hand. The smirk smeared across his mouth still remained, almost as if he couldn't believe she had dared cross him. In a flash, Maggie was out of the room, running down the hallway, her red shoe abandoned in flight like a desperate Cinderella, racing against time.

She thought she would hear the gun explode behind her, but she neither slowed nor swerved, flying down the corridors she had seen engulfed in flames in another time. And she wasn't running from her prince but to him, hoping against hope that time was on her side.

The main hallway on the third floor made a large circle, looping from the center rotunda's highest balcony. Maggie wanted to scream but knew her cries would only call Johnny to her and toward the threat that pursued her, so she fled silently, her legs pumping and her bare feet slapping against the glossy new floors.

Johnny stood by the balcony rail. His back was to her as he tried to usher his frantic brother down the stairs. The hallway in which she ran was dark; the brush of moonlight filtered in from the high windows left shadows all around. She thought she could hear Roger behind her but couldn't separate his breathing from her own. She tossed a glance over her shoulder, expecting to see that he was within an arms length of bringing her down. The hallway beyond was silent and completely empty.

"Johnny!" Billy cried out, pointing at Maggie as she hurtled down the hallway toward them. Johnny swung to greet her, and his face was grim and hard.

"Maggie!" The relief in his voice echoed down the hallway and into her heart.

"Go! We need to go, Johnny." He swung her up against him, his arms around her, his face in her hair.

"Maggie, where in the hell have you been? And what the hell are you doing here?" His voice was angry, but he held her tightly, contradicting his tone.

"Johnny!" Maggie sputtered. Billy looked dumbfounded, watching the ladies man that was his big brother embracing the mysterious brunette in a siren red prom dress...and no shoes.

"Johnny!" Maggie wrenched herself from him and cried out as Roger Carlton materialized out of the shadowy hallway beyond. He had circled around and come out on the opposite side. Billy and Johnny both stood with their backs to him, unaware that death had come to call. He raised his gun, aiming for Johnny's back.

Maggie didn't consciously decide in that moment to do what she did. It wasn't an act of heroism or sacrifice. It was simply the instinctual nature of a woman to stand between death and someone she loves, and that is what she did. She stepped around Johnny, covering him, her arms extended like wings to shelter him. In the same instant, Johnny swung around and, seeing Roger, cried out a warning to his brother. But Roger wasn't aiming for Billy. The gun exploded, and Roger's bullet struck Maggie, throwing her back violently into Johnny's arms.

"Maggie!" Johnny cried out in horror as she collapsed against him, causing him to fall back heavily and struggle to keep his feet. Roger shot again, but his aim was skewed with adrenaline, and the bullet veered just right of Johnny's left shoulder, embedding itself in the wall beyond him.

Johnny wrapped one arm around Maggie, easing her to the floor, sheltering her with his larger frame as he warded Roger off with his left arm extended.

Roger just smiled and leveled the gun at the wounded girl. And then her image flickered. For the briefest instant she was gone, leaving nothing but a pool of blood beneath her. She reappeared almost instantly. Roger stared, the hand that held the gun wavered as he blinked his eyes and shook his head vigorously from side to side. Johnny didn't see Maggie shivering in and out like a mirage. His eyes were trained on Roger and the gun in his outstretched hand.

Without warning, Johnny lunged for Roger, reaching for the gun as he barrelled into his chest. Roger was caught completely unaware, his attention riveted on Maggie. He flew back, squeezing the trigger once more as he collided with the wooden balustrade that separated safety from space and life from Purgatory.

The momentum carried Roger up and over the railing, and Johnny scrabbled to extricate himself from Roger's clinging limbs, only to find himself hurtling beyond rescue with his enemy wrapped around him.

Their eyes locked for a split second, maniacal green on sky blue, and then they were falling, tumbling through the air in a sloppy cartwheel. Maggie's scream punctured the air as yet another shot rang out, drowning out Billy's cry of horror as he watched his brother plummet to the tiled entrance two stories below.

~24~
A Time for Peace

Roger Carlton lay with his legs twisted beneath him, his head cocked at an odd angle, staring blankly at the domed ceiling high above. Billy had never seen death before, but he had no doubt that Roger was dead. He had definitely taken the brunt of the fall. Johnny had fallen on top of him and then rolled to the side. But Johnny wasn't moving either. Roger had managed one final shot as death rose to meet him. The gun was still clutched in his hand, resting on his abdomen, his finger curled around the trigger. That last shot had pierced Johnny high on the right side of his chest.

Billy didn't remember running down the winding stairs to his brother's side, but he was suddenly there, kneeling next to Johnny, begging him to hold on, begging him not to leave. Johnny's breath was labored, and blood soaked his shirt and pooled beneath him. His eyes were wide and scared.

"Maggie?" Johnny groaned.

"She's hurt bad, Johnny!" Billy cried, tears dripping down his young face and onto his brother's heaving chest. "I've got to go get help. For you and for her! Hold on Johnny, please hold on!"

***

Maggie eased herself down the stairs, clinging to the railing with her good arm, her right arm useless where the bullet had sunk into her shoulder. She could hear Billy talking, begging. She had to get to Johnny. She wouldn't look, wouldn't allow herself to turn her head to see the bodies of the fallen boys. She had to focus, had to get down the stairs. She was weak and dizzy, but surprisingly free of pain, as if she had physically passed beyond the earthly plane and existed somewhere between time's layers. The wrenching, pulling, pounding at her core demanded she succumb and fly away. She fought it desperately as she focused on one step and then one more, moving faster than she thought she could, letting her need to reach Johnny fuel her efforts.

And then she heard Billy leave, racing through the double front doors, out into the night beyond. Maggie cleared the bottom step and let her gaze rest on the figures sprawled in horrific display in the center of the rotunda. Maggie's legs buckled at the sight.

"Johnny!" Her keening voice echoed through the stately entrance like a death knell. She attempted a step forward, but gravity swallowed her whole.

***

Johnny tried to keep his eyes open and resisted the magnetic pull that fought to wrench him from himself. It was like the pull of the undertow, and for a moment Johnny thought he was dreaming. He thought he was back at the beach -- ten years old -- feeling the sand being sucked out from beneath his toes, his mom and Billy back on the blanket, the sun bright overhead. But the pull was much stronger, and Johnny fought for something to anchor himself to. His hands didn't want to work, and his legs felt like they'd fallen asleep. His chest burned like he had been too long underwater. He curled his toes inside his boots and fought against the pull with all his might. Why was he wearing his boots at the beach?

In terror, he realized what the pull was, and he forced his eyes open to find his brother. But it wasn't

Billy that lay beside him. Billy had gone for help. Billy was okay. Billy was safe. But Maggie wasn't .

"Maggie?" He tried to form the word, but he could not.

"Maggie!" He tried again and heard only a whisper of breath.

Johnny screamed inside his head. He screamed, and he fought the pull and demanded an audience with the source of the power trying to disconnect him from his body.

"I'm not going anywhere!" he raged over and over, over and over, until the pressure built and exploded in white light and brilliant sparks like a blow torch on metal. Johnny felt a snapping and a shredding. But there was no pain, only pressure, and then a giant crack, like a million balloons simultaneously popping. And then...nothing.

***

2011

When Maggie again became aware, she was lying across the front seat of the pink Cadillac. For a minute she didn't know where she was, or more specifically, when she was. The pain that had been held at bay by time or adrenaline was now almost unbearable, and the seat beneath her was slick with blood. She eased herself to a sitting position, and her head spun and unconsciousness rose to claim her again. She protested loudly, crying out against oblivion's lure. She struggled to maintain her grip on reality, whatever that was, and find a clue as to where she had landed.

"I'm in 2011," she moaned, seeing the blackened shell of Honeyville High School through the car's front window. The silk trees that lined the Prom's dance floor stood like a sentinel between the hope of before and the despair of after. Her small purse and her phone lay on the floor where she had tossed them earlier. She stretched, whimpering, and wrapped her left hand around the shiny gadget. She pressed the button to turn it on, breathing through clenched teeth. It lit up briefly and then gave the cascading tones of shut-down mode. It was dead. Maggie moaned again, lying back against the seat, pressing her palm against the flow of blood below her right shoulder. Her dress was useless, the fabric completely unsuitable to staunch its flow. The flesh of her palm would have to do, but it hurt too much to press as tightly as she should.

She was in trouble. And she was too tired and heartbroken to care. The image of Johnny, bloody and motionless, with Roger Carlton lying in a twisted heap at his side filled her head, and she turned her face into the seat, letting her tears flow with the blood that wouldn't be stemmed.

Suddenly, the passenger side door was wrenched open. Maggie lifted her head wearily, unable to find the energy for surprise. Johnny was framed in the opening, moonlight at his back.

"Johnny?" Maggie whimpered in disbelief.

"Maggie!" Johnny flipped the key in the Caddie's ignition, illuminating Maggie where she huddled against the seat.

"Come on, baby! We've got to get you to the hospital." His hair was disheveled, his white sports coat abandoned, his dress shirt untucked, and his tie dangling.

"Why does Heaven hurt so much?" Maggie whispered, wanting to embrace him but unable to move.

"Maggie. This ain't Heaven, baby. Come on, Maggie! You gotta stay with me." Johnny was frantic, his eyes never leaving Maggie's face. He didn't know if she would survive the drive to the hospital. He had to stop the bleeding. Her skin was pasty white, and her body was limp. It was probably a miracle she was conscious at all. The Bel Air was waiting, the engine rumbling, ready to transport her to wherever Johnny wished, but she was out of time.

He didn't know if he could do it. But he had done it before. He slid Maggie so she was lying flat against the front seat. Then he knelt at her side, his legs folded awkwardly in the foot-well, and pressed both of his hands into her wound, remembering how it felt to gather energy, to feel it flooding his system like a hot white light. He remembered it so clearly now. Every moment of the last fifty-three years was stamped on his memory like a prison tattoo, permanent and fixed.

He had been riding in the back of that overcrowded truck, instruments and equipment pressing against him. He had known leaving Maggie was a mistake, and the farther from her he traveled, the greater the overwhelming sense of wrongness became. They were almost to his sister's house when something had yanked at him, loosening him from his physical surroundings, as if he were tied to an anchor and dropped into a weightless sea. And like water, the knowledge of what had been drenched him in memory.

He was suddenly, acutely, aware. He remembered the loneliness of the last fifty-three years. He remembered the despair, the intense anguish, and yet...the opportunity. In Purgatory he hadn't aged, but he had grown and changed. He had discovered an inner power and an inner strength. He had developed fortitude, patience, and perspective. He remembered it all. And most of all, he remembered Maggie.

He flew through their time in Purgatory, watching the relationship unfold, remembering the wonder he had felt at her friendship, letting the desire he had felt to join her in life resonate within him.

And then he had flown beyond Purgatory to the final moments of his old life, when he lay at Roger Carlton's side, at peace in the knowledge that he had saved his brother. He and Maggie had saved Billy. *"It is a far, far better thing that I do now."* The words of Dickens echoed prophetically in his head.

He watched Maggie as she struggled to descend the stairs, her blood spilling across the bodice of her dress, her attention riveted on the next step. She was doing everything in her power to reach him. In that moment, he had been well aware of his choice and what that choice would mean. Paradise or Purgatory?

He saw Maggie stagger as she reached the main floor. She cried out his name, and then she was gone. She simply vanished. Nothing remained but the trail of blood that stretched beyond her to the third floor, marking her path, verifying her existence. He knew where she had gone.

Paradise or Purgatory? The choice was easy. He chose Purgatory.

***

2011

Johnny bore down. Maggie hissed, the pain keeping her tethered to the present. He pushed away the doubt that said he had relinquished Purgatory and all that had gone with it. He remembered the spark that had shorted out Jillian's computer. He remembered how quickly he had healed in the hospital after escaping Purgatory. He acknowledged the fire he felt burning just beneath the surface. Surely *something* from Purgatory remained.

Johnny called on that heat that lay beneath his skin and gathered it, coaxing it forward until it seared the skin on his palms where they were pressed into Maggie's wound. The pain was shocking, but he used it. He used the intense pain in his hands, the overwhelming love in his heart, and the bottomless faith that there was purpose in Purgatory, and turned it outward. Light began to seep out from the edges of his fingers, as if he held his palms over the beam of a flashlight. The intensity grew and grew until light filled the interior of the old car and spilled out of the windows. The Cadillac, marooned in the dark parking lot, became a lighthouse to the lost, guiding Maggie and Johnny home at last.

Epilogue

Matching scars might not be much to build a future on, but Maggie and Johnny had earned theirs. And if scars are the reminders of the past, then the identical puckered pink circles high on the right sides of each of their chests bore witness of the hard fought battle they had waged through time and space. And Johnny and Maggie remembered all of it. The sacrifice, the sorrow, the race against time, all leading up to the moment Johnny chose Purgatory.....again. Like a movie with alternate endings, they not only knew what the world had become, but what the world had been like before, when two people, two worlds apart, had found each other and fallen in love.

No one in 1958 ever knew what happened to Johnny -- or Maggie, for that matter. Billy had gone for help, only to return to a bloody trail leading down the stairs from where Maggie had been shot and a pool of blood where Johnny had lain. And Roger Carlton, of course. He was dead, and very few grieved for him.

In the space of a few hours, the world had changed. At least a small corner of it. Billy didn't die, and Roger did. Irene didn't marry Roger, but many years later she married Billy.

And there were some things that didn't change. Sadly, Irene still gave birth to a stillborn baby, and she and Billy never had children of their own. Dolly Kinross still suffered, Chief Bailey still searched for answers, and the years still passed while Johnny Kinross languished in Purgatory, waiting for the day when Maggie O'Bannon would help him break free.

When a young Maggie came to live with her Great Aunt Irene and her Uncle Billy when she was orphaned at age ten, Billy commented on the coincidence that she was named Maggie and that she resembled the girl that still haunted his memory. But it had been so long ago, and it was beyond comprehension to think the two girls were one in the same. Billy, Irene, and Maggie traveled quite extensively with Billy's work, but Maggie's last year in high school found them back in Honeyville, back in the old family home, back where the story truly began. And then time resumed its track, Maggie found Johnny in Purgatory, and what was became what is.

After all, that which has been is now, and that which is to be has already been.

The End

Author's Note and Acknowledgements

Thanks go to my mom for being my sounding board and for reading even when she was solving the world's problems - or at least the world's math problems. Also, big thanks to Lorraine Wallace for being the best English teacher and editor a girl could have and for volunteering to help a starving writer. Big hug. I promise you, someday you <u>will</u> get paid. Maybe.

Thank you, kiddos -- Paul, Hannah, Claire, and Sam -- for putting up with your crazy writer mother, and the foggy brain and sometimes messy house that accompany each book. Ditto goes for the big guy. Travis, thanks for hangin' in.

Finally, a big thanks to all who read my first two novels and gave me the encouragement to keep writing. Terri Bailey Clark, Mary Purdon Stevens, Shauna Harmon, Cindy Joy Wilkerson, all of Juab County, and so many of my Saints Unified Voices friends, so many of you went the extra mile for me. To my siblings --- particularly you, Joey Sutorius -- you guys rock. And thank you, Dad, for always making me feel like my success is never a surprise. Thank you!

The song, "Where or When" was written in 1937 by the songwriting duo, Richard Rodgers (1902-1979) and Lorenz Hart (1895-1943). They worked together on 28 stage musicals and more than 500 songs. Thank you for your contribution, gentlemen. Your lyrics were perfect!

Amy Harmon has written three novels, all available in paperback and e-book on Amazon.
www.amazon.com/author/amyharmon
Books by Amy Harmon:
Running Barefoot
Slow Dance in Purgatory
Prom Night in Purgatory

Visit her at www.authoramyharmon.com

.

Made in the USA
Charleston, SC
01 October 2014